INDIGOS

Edward Fahey

Indigos
Copyright © 2021 by Edward Fahey

All rights reserved. This book or any portion thereof may not be reproduced or used in any manner whatsoever without the express written permission of the publisher, except for the use of brief quotations in a book review.

This novel is a work of fiction.
Although parts of this story might have been inspired by the author's sometimes rather fanciful ways of looking at certain people and events, the characters and scenes in this book live only in this writer's imagination. This tale is fictional, and not intended to be seen as any kind of history or revisiting of actual events. Unless someone in real life has herein been specifically quoted and/or cited by name, any resemblance to real persons living or dead should be seen as coincidental.

Printed in the United States of America

Luminare Press
442 Charnelton St.
Eugene, OR 97401
www.luminarepress.com

LCCN: 2021922595
ISBN: 978-1-64388-892-7

*This book was Lynden's idea.
If it works, she can take a lot of the credit.*

*Deep gratitude also for my dear friend, Nancy Bragin,
who introduced me to the term Indigo Children, and who
insists that levels of consciousness worldwide
are generally kicking up a notch.*

*This is for Dora, and Dee, and for gentle John Coats.
All of them now gone from this plane. I miss those times dearly.
I pray their positive faith in the youth of today
can blossom in the hearts of my readers.*

*And for St. Francis of Assisi.
A young man who stood strong against the elders in power.
He has reawakened our love for all life everywhere.
For that greater life which is our true family.*

*But mainly, this book is for Dr. Barbara Hebert.
Neither I nor this story would be anywhere without her warm,
constant, loving, and long-term support. She has dedicated her life
and her spirit to helping children, and to living theosophy. Along
the way, she has always been there to help me accept why I am
so different from most folks, and what a good thing
this can be when turned toward service.*

*So Barbara, dear one,
this is for you.*

*L*ooked like it was all over for humanity.

There were a few people left who wanted to believe maybe the world still had a chance. Maybe fate, karma, disease, politics, and violence were only bulldozing a clearing. Making room for something better. Destroying pretty much everything so we could start over.

But there was so much sorrow and darkness. Everywhere we turned. Our dreams for a better humanity had been ravaged. Any sweet lingering hints of innocence torn bleeding out of our hearts. We needed hope so very badly, but there just wasn't any.

We ached to believe that the little guy still counted. That he could stand up for something worthwhile and make a difference. But we marched by the millions, and were not heard.

Our taxes were handed over to billionaires as we starved on the streets. As the pandemic crushed through us, they offered us only denials. Blocked anything that could have helped. They watched us suffer and starve as they riled us up against each other.

After a while, we grew numb. To everything but the slow, rotting cancer of our spirit.

Some of us had tried to hold on. To stand up against all that ugliness and devastation. We had tried, but we had failed.

And now it was too late. The bad guys had taken everything from us. What good would it do to even want anything anymore? All was lost.

But then came these children.

Children live in a much larger world than we do;
though ours may take up more space.
We have closed so many doors, let our burdens bear us down
into the dulling gray torpor of life.
Children fly through open fields of brightness and wonder.
Clearly remembering what we have lost.

Chapter One

It was a time of darkness. Not a world for more sensitive souls. No place certainly for children born feeling the pain of others. And yet, empathic children seemed to be popping up everywhere. Brilliant and gifted children. Strange kids who didn't fit in. Child geniuses. They were showing up in nations and cultures all around the planet. Almost as if they were answering some kind of a call. Following some higher guidance into these ugly and desperate times.

Little Benjie hadn't started talking as early as toddlers were generally expected to. His mum had worried about him at first, though their doctors and specialists had told her many times these things sometimes just happened. To just give it time.

They had the money to pamper him with nannies, special tutors, and all the best toys and educational tools. Their boy would be bright, even if he never spoke a word. She had worried, but would never tell him that. Everybody knew, she told neighbors and friends, that Capricorns started life off as very serious, intelligent, wise old men even as children. If he was quiet it was because he was thinking.

But the details and extent of his silence were a family matter not to be brandished about. She was British and there were rules as to what should and should not be discussed. There were traditions. There was propriety.

If Benjamin hadn't learned to talk quite as early as most, still his mum had never worried that her boy wasn't bright. That he might have been dull-witted. She knew better. It was obvious. Or if she had ever held such thoughts, she would have kept them to herself. Certain issues were simply not to be spoken of, even to oneself.

Benjie was quiet, but she could tell he was thinking deep thoughts.

The land that day was splotched with patches of snow, stretches of gray melt, and layers of brown land poking through. "Just like one of those Apple Splootchie horses," little Sylvie told her friends of the forest as she gazed about her in wonder.

There were no humans around to correct her, nor would they have wanted to. Sylvie had her own ways of seeing things and her own ways of saying them. She lived in a world of stumblebees and flutterby's. There was a very good chance that in most cases she had learned the names things were *supposed* to be called, but deemed them unworthy. And so, she had needed to rename them. Adult peoples rarely thought things all the way through.

Sylvie was a bouncing, spinning vortex of wonder and delight who saw things adults generally missed. Even stuff about themselves that they apparently hadn't noticed. But when she just walked right up and told them what they didn't want to see, they didn't always take it very well. She figured adults would just have to grow up on their own some day, with or without her help, when they were ready. So for the most part she didn't pay them much mind.

It was one of those days when the sun was dull and fuzzy, but the land was all shiny and clear. None of that was lost on this small child playing along the edge of the forest in great big green rubber boots.

She'd been named Sylva by openly hippie parents who'd seemed to know even before she'd been born that their little girl and big

Mother Nature were always going to be the best of friends.

Today she was poking around, trying to decide if snow lived and died like animals did, and she kind of figured this wasn't so. Snow was more like the clouds. Clouds sometimes looked like one thing and sometimes like another. Where the snow had melted and left a puddle on a rock, that snow hadn't died. You just couldn't really call it snow anymore.

Sylvie always had deep thoughts she had to think, so she was really glad Mama Nature had given her such a big head to do it with.

Even if most of it was hair.

She was exploring her Auntie Ailana's magical gardens and her auntie probably knew she was there. Auntie was a lot like Mama Nature. Between the two of them they knew pretty much everything. When Sylvie had questions; which was most of the time; she could always just ask her aunt, but it was more fun finding out on her own. She was never going to learn things properly all the way through if she kept taking shortcuts by asking somebody.

She was a happy child with a deep sense of purpose. Her giggles rose like bubbles into the air and it was as though these barren branches reached to catch them.

It was winter. When the trees drew inside themselves and rested for a while. Nature had been trimmed to its nubs. The sun rose high above her as some deeper light played softly through this little girl's heart.

Sylvie was a child of Nature, and Nature was a loving mom who enjoyed playing along. The two of them sat together, ran together, and read each other stories.

She and Mama Nature were buddies.

She hopped with bunnies and fawns, sat quietly with trees, and spun with the "whirlybubs", which seemed to be pretty much any kind of bug that liked to fly in circles.

"God sings to us through the flowers, you know," she had once told her slightly older brother, Renn. "Only you don't hear it with any part of your head."

And Renn had only kinda sort of understood.

But, truth be told, Renn understood her better than most folks even tried to. The trees, and the squirrels, and the bunnies, and the deers; these were *her* people. They were much more real, and honest, and true than human peoples tended to be.

Except for her Auntie Ailana.

When her parents were away and Auntie Ailana was in charge, it was "okay, but not excellent" if Sylvie sometimes wanted to feed herself chili for breakfast and have a little cake with her lunch. But then she would have to eat a really good dinner, so it was a trade off.

Her Auntie liked to call her "Little Flitter," though Sylvie didn't know why.

But then again she hadn't really given the matter a whole lot of thought. She had deeper things to learn, and this apparently wasn't what Mama Nature wanted to teach her right now.

Somewhere far away (by little kid standards), Benjie was another kind of person entirely. Sylvie could see, talk to, and dance with the fairies. If Benjie saw a flickering light that shouldn't be there, or an eerie moving shadow off to his side, his heart really wanted to believe something mystical was going on, but then his logic got in the way with a more realistic explanation. He wanted more than anything to see spirits. He wished all to heck they'd give him special messages like they had with Mr. Edgar Cayce, "The Sleeping Prophet." Or Nostradamus; writing things down that nobody would understand for hundreds of years, but then people would see what a great genius he had been. He had seen things that were going to change the world.

Benjie only got this vague feeling sometimes that he wasn't alone. But then he figured he was maybe only making that up just cause he wanted to talk to spirits so bad. He probably really was alone, and nothing important was ever gonna happen cause of him.

He thought about that kind of stuff a lot. He read all the books he could about ESP, and UFOs, and ghosts, and special people like

Mr. Cayce, and magic yogis with special powers. He tried to bend spoons with the power of his mind, or at least move them a little, but they just sat there. He tried so hard, and read pretty much everything, but it never did him any good. He was nobody. He had no special powers. The spirits didn't care about him.

Sylvie, on the other hand, understood what Mama Nature wanted to show her. She was convinced she could see fairies, and the glows around people when they changed moods. If she didn't know what things meant right away, she figured Mama Nature would help her understand them eventually, or she wouldn't have shown them to Sylvie in the first place. Sylvie and Benjie lived maybe only a couple of hundred miles apart from each other, but might as well have lived on different planets.

Benjie may have been odd, and maybe didn't talk very much, but that didn't mean he was troubled. He was quiet in a way that even birds and squirrels gathered around him to share in. He was an awkward, unpopular, skinny child; all bones at odd angles, and patches of thick, dark hair where he would rather not have them. And yet there was a certain kind of a presence about him. Maybe animals noticed it before kids his own age did, but there was something about him.

Sometimes he thought he could feel other people's deepest pains in the air. Air that other folks just walked through in blithe incoherence. His had never been the innocence of the unseeing. Even as a baby he'd peered out at those around him with sometimes unnerving seriousness. An intense level of focus that had made visitors want to hide their hearts under their hands, or run home and burn their diaries. It had been like he could see what they'd been up to, but loved them anyway. They'd want to protect him from a world that was going to be hard on anyone this serious; any little being this aware. Anyone who stood out as so clearly not like others.

But that had been years ago. Now he was just another awkward kid working his way through his first years of schooling. He read way too much about things that had nothing whatsoever to do with his classes, but then ran out of time to do his homework, and only got mediocre grades. He also wasn't making any friends, but wasn't really sure he wanted to.

Today though, Benjie was wandering the woods behind his family's estate in a posh, gated community. He touched leaves and fallen branches with the toe of his sneaker as he pondered. He picked up a few rocks to study now and again, but then put most of them back, positioned just exactly as he'd found them. Others he planned to take home with him. Like a lot of little boys who read a lot of science fiction, Benjie felt he'd been put in this body, in these times, to learn some very important things about life on this planet. This was very important. It gave him a deep sense of purpose.

And he wanted to believe there might be others around him somewhere, watching him learn.

It was winter, so Sylvie wasn't running around barefoot outdoors as was her norm most of the year. She was bouncing about in huge rubber boots. Big enough, she said, to fit three more legs into.

Just how she liked them. She could at least pretend to be barefoot anyhow. Feel breezes where her toes needed to feel them. No part of her could have dealt with being confined. Every bit of her needed to flow freely like the streams; or the winds; or those teeny tiny white bugs that flew in circles like a slow dancing whirlwind until she couldn't help but join in and dance along, with her arms flying off to her sides.

This was just Sylvie being Sylvie.

The child was a giggle of light.

She loved glomping around in her Giant Boots because she could still make that squishy sound with her feet even when she wasn't actually standing in mud barefoot like she liked to do. The boots made their own squishy sounds, so she could pretend.

Today, her Auntie Ailana was letting Sylvie carry the bucket. It was awfully heavy, the little girl told her, but still insisted on half-lugging, half-dragging it around as they carried dry corn to various feeding spots that Sylvie had picked out. It did look to be about half her size as she hefted it. But she liked helping Mama Nature out with her deer. Sometimes they needed a little extra nutrition in the winter when greens weren't quite as lush as they liked to be. She'd planted some of the dried out corn in open areas of soil she'd selected, so the deer could eat all they wanted to once those kernels grew up into plants. But Mama Nature must've decided she maybe didn't want it there. Or else the squirrels came and stole it.

From time to time Ailana leaned in to offer an extra hand with the bucket, and sometimes Sylvie let her, but mostly she batted her hand away. She liked taking on challenges that made her stronger. And anyway, they could rest whenever deer came by to eat out of it, and Sylvie could set it down for a while and the two human ladies could have a nice human ladies chat.

This was one of those moments. Freddie and Scar Butt chomped away as they watched.

Sylvie had named many of the local fauna.

"I can never figure out if they're brother and sister, or boyfriend and girlfriend," Sylvie said, listening to all that grinding noise they made when they ate.

"Or maybe both," Ailana suggested. "I've wondered that myself."

"Are they allowed to do that?" Sylvie's eyes were wide with wonder, but there was no trace of judgment in there.

"I don't write the rules," Ailana told her, and she laughed. She did that a lot. The deer looked up at her for a moment, but then Freddy went right back to crunching out of the bucket. Scar Butt kept watching them for a couple of minutes, and then gazing around through the woods, and twitching her tail.

"They're probably at least cousins," Ailana mused. "When they keep making families every year, it must get awfully hard keeping that straight."

"Yeah, I guess so," Sylvie said, and then she pondered it for a while.

There was quiet except for the crunching, and a little bit of twittering from birds here and there.

"They must have awfully strong teeth," Sylvie said.

"Guess they must," said her Auntie.

They both stood and listened.

"I found a dead puma the other day," Sylvie mentioned to her after a while.

"Are you sure it was a puma?" Ailana asked. "This far east?"

"Well, it mighta been a groundhog," Sylvie answered only after giving the matter some thought. "I'm not very good at naming things sometimes."

"You did a good job naming Freddy and Scar Butt here."

Sylvie explained, "But that's cause I've gotten to know them for a while. Once we find out their real personalities and what makes them special, people should always have new names. They have earned them.

"Including deer people," she said.

Then she thought some more. She added, "Some just aren't ready yet. Most don't know who they really are. They may not even be trying to find out yet. They're still okay with only being part of the herd."

Some more thought then.

"I meant that for human peoples as well," she clarified. "If they're not ready to stand out and be themselves yet."

"I caught that," her auntie told her.

Sylvie added, "Unless they're bugs. Then it's okay to be only part of the herd."

"That makes sense," Ailana said. "But you make friends with stumblebees and flutterby's," she pointed out, not laughing quite so loudly this time. "And they're not yet fully individualized."

"Indiv…" Sylvie started, but then she changed tracks because that word was too hard. She would have to learn that one later. "Yeah, I guess" she agreed. "But not with the whirleybobbles." She didn't explain what those were, or how that related.

They watched the two deer a while longer.

Then Sylvie asked her auntie, "How come when you sit on the bench I've seen birds come and sit on your head sometimes, but they never sit on mine even when I put seeds on it?"

Ailana suggested, "Maybe it's because you don't hold yours still long enough".

"Yeah, that's probably it," Sylvie said. And she thought about that.

"But I've tried to hold it still for them," she told her auntie.

"Well then," Ailana said, "Maybe it's because my hair looks more like a nest to them when I forget to comb it sometimes."

"Yeah, that's probably it. My hair looks more like clouds when we're having a thunderstorm."

"Hmmm," Ailana said. "I guess it does at that." She reached her hand over and ruffled it up even more. She stopped, and smiled at her young protege. "And birds don't like storms quite as much as they do nests, I guess, huh?"

"I think you have found the solution," Sylvie told her.

Ailana laughed. The little girl didn't understand why, but she knew her auntie did that a lot.

She told Ailana, "But at least I can get deers to eat corn out of a bucket."

"That you can." Then she offered, "I can try to have a little talk with the birds for you, if you like. See if they could try to be a little more sociable."

"Naaah," Sylvie told her, shaking her head. "They'll come if they want to."

They let the deer eat for a while.

"Do you think they've had enough?" Sylvie asked.

"Do you think *they* think they've had enough?"

"Oh, they will almost never think that," Sylvie answered. "They will make themselves sick, and still they won't stop. Some deers are just pigs."

Sylvie visualized what she had said, and laughed. So then her auntie laughed at her. They were making so much noise the deer got tired of all that racket and wandered off.

"Even deer I guess sometimes prefer a certain ambiance with their meals," Ailana observed.

Sylvie looked up at her and studied her face. "I like some of your words," she said.

Then she bent down to pick up her bucket again. It was a little lighter now, but still a struggle.

Benjie liked to imagine there were Indians around him in the woods. Friendly Indians. Or at least their *ghosts*. If he worked at it, maybe he could learn to talk with their Great Spirit like they used to do. When he came across a pile of big stones he liked to pretend it had been a fort long ago. But it had been a friendly cavalry; not the kind that kept hunting the natives down and killing their whole tribes. Why would anybody want to attack friendly Indians?

He also liked to imagine there were other kids around who saw things the same strange ways he did, but he just hadn't met any yet.

He watched a chipmunk sitting straight up, spine erect, not moving, or even seeming to breathe, in a perfect meditation sort of posture. Holding perfectly still on a mossy stump a little ways off. Like a tiny brown-robed monk on a lush green mat, lost in contemplation.

This got the boy picturing natives in sweat lodges, monks in their temples and caves; hidden mystery places almost nobody could find, but with doors left just a little bit open for those who were ready.

The world breathed softly, breezes came and went, the chipmunk sat, and Benjie took it all in. He thought about how the natives had taken Nature as their guide. They had opened their hearts and their lives to the flowing waters, to the skies, and to the animals who came to them. Through ceremony, dancing, drumming, and song, they had spoken to each other; Nature and man. They could sit alone in a field, on a tree stump or a rock, and just listen. To the sunrise and sunset; to starry night skies, and to winds across the prairies.

Back in the real times, he thought, they could listen and probably hear things even when the air had gone silent. Even when their ears told them nothing. Even then, Nature probably murmured to them, shared with them, and they learned. Everything was connected. Everyone knew it, and cared.

He found his favorite fallen tree and sat down on it. It had broken over close to the ground and now rested sideways, like a bench of soft wood. Old times and new times softened, letting go of the edges between them. He was no longer just a rich kid in a rich people's paradise, looking at trees. Times and places melted together until all things since the beginning seemed to rustle, like a vast silent murmur. A motionless stirring. A dance without form.

He felt called into the eeriness and tried to listen even harder.

He sensed something rising up everywhere. Coming at him from over the hills. Much of the world was aching. People were crying. It was as if those old spirits were warning him of a world going terribly wrong. Something bigger than all of mankind would be striking back soon to rebalance things. Many humans would die.

He felt the weeping and the loss. Growing stronger, and louder. Reaching out through every community. It was as if someone was holding a curtain back so his heart could hear that gathering, crushing pain for just a moment. He saw no actual visions; heard no real sobbing; but the anguish he shared with millions of the unseen tore into him. Some darkness had been eating through much of humankind, leaving a trail of overwhelming anxiety. And the worst of it hadn't even hit yet.

Soon, the world would have to strike back.

People everywhere would be forced into hiding. They'd feel terribly alone. Have to let go of everything they'd learned to rely on. Nothing would make sense anymore. A few special souls were already being prepared to help them find their ways out of it. To seed hope through this coming rain of ashes. There was much work to be done.

But all of this was only a feeling, his more logical side tried to tell him. It wasn't like someone was actually standing there showing him movies from the future. Probably just his imagination acting up again because he'd been reading about Nostradamus predicting Hitler and atom bombs hundreds of years ago, and now Benjie wanted to find something dark to warn the world about himself. Because that would make him special; not just some dumb little nobody kid. He was probably just making this up. At most, these were only vague hints and maybes. Just his imagination acting up again was all.

But it felt so real it terrified him. Like he really was being warned.

Yeah, but so did nightmares feel real, he argued back. Nothing was scarier than nightmares, and they never came true.

He tried hard to not believe. He wanted to turn away, and shut down, but some part of him just couldn't stop listening. He couldn't help but feel bad for all those people in pain.

He got up and started pacing. Slapping at trees and kicking rocks to blow off pressure. Anything to distract him from what he didn't want to feel, and wouldn't let himself believe.

Light and shadows shifted. He thought he saw a path opening before him through the woods. He wanted to follow it, but as always, he hesitated. He had always been this way. Always held himself back.

He hated himself for that.

And so then, in that next instant, those shadows shifted again. Nothing there but trees and undergrowth.

The light, the path, and the invitation had been withdrawn.

"Our civilization is being sacrificed for the opportunity of a very small number of people to continue making enormous amounts of money."
—Greta Thunberg

Chapter Two

Laurence Beaufort had an autistic child.

Or at least that was all his expensive hired "experts" could think to call the boy. No more than a convenient catch-all diagnosis they were pinning on everyone these days. No one really knew. All they could do was analyze their data, but did they see what made him so special? Could they see him as more than just one of their files, someone to probe and talk over with their colleagues, cram into their analytical cages, tally up similarities, average him out with others of his "type", throw some numbers around, then maybe they could put a name to his syndrome? Prove for themselves that he had after all been just like so many others. We all have to be labeled. We need to fit in somewhere, or their whole pompous methodology comes apart.

But what if he didn't? What if there was no category that could hold him? What if there was something very special about him; something outside their precious stereotypes? What if there was more to him than just their all-seeing, formulaic constructs?

There had to be other kids out there they couldn't squeeze into their pigeonholes, but who weren't necessarily pathological just because they were different. Maybe they weren't like other kids, but so what? It shouldn't be all about proving their theorems. This was a human soul they were trying to cut all the corners off of. Trying to cram into one of their neat little packages. How does that help Madison? They could keep ramming, and cramming, and prodding all they want to, and still not figure him out. Real people can be damned inconvenient when they refuse to be categorized. His son was not just someone else's damned pigeonhole.

But even as he sat there, stewing over his desk at work where he had other matters he should have been attending to, Beaufort knew he was being unfair. He was over-reacting. They had always been nice to Madison. They treated him gently and with respect. They had suggested to Laurence and his wife that maybe their boy just found too many things over-stimulating to the point where he'd had to pull away, not having the words or means to talk to them about it. They had assured them this sort of behavior wasn't unusual these days. That more and more children were being born with exceptional sensitivity. But even knowing that didn't solve anything. He felt so shut out of his son's life.

Beaufort sat in his executive offices suite on the top floor of corporate headquarters, but felt like he might as well have been unemployed and uneducated for all the help he could offer his child. He could think of himself as a sort of a corporate negotiator who needed to stay calm, clear, and more or less objective, but he couldn't play neutral on this one. A child's life was too important. He needed to know what it was that poor Maddie held dear in his heart, and find some ways to share that with him. Not leave the boy hanging out there, isolated, and alone.

Beaufort twisted his coffee mug around and around in its tight little circle. It grew cold, but he didn't call for another. He stared at the bronze plaque on his desk but didn't read it.

Madison would be turning nine soon. A boy should have at least one friend by that age. Someone who understood him. Some other little boy who maybe didn't himself spend so much time staring at things that weren't there, but could at least understand why Madison chose to. Staring like he was actually seeing something. Like there was something or someone actually there. Like he was almost expecting those bare, empty walls in his room to start speaking.

In a suburb just a little ways outside the city, storm troopers had crashed into the offices of one of his subsidiaries. "One little call," a thug was telling an accountant he had trapped up against her own desk. "We'd be loading your kids onto trucks just … like … that!" He snapped his fingers right in her face. She jumped in terror. Her face went gray. He might as well have been pulling a trigger. He was going to kill them.

"Next time you look under your bed, I'll be there."

He paused to let that wreak its havoc inside her. Her mind wept with stories from the holocaust. Jewish ancestors had warned her, "Such evil never dies. It is only hiding, and waiting." And now there were racists in the White House. Nazi's and KKK everywhere. How can hearts carry such twisted and horrifying ugliness without tearing themselves apart? She couldn't understand. This couldn't be real.

He told her, "The boxcars are waiting. Only need to pick who to fill 'em with."

She wept from the relentless depravity. Her forebears had been starved, crippled, and burned alive. Whole families, with babies and old people, buried by the thousands in unmarked pits they'd had to dig for themselves. Soldiers all over Europe had fought, bled, and died to drive these devils back down to Hell, and that should have been the end of it. This can't be happening again. It can't be real. Tears ran with saliva down her face, staining her white lacy blouse. She gasped from pain and disbelief. But this is America! Twenty-first century. This can't be real.

She felt trapped. Trembling. A cornered little sparrow with a broken wing that could only flap and slam itself around as that horrible cat toyed with it, knowing it could never escape.

They'd charged in and suddenly were everywhere. Snarling, threatening, flipping papers just to intimidate those poor workers who had so carefully organized and stacked them. Armed with mean-looking weapons, proudly on display in shiny black belts with ammo clips, tasers, handcuffs, knives, and cans of something that could probably eat your face off for all anyone knew.

Someone in a side office wailed.

"I was born here. My ancestors and their ancestors were born here," an office worker told one of the intruders.

"Don't mean we have to let you stay," that invader shot back.

He pulled out his key chain and toyed with it in front of her face. It was shaped like a noose.

Workers didn't dare look around at each other. These were their friends. Nice people, good people, people they'd had over to their homes for quiet evenings. Weeping, blubbering; begging for their lives and their children's lives. Saying and doing things they would never want anyone to see.

Why them? They were just your usual, nothing special, desk jockeys for some nondescript company in a not very interesting part of everyday America. Working their boring jobs for a company that most of the time no one paid much attention to. Why would some militaristic branch of their own government come storming in all over *them* like this? How could that even be legal? The world had gone mad.

In High Towers Building, Beaufort could feel the stress in his receptionist's voice. She was normally warm, but professional. Unflappable under the most challenging situations. Now she struggled to hold back her panic.

"It's… It's… It sounds like they're tearing the place apart, Sir. Threatening to haul people out to the cages. Black bagging them, or threatening to. I could hear them screaming. People sobbing. Pleading. I could hear it. These poor people have nobody."

A crisis team was assembled in Exec Boardroom 3. Beaufort headed there as his secretary cleared his schedule.

Details were few. Some sort of disruption or takeover on twelfth floor of Peterby's. Mostly just quick, broken messages and conjecture. Phones were down. Dropped connections. Like one of those armed, middle-of-the-night raids; barricading streets, everybody hitting at once.

Around the table, each exec was trying to throw in what they'd heard. All of it together didn't amount to much.

"Rumors are, kids are somehow involved. Children held hostage. We aren't putting much juice into that one since there shouldn't have been any children onsite, but we can't rule anything out. It might have been *Bring your child to work day*, or something. They wouldn't have had to clear that with us."

"Might be nothing we can do but have engineers check connections and wait until somebody knows something. But on the other hand…"

"Sounds Federal."

"Sounds White House," one suggested. "They don't clear their ugly, illegal shit with Congress anymore."

Beaufort couldn't push past the fact that children were being tossed so casually into this hubbub of theories. Whatever else may or may not be holding water here, it seemed at least possible that young, helpless children were in danger.

He couldn't shake the horror, the sheer ugliness of that. He might have missed some of their other theories because he'd dug in right there. That had hit him very personally. He'd lost all professional objectivity even as he kept telling himself he had damned well better get it back. Get a hold of himself.

But he couldn't. He couldn't let that go.

He heard himself telling them, "I'll take this."

"You'll what?"

"I'll go. I'll head over there. Check it out for myself."

They stared at him from around the table but no one spoke.

"The manager is a very old friend," he explained. "I owe him." Which was true, but what he was really thinking was that he'd have wanted someone going to bat for his own kid.

In this crazy, goddamned, going-all-to-shit world, someone had to stand up for something.

They'd slammed in like the FBI busting doors to grab terrorists they'd rather kill than take alive.

Then they'd scattered, filling the air with the stench of their overpowering presence. Towering over ordinary citizens like military elite, but smashing through like common back alley street thugs. Like snapping, slobbering dobermans broken through the gate.

A few were waving blackjacks or clubs around; slamming desks, threatening facial bones, but not yet making disfiguring contact.

No one flashed credentials or gave their names. It all seemed so much more horrific that way. Not knowing who was doing this to these poor innocents, or why.

The head thug had called out, "Terrorist Patrol" when they'd first exploded in. Or it might have been "Border Patrol." Those who'd heard even that much in that first flare of violence wouldn't agree on much later. And besides, they were hundreds of miles from any kind of a border. Nothing made sense here. Others in the gang were saying "Immigration" or "Homeland Security." Even they didn't seem to know whom they worked for.

Like wranglers charging into a herd, they culled out the weakest to break first. One agent headed for the cubicle of a mousy old lady. Another zeroed in on a guy standing at a filing cabinet who could be easily backed into a corner.

Another went straight for a lady with photos of her children and grandkids splayed lovingly across her desktop. He had the same proud military haircut as the others, but had let it go greasy since his army days. He stormed up on the lady from behind. She had heard them smash their ways in; everyone had flinched from that racket; but now she jumped when his arm shot past her head. He grabbed up a picture of her thin, pale-skinned grandchild, Lee Anne.

The towering beast leaned into her, penning her in as he went for the photo. She couldn't back out of his way, couldn't get up, couldn't maneuver; he had her trapped. She had to twist her neck at a painful angle just to see him, and even then could barely make out his features. She imagined way too much from his voice. Felt his foul breath on her face.

He snatched up that picture of innocence, clutching it close like he was getting ready to lick it. He held it so hard; such a long, unnerving time. She felt herself coming apart, but said nothing. She sat rigid, face contorted, eyes fighting for control, to not let him see her sheer terror.

"This kid's gonna be a real hottie!" he told her.

She spoke, trying to reign herself in; knowing she was treading deadly ground.

"May I help you?" was all she dared say. She'd have to select each word with excruciating care.

"Who's this little beauty?" he asked. It was clear he hadn't showered in a while, and had long been a heavy-duty smoker and drinker. He held the photo close to his face, his hands trembling as he leered at it. He started sniffing it.

Lee Anne had barely been five when that had been taken. Her grandmother wanted to snatch it away from him so badly it took everything she had in her to hold back. She wanted to grab it away; grab back those last stolen minutes and any ugly, scarring memories that could grow out of them; but she could only sit there trembling.

His eyes; those dark and horrible eyes as he ogled the child; that savage, dripping lust.

He stared hard at the photo; his hands flexing, releasing, crawling all over it. Sweating heavily; his eyes glazing.

That poor child's grandmother sat jammed against the edge of her desk. Like a mummy wrapped in layer after layer of binding. Embalmed while still alive. Wanting to cry out, but crammed in too tightly; sealed up, and running out of air.

Across the room from her, two agents had descended on an accountant whose name tag read, Buonosiglio.

"That's a pretty foreign-sounding name," they were prodding her. "What's that? Mexican? Muslim maybe? You got papers?"

That slender fellow they had penned in behind the cabinets was being interrogated because of his neatness and wardrobe.

"Pretty fancy cuff links you got there," one of them told the frail and whimpering little man. "That's the sort of thing a homo wears, ain't it?"

"We can call the vans in right now," another was saying. "Whole fleet of 'em. We'd have you and your kids all boxcarred and shipped out by sundown. No one know where we send 'em. Haul off every fuckin' kid at their whole fuckin' schools if we wanna."

"What school you say they go to?"

Massed bedlam. The air lay thick with helplessness and distress. With pure, dripping evil.

"Just gotta snap my fingers," one said. "And they're gone."

"You have three children?" another asked. "They all full citizens? Can you prove it? With a name like yours, law says regular Americans have a right to protect themselves from dangerous foreign influences. Gotta keep America safe. Make it great again."

"Romero?" they heard men asking. "Busemi?" "That's kind of a foreigner name, don't ya think? You got yourself a little mosque in your neighborhood, do ya? You from South of the border? Got a little mixed blood in your family, I bet."

"Got any kids?"

It was that last part kept slamming home hardest. Foul, sweating brutes tossing it out so casually. Like ordering treats at some back alley dive. Like it was nothing. It came out so twisted. Seeping like a swollen red pustule. Like someone on *Criminal Minds* making sausages, and you'd loved the college girl he was making them out of.

"Bodnachek?" they'd taunt. "What kind of a name is Bodnachek? I can't even say that."

Workers' faces blanched or turned red. Some tightened in fear, all blood leaving them, while others swelled to crimson from suppression of their own hatred and rage. Forced to swallow what they could not tolerate, but dared not give voice to.

They wanted to run, but there'd be no place to hide. Some hid their fists under their desks; or dug their fingernails into their own legs. Standing up for their rights could get their whole families thrown into cages. Sent off to countries where they might not survive interrogation. Sold for the sickening carnal delight of ugly, evil, horrible men. Their imaginations darted wildly through horrifying scenarios. They locked their jaws tight and said nothing.

How had America fallen so far?

"Wanetka? You Injun? Sounds Injun to me. Go back to your tribe. I can help you with that." He laughed hard until she choked from the fumes of his cheap cigarettes.

And then they always kept asking, "You got any kids?"

One slime in particular smelled like he was rotting inside. He had a military-style hat and a red swollen face. Huge shoulders like he'd spent much of his lifetime in gyms, even as his gut showed he'd lost just as many hours in bars.

The whole place now smelled rancid and sweaty. Someone had eaten old fish after it had turned. Someone hadn't changed his underwear in a while. The room had gone rank and could never be cleansed now.

At least not from their minds.

From their guts.

Future generations; children and grandchildren; would carry the stench of this one fetid moment. Even if never mentioned again, this could never be scrubbed out of the family.

The floor beneath them, the world around them, was giving way. Sinking irretrievably into morass. They felt even their bones cringing to grit as the dark, putrid cancer of these horrible creatures ate through them. It hung, heaving and oozing in the air; twisted in the pits of their bowels. Even the most kind, gentle, and forgiving of them felt they were rotting inside.

That utter and degrading futility. That unshakable knowing that all innocence was lost. Everything they'd cared about had been stolen from them. Any sweet and gentle connection they'd ever had with anyone they loved, dragged through disgust into horrors they could never leave behind. Each and every one of them plunged so deeply and irretrievably into a sickening sense of unworthiness. They could do nothing to stand up for their families. Before they could even get home today; *if* they ever got home again; their beloved children and grandchildren could be gone.

Laurence Beaufort stopped to settle himself in the entry hall. He was angry. He was scared. But it would do no good to show the other side any of that. He could handle this.

He took a few calm, clearing breaths. He smoothed his tie, then his jacket. Basically though, he just stood there. He had fumed all the way over, venting what he could quietly as his driver had taken the quickest route. He had to bring himself under control. A luxury these poor office workers hadn't been allowed.

But now he was here. Anything he'd been wanting to say and do to these guys would have to be set aside for reality.

He barely rapped on the door of the makeshift command post Ralph Santorio had set up on ground floor. He rushed in, nodding a blank and distant smile at the secretary, barely noting five or six others in her room.

"Speak to me," Beaufort told Santorio. "Done all the usuals, I suppose. Called the cops, heard their lame excuses, got the run around."

"Right. All your usuals checked and double checked. Building security is of course nowhere to be found."

"Okay. We can deal with them later. Sudden flu or something, I suppose." Beaufort made no real effort to hide the sneer.

"Or something," Santorio agreed, nodding. He and Beaufort had known each other long enough to sidestep pretenses and formalities. No need to pull punches when it was just the two them in that quickly emptied room. "I'll handle that. These pussies won't be working anywhere for a while."

"Sure they will," Laurence snapped back. "President'll probably give them medals."

"Right."

"So, what's next?" Laurence asked.

"Well, I figure they want something. They haven't hauled anyone out of there yet. Don't seem to be looking for anyone in particular. Haven't done their homework enough to even agree on what branch of the bureaucracy sent them, or how many kids each clerk has. Seems to me they just came storming in here to make a whole lot of racket and draw attention to themselves.

"Or at least that's how I read it, anyhow. So maybe what they *claim* to be here for isn't really much of a clue.

"But this also doesn't appear to be random," he said. "They came here for something.

"It's just that so far they haven't tipped their hat on just what that might be."

"So, some of what they've been saying sounds to you like it's been ringing a little hollow?" Beaufort asked. "You think they might settle for something else?"

"Just a guess," Santorio told him. "Border Patrol's always got some sort of angle. Buncha cretin, lowlife scum open to any kind of filth they can turn a little profit from. Ain't doin' what they do for pride of duty, and God bless America."

"Right." Beaufort considered what that might suggest.

"So," Santorio started in again. "I figure either they really do have the hots for kids-in-cages like a lot of their buddies; that is always a possibility with these bastards; or… Or, they maybe think they see some way to make a little side cash. Maybe shake down some parents.

"Or, they are trying to shine for The Boss is another possibility. Show off for the capo. Maybe get a job higher up.

"If we can figure out what they're really up to; what's the real reason they come blasting in on us like that…

"All that high drama; dialogue lines straight outa Scary Nazi's Playbook…" Santorio had to pause as he thought more of that through.

"They have obviously been trying to put the fear of God in us," he said. "Until they figure we can't possibly say no.

"None of us. Even those't don't have kids. Figure we gotta give 'em what they want, no matter what.

"They're up to something. They want something. It might be the kids, and it might just not be."

"Or…" Beaufort started off on a thought, but never finished it.

"Or?" Santorio asked.

"Or maybe this isn't their doing. Maybe this isn't about what *they* want at all.

"Maybe this comes from the top."

"Shit!" Santorio said. "And in his fucked up tiny head, he always has to get everything he wants."

"Yeah," Beaufort agreed. "But you're the one who's been out here getting bullied. I'm just throwing ideas around. I want to know how you see things."

"Thanks, Laur. I appreciate that."

"Sure.

"So, just between us, what's your real hit on this mess?" Beaufort asked. "No holds barred. Tell me what your heart says."

"I'm afraid my heart is saying you might've nailed it. It makes a lot of sense when you think about it. Taken man for man, these guys are mainly just bullies. Common street thugs easy to wind up and push at anyone you tell 'em's the enemy. Loudmouth cattle. Point them at some easy marks; a bunch of nobody office workers who're gonna piss themselves before standing up to the likes of them; and…"

"So, what we could do is just stand up to them and see where that gets us," Beaufort suggested, "But that wouldn't help much if they're only following orders."

"Right," Santorio told him. "Which leaves us nowhere."

"Yeah," Beaufort said. "But if we can figure out who they might be trying to impress, it could maybe at least give us a shot at backing a few of them down anyway. Set them back on their heels for a moment. Get them thinking they're not handling this well, and the don's gonna be pissed. Something like that.

"But then what? We maybe buy ourselves a moment, but then what do we do with it? How do we take advantage of that?

"If we can even manage to pull that much off in the first place."

"Which is one might big *if*. No disrespect intended."

"No, that's fine. But we also can't be just standing around down here for the next couple of hours weighing all the pros and cons Those poor people are up there pissing their pants, thinking nobody's coming to help them.

"We have to move."

"Yeah," Santorio agreed. "Thanks for coming."

"Sure."

Santorio told Beaufort, "I think we both know who their God is. Up there calling himself The Second Coming and being slobbered on by all them fundamentalist numbskulls."

"Yeah. We probably have that much anyway."

They took only a short while longer to think through what they could, but then Beaufort rode the elevator up alone.

He stepped off the lift and squared himself again best he could. He was just about to go pushing through those steaming gates into Hell.

He took a moment to look around. To establish himself, at least in his own mind, as someone who hadn't already lost hope.

He was a corporate force. He had earned it. He'd fought his way up through better men, and tougher men, than these guys. Laurence Beaufort was someone they had every reason to respect, and someone they would just have to deal with.

If only he could believe that in his own heart. What would they see in his eyes in those first crucial moments? Someone already yielding? Or that powerful corporate exec who'd helped build and crush empires?

But he wasn't dealing with corporate raiders this time. Just unpolished street thugs. With the full backing of their emperor and god, and no reason to back down. He had nothing to threaten them with.

It would do no good to just stand there. He didn't dare let the full impact of what he was up against haul him under.

He made his move.

He stepped into orchestrated chaos. Sheer and intentional mayhem. Tension hung thick and wretched in the air. An inaudible screeching, barely held in, ready to break.

Looking around to assess the situation, he saw the damage already done. In the eyes of innocents he saw deep and lasting crippling of their spirit.

One of the men kept rubbing his hand against the grip of his holstered, government issue pistol like he was making a wish on a lamp. His eyes afire with lust. But for what? Domination? Some of these secretaries in tight blouses or short skirts? For what he could do to their kids?

"Silverberg?" he was asking one of the women at one of the desks as he looked around, ogling others. "You a Jew? You marry one? Got any Jew kids?"

Everywhere Beaufort looked, ordinary people who had only been doing their jobs were cowering, many of them broken. And these men were feasting on it.

The gang leader appeared to recognize him, stepping forward as though Beaufort had been expected. This rattled him even worse. If he'd been hoping for the element of surprise, that had just been yanked out of his hands.

He tried pulling himself together, stood tall, and commanded, "Who's in charge here?"

"That'd be me," came the instant response. Beaufort knew any kind of hesitation was a loss in a battle for one-upmanship. But there was more to this guy's voice, to the thrust of his jaw, to his attitude, than just a chess player making his move. This street thug was showing him who was really the boss. Setting terms before they'd even introduced themselves. Getting his hands on an executive might have been the plan all along. And Beaufort had just thrown himself into their trap. He had made their move for them.

"Mr. Beaufort," the man said, "We've been waiting."

Any time he'd spent girding himself scurried off into hiding. The ball was immediately in this other guy's court, and he was running with it before Laurence could recover his balance. This guy knew his name.

He didn't offer his own. He didn't extend his hand. He commanded. "Follow me. They cleared me a room for our talk."

Had they chased someone out of it? Had someone been hurt on account of him? Dark images burrowed through Beaufort's mind.

The leader of this gang of Federal marauders led the way. Not even looking behind him to see if this fancy guy in a tailored suit was following.

He had to.

They both knew who was in charge.

It was probably forty-five minutes before they came out again. Thug leader had taken his time breaking Mr. Fancypants down, and enjoying every moment of it. Which also gave his men plenty of time to play with their own prey outside the shuttered conference room windows where Laurence could worry, and imagine the worst, but couldn't see.

Boss thug knew this would be screwing with the head of Mr. Big Guy Executive here. He'd planned it this way.

He ultimately got what he'd come for. There had never been any doubt about that.

Beaufort told him they'd double their contributions to the President's re-election campaign. "Off the books. Where the tax guys don't need to know about it." Said they'd, "Spread some cash around at that great golden throne of his down in Florida."

But only after he'd had his fun and was good and ready to stop batting his prey around, did the thug call negotiations completed. He walked out and told his men, "Let's go, boys. We're done here. We have reached an agreement."

"But what about the merchandise?" one greasy creep all but whined. He was still clutching that pink-framed photo of a tiny child named Lee Anne to his chest.

"We'll come back for it," his boss told him.

"Don't," Beaufort commanded the guy holding the picture. He'd pulled as much firmness into his voice as he could still muster.

But who could fight Federal thugs anymore, he thought? Those days of checks and balances were over. The world had gone mad.

The gang boss looked Beaufort right in the eyes. Held it as he let Beaufort squirm. He stood there, locked on target as he told his cringe-worthy subordinate, "Bring the picture."

Beaufort wanted to scrub his whole body with raw sand. He wanted to burn his clothes, and move in with a therapist. He stayed in his car a long time before heading back up to his office. Couldn't talk himself into heading home until well after midnight. He didn't want to be seen. By anybody. Most especially his family. He didn't deserve them.

Everything had all turned so ugly. The world could never be made right again.

He didn't tell his wife what had happened. About any of the horrific evil of that day. About those vile, disgusting creatures. How he'd just buckled. Given them everything they'd wanted.

He didn't want Danni to even suspect what he felt crawling around in him. Like some turgid, foul stench, rotting his insides.

Eating away at him.

Sometimes telling what was real from what he was only making up was like watching a rabbit in the undergrowth. Just when he thought he was getting a good look at it, the truth would find a better place to hide.

Chapter Three

Benjie's mom was like that White Rabbit in Alice in Wonderland, but with a Fitbit, and spreadsheets. She was a relentless organizer and planner. Her closest friends appreciated her detailed preparations, and let chunks of their own lives fall into place around Reenie's calculations and calendars. They liked stopping by for visits or inviting her out to tea, but would let her orchestrate the dance of that with careful timing and precision.

She always remembered the servants, keeping track of their families and anniversaries, buying them presents from high end stores. Maybe it was the birthday of one of the granddaughters of one of the maids. Or maybe she just happened to come across a scarf with pink frogs on it and remembered one of the cooks telling her she had a niece who loved frogs and unusual scarves. So Irene would just have to buy one for her. She was a sweetheart. A very efficient sweetheart with tightly constrained manners.

Servants liked to cluck fondly amongst themselves (often right in front of her) that she did have her ways. She maintained that there was a precise order in which things must be done, and a clear and consistent way to go about it. English people had their traditions, she would insist, and a thing had always to be done in a certain manner.

Folks loved her for that quirkiness, felt free to make sport of it, and she could laugh along with them when they did. This too was part of the woman's odd charm. Sometimes, with a wink and a smile to little Benjamin; just a little joke between friendly conspirators; one of the servants would try something just a little outside the established way of things. She might add the milk to "herself's tea" *before* the teabag, rather than after. Or stir it thirteen times rather than twelve. "Oh my, it must never be thirteen. This is clearly bad fortune. It has never been thirteen. We English have our rules you know. We have our traditions."

As for Benjie's dad, Frank Squirrelmann was a corporate CEO, and a force not to be reckoned with casually. At least not in boardrooms. At home he tried to let some of that go. He did his best to smile and chat with his family. He loved his young son, and his British Lady Irene; the queen of his household. He just had to love them through a fog of distraction.

Everyone loved Reenie Squirrelmann, though she gave the servants much to talk about. Frank they respected, but tried to stay out of his way. Probably one of the main reasons little Benjie was starting to seek solace out in those thin stretches of woods behind their estate was to take a breather from the often unspoken dynamics of this rather strange home. He could find his own quiet pace in the slow rhythms and unforced, natural flow of Nature in its essence. As he grew older he also seemed to be growing more sensitive. And as he grew more sensitive he liked spending more time in the woods.

Perhaps somewhat surprisingly, his mum was all for it. She thought it healthy for a young man to get outside and scruff himself up a bit. Bring a few germs in from the lawn. It helped build his immune system. Benjie, being how he was though, wasn't drawn to rolling around in the mud and rough housing with the other kids. He didn't understand scrapping for turf or dominance on a ball field. Why attack each other over some silly ball? Just let the other team have it. You can always go out and buy yourself another one. Why fight over stuff? But despite their different ways, he and his mum reached a kind of agreement when he went off to sit among the trees quietly by himself for a while. And maybe even come home with a splinter.

They all three of them grew closer as a family when they could find a little time to rent a cabin in the mountains. One so remote, his dad liked to say, that "even bears couldn't find it."

This had to be carefully thought through and planned out of course, which called upon the talents of the mum. "The Mistress of all She Prepays", as Frank liked to call her. She really came into her own from the instant the decision to head for the mountains had been made, and her husband's schedule cleared. She took detailed control right up through those first hours of their arrival. She guided them as groceries and supplies were arranged on their appropriate shelves, all lists checked, and maybe fires and lamps lit. This was all a part of settling in as a family, she liked to remind them. A man, a woman, and their little boy in a world far away from board meetings, tea socials, and restaurant reservations.

This empty cabin in the middle of nowhere was now a home again, and there they were, all together. At their beloved *La Maison Sans*. The home without … (and pretty much anything could fill in that blank). The home without city plumbing. Drawing their own water from a well, and who knows where their sewage went? With no pizza delivery or take-out foods of any kind. A home without even much of a town nearby, and quite clearly no fine restaurants or clever little bistros. *La Maison Sans*. Their sweet home without.

But here, the air was fresher. The breaths they took were deeper and more rewarding. They learned which direction was east and which was west, taking the sunrise and sunset inside them. "Ahhh; this is how to do it", the dad often said, usually when he didn't seem to be doing much of anything.

In *La Maison Sans*, life flowed gently.

Little Benjie could spend hours quietly but intently sorting through the different fragrances. Leafy greens. Mountain laurels in bloom. Pine sap and fallen needles. Noticing how each had its own texture. Some smells lifted gently and softly over others. Pines bit in sharply and hung on. More subtle aromas floated through, hardly noticed, and were gone, while others came in heavy, and sank. Some were smooth, and rich; almost milky; but others were pungent and harder to ignore. Some stayed with you a while, while others passed quickly.

And yet, all in all, they blended. Until, if you didn't really think about it, you could almost believe there was only one "smell of the forest" as his dad liked to call it. One of his father's favorite parts of visiting this cabin in the middle of nowhere was to "get me some of that smell of the forest!"

Benjie was wandering among the trees one day; pinching leaves, touching wood, and smelling smells. Thinking without really knowing he was thinking. The forest can do that to a fella. As he breathed, fully and richly, he raised his arms high and turned his face toward what little jabs of sunlight filtered through. He felt like he was breathing in the golden light itself.

The world was full, it was meaningful, and it was alive.

His rich imagination kept adding more details. He could almost hear chanting through the flickering shadows. Men working magic who knew the secrets of the universe. Spirits lived and moved among the trees, and in the rivers. Spirits who could walk with you and teach you things. He heard a voice telling him, "This was a time and a place not so very long ago or far away as you might think."

That next breeze then carried a hint of burning sage.

Ahhh—there was nothing like the smell of early morning coffee in the forest, Frank thought. The sun wasn't up yet. The world was quiet, but alive. Out here, far beyond that strangling bustle of the cities, he could feel birds and creatures awakening. Holding their silence as though in reverence. All the land was still, and yet it wasn't. Everything everywhere gathered in silent awe of itself, and nothing moved.

If there was a God, he thought, opening to a level of veneration he'd rarely known; if there was a God, He lived here.

Francis Jerome Squirrelmann; adviser to powerful corporations; Irene's husband, and little Benjie's dad; held silent and rapt in that moment. A man notorious for never standing still; who let no grass grow under his feet before the next deal was made, the next meeting confirmed; that next company built or torn asunder; now he held his hot mug high before his face with both hands, but made no move to sip from it.

The world in that moment was complete as it was.

Steam rose up from his java, intermingling with early morning mists. Wisps of fog passing by; lifting and settling through the woods. Lingering everywhere so beautifully just beyond these porch screens. The fragrance of fresh greens intertwined. The rich, delicate, inviting aroma of his freshly ground and brewed Jamaican Blue Mountain with just a touch of Sumatran. He'd ordered the beans just for this trip. It was his special mountain brew. He never drank it in the city. He needed it here to shake everything else loose. To leave all that chaos behind.

Standing on well-weathered floorboards, he opened his heart to the forest; inhaling full into his soul. Deep tears of gratitude, of release, formed in his eyes, blended with early day fog.

In a world no man could ever truly own, he struggled to just be with that gently for a moment. Enjoying Nature so wild, so natural, so free. That special essence he could never write into a contract and small print the life out of. He worked hard to let the pleasures of freedom come alive in him. To lose himself inside them for a while. Break free of all his spread sheets, analyses and projections; all those quantifiable projects in all those flashy but sterile offices and boardrooms he'd so meticulously arranged to schedule himself out of for at least these few weeks. To just *be* for a while. To just breathe.

But that stress that followed him everywhere just would not release. It crawled through him like snakes, rising up to strike. Even when he thought he had everything under control, he could feel it writhing in there. Crunching through his nerves. Chafing at him. Background chatter he could not ignore. Hitting him in spasms, tearing everything else loose. His more hard-driving persona couldn't relax even here. Conferences, decisions, pressures held tight their grip on him. Anxieties he could never completely leave behind and be done with. Not even here.

Frank took tighter hold of his hot, green, earthenware mug. Fought to chase everything but this soft, unseen stirring out of his heart and his mind. Floating aromas of mountain laurels and evergreens whispered, and he tried so hard to hear them.

He was out on a porch in the forest. Far, far away from his offices. Everything was in competent hands; things would be handled; he could let go. All he had to do for now was just enjoy this rich coffee. Hang out with the quiet. How hard could that be?

The steam from his early morning java rose up through the air. Through his nostrils. Through his heart. Deep, soothing heat. Seeping though his palms. He held his huge mug; taking everything in; all of it. He held on to that fresh wilderness for just as long as he could manage; and the heart of the forest was everywhere.

The peace of the woods drifted by, languorous, and friendly.

He would try for a while, but then lose it again. He'd thrill to this long, enticing, wonderful taste of peace, but then get dragged right back into the office.

He could tell himself he'd at least tasted it for this one moment anyway. And each time, when he reached the point where he finally just had to give in, when he just couldn't wrench all that stress out of his heart for one moment longer, he'd at least know he'd had that for a little while. For a few minutes anyway. He would take what he could when he could wrestle it loose.

Eventually though, he had to quit trying.

He released several sighs and gave in. For a few moments he had felt cleansed and pure. But through that last sigh, he yielded to exasperation. The office had won another round.

Faking a smile, he headed back inside. Carrying his cup and his stress back into the cabin, he passed a clock that tried to tell him he'd been out there for over an hour. His coffee had gone cold while he'd barely noticed.

He found his wife scurrying around, checking closets and shelves she'd stocked herself. It seemed to be getting her nowhere.

Frank opened his arms to her. They melted together into a wondrous soft hug.

"Welcome to *La Maison Sans*," she told him. "Where you can't find a thing you've been looking for."

"But where you learn things you're not sure you want to," he added.

They held in that moment a long while, cherishing that freshness between them.

The battle continued between Francis Jerome Squirrelmann, corporate terror; and Frank, the loving husband and dad. Less traumatic perhaps were those awkward moments of disconnect between Reenie in a rustic mountain cabin, and those inflexible British traditions of hers that did not always work so well here. Benjie felt like he was being sifted through other times, when there had still been magic.

This vacation home had been designed to house extra guests, or be shared by several families. There was a hide-away bar in one of the cabinets. Fold-up chairs in the closets. The sofa could pull out to sleep two more people with relative comfort if they weren't excessively large. One of the guest rooms had a bunk just big enough for children, and one had a trundle bed. The trundle had an extra mattress on springs that rolled out from underneath it. Offered a choice, Benjie started sleeping on the roll-out. He said he liked lying close to the earth.

All of this naturally set the wife to planning out whom they could entertain there, and for how many days, while Mr. Squirrelmann was more of a mind to dwell on those he was glad he wouldn't be seeing for a while. Bj was more like his father on this one.

But for as long as it was still just the three of them, they bonded like never before. They learned to play, and grew lighter in spirit toward each other.

They were sitting around the dining room table one evening when young master Benjamin started wrinkling up his nose. Out here in the wild; where pretty much any kind of animal could have been doing his business somewhere nearby; he could have been smelling just about anything. Maybe a skunk had been startled outside an open window. Perhaps some large animal had been marking his territory. Some pungent nighttime plant might have released. But whatever it was, Frank leaned in toward his son and told him, "Right. I was thinking I smelled the same thing."

He paused for a moment.

And then, completely out of character, he added, "Somebody cut one!"

Well, this of course set the nine-year-old off into bursts and sputters of laughter as only a good fart joke told in mixed company could.

He hadn't known he could snort, but apparently he could, and he did, and then his dad started making these really shocked and offended faces at him, acting like he was wiping the boy's spit off Dad's shoulder every time he did it. Which only made him snort more, trying to suppress it. And then that made him laugh harder still, out of embarrassment, thinking he might actually have spat on his father.

And soon, he was helpless. He had never laughed that hard before, and wasn't sure he liked it.

His mom and dad watched; in both surprise, and parental adoration; as their son broke free of that rigid self-discipline he'd been born with. They'd always thought him too hard on himself. That he needn't be so brooding and serious all the time. But now this was carrying it all to the opposite extreme.

Benjie had never really thought of himself that way. Not really. He just had important matters to think about. You were in this world for some reason. You had responsibilities. He didn't see these as unusually deep and serious thoughts for such a small boy. It was just how things were.

But now here he was, guffawing and spitting all over his father. He collapsed onto the table, terribly embarrassed, helpless in laughter, fighting to get himself under control.

His parents just sat there, thrilled that he couldn't.

They were doing everything they could to make it worse.

Just as he was finally starting to calm down a little, wrestle control back to his more disciplined and serious side, his dad leaned in again.

But then he didn't say anything.

He just waited. Letting anticipation build.

His son studied him eye-to-eye. He waited, but his dad wasn't saying anything. They just sat there. It built up.

Benjie snorted again.

Even Irene started sputtering, which didn't help Benjie at all.

Father and son stared into each other's eyes.

Frank opened his mouth to say something, but then just stopped.

His son watched his mouth. Studied his eyes. Watched his mouth again. Spluttered a little. He waited.

He started to spit. Even with his mouth tightly sealed—or so at least he had thought. He felt another laugh start bubbling up from his belly, but tried to hold back. The added pressure only made it louder and messier when it finally broke free. He wasn't even laughing at the fart joke anymore. Something else had taken over. He couldn't stop.

His dad finally spoke.

He told his boy, "Yup. Somebody definitely farted."

Benjie bit his own lip. He only spat just a little at first, as he fought against everything to hold the rest of it back.

A splutter broke loose. With a little more spit.

His dad was still leaned in really close to him.

He told his boy, "And I think it was your mom."

Benjie exploded.

Then his mum, with all her proper mannerisms and crisp British enunciation, tried to tell them, "Well, I should certainly think not", but she was acting way too melodramatically offended. So now, all the boy could do was dart his eyes back-and-forth between his mum and his dad, his eyebrows arched as he sputtered and spewed; held for one long, aching, high tension moment; but then busted loose again.

His mother tried to explain, "That would be highly improper. British ladies never do such things."

Dad held for effect as Benjie waited, but then asked, "What?" He sounded shocked. "They do not fart?" But he had dropped the "r" out of the word, mocking her English pronunciation. It came out sounding more like, "Whot? They do not faht?" As he repeated it, he dragged this last word out even more, until it sounded like, "They do not fahhhhhht?" The word itself was starting to sound like one. He asked, "But, Heavens! Can this be so? Can it possibly be that proper British ladies can not fah-hhhhhhht?"

The whole family was convulsing. Benjie had never seen his father act like this. Dad placed his arm around his boy. They were a team. Co-conspirators against Mum. Deliciously irreverent. Father and son. Openly mocking the Brits.

Then it was Benjie who threw in the farting noise.

And he made it messy.

His parents both looked at him in mocked offense. And stunned delight.

The rest of that night was a hoot. Not one of them could be serious about anything for very long, no matter how hard they tried.

But then, truth be told, by that time they really weren't trying very hard.

The cabin was loaded with hand-crafted furnishings. Baskets woven from tree bark by what one was supposed to believe had been Native Americans, and in some cases may well have been. Lamp bases, candle holders, even salt and pepper shakers formed from antlers. Elaborate dream catchers nailed to walls where anyone knowing anything about how they worked would have known they could never catch dreams. Drums that could manage only dull, weak, dispirited thuds that could never have summoned any actual spirits, or revved up one's passion for war; but at least looked exotic, and complemented the general decor.

Benjie was falling in love with anything Indian. This exciting summer cabin in the woods had come prepackaged with books and artifacts from other times, species, and cultures. Lots of books. He hadn't really needed to bring his own. Books on local animals, birds, trees, and flowers, and special pamphlets on how to act around bears. His favorites were the ones about the natives. He spent hours poring over them; carried them outside to sit on the steps with. He held them as he looked out over land where they had once probably hunted, and camped. He brought their stories and pictures along with him to his favorite fallen logs or flat-topped boulders, where maybe these Indians themselves had long ago sat and wondered what the future—what his world—would be like.

His parents stood back and watched him quietly. They vowed to start spending more time in the mountains as a family. Out here where their son seemed to come so much more fully alive

Benjie could lose himself completely imagining other times. He liked to put himself right in the middle of them. It was like he was starting to see through "other eyes." He pictured tribes, cultures, and places he'd never been. Natives chatting together under stars. He heard their quiet, friendly rhythms. Smelled campfires out on the plains; heard them crackling, and sparking. Spitting out puffs of deep woodsy aromas.

He found feathers in the forest; treasuring them; almost reverencing them as mementos. Connections to richer, more interesting times. His world was coming alive.

He started carrying bags with him when he left the house for a trek out into Nature. He might fill a couple of them with nuts and special treats (sometimes even oatmeal cookies with giant raisins) for the chipmunks, gray squirrels, and blue jays. On the way back he'd have maybe exotic bits of bark, colored stones, or special leaves in odd shapes. He'd collect thin sheets and thick tablets of mica. Quartz almost formed into a crystal. He gathered up all sorts of really interesting stuff, and then carried it back to the cabin in his bags. His mum told him she would have to go shopping for more luggage if he intended to bring all of that back with him.

It was as if someone brand new had been born in those woods that special summer.

Or maybe someone from long ago had reawakened.

The air was a gentle spritz that morning. Thicker than a mist, but not quite a sprinkle. Each deck had its own porch swing and rocking chairs. Mom, Dad, and son had their own individual rhythms, but every one of them loved rocking. To the soft flow of days, and the stillness of evenings, they rocked quietly.

For Benjie, just being there had been opening windows to other times. Immersing himself in everything he could read or think about them, he could reach into the past. They had lived and walked where he now did. Touched some of these same rocks. Maybe even sat on them, trying to imagine what he and his own times would be like. He rocked on the deck that morning, feeling connections.

It was as though their spirit was reaching in through those porch screens for him. On this lovely, wet, gray, miserable, wonderful morning, he could just about hear the faraway chant of some loving and powerful keeper of the old ways. A caring and wise guide or shaman offering him wonders and deeper ways of knowing.

Near beside him, his mum was simply enjoying this moment, and breathing.

Frank was fighting his darker inner nature to be there with his family and leave the office behind. He couldn't help but think about what a cold, cruel world it could be out there, and how could he ever hope to protect his family from that ugliness mounting up everywhere?

Every new law, every big business decision he helped orchestrate, took food out of somebody's mouth, or caged them in unsettling ways. As head of household and bread winner, it was his job to make sure his own family didn't go hungry, but did it have to be at the expense of so many others? This whole system was cruel, but did he himself have to be? At work, he buried himself in paperwork, details, and decisions he didn't dare look too closely at. Patterns of at least heedless, sometimes intentional heartlessness. He had tried to ignore the worst of it. America had degenerated into a nation where you either ate or got eaten, and his were among that top few who could feast. It was just how business was done. He'd been finding little comfort in that lately.

One of their subdivisions had been buying up water rights while local farms, families, and whole communities were running dry. It had been profitable. Stocks were rising. But was it right? That was how business was played these days. It was a game, ordinary citizens were pawns, and everyone knew this was a rugged sport that hurt people and cost lives. But did it have to be this way?

That had been a lot of why he'd needed to get away. Head off into the mountains with his loved ones. Let someone else sign off on some of that for a while. He'd turned tail and fled into the hills like some wild west bandit pursued by the posse of his own conscience. He'd gathered up his clan and headed off into the wilds. Or at least into these rich guy, second home wilds.

No. That wasn't all of it. It hadn't been *just* that anyway. He should probably give himself a little bit of credit. He'd also wanted to spend some quality time with his family.

He wanted so badly to just leave things right there. Stop picking at it. He was here to spend time with his loved ones. That's all it has to be. Leave it alone. No need to keep poking around in ugly matters he should have left at the office.

But in his heart he knew he couldn't. Something had changed. He felt all twisted and knotted up inside. Somewhere deep where he couldn't get at it. He couldn't just shake these matters off anymore. Wrench them out of his guts. Some things were just wrong.

This was a very special summer. A season of very personal lessons for each of them; even as they were bonding together as a family. A time that set a lot of things loose. Drawing their attention to threads of long-spreading darkness; as deeply good things inevitably must. Darkness and Light always thrive one within the other.

But for now, they were just a family on vacation. Discovering themselves, and learning to love.

Dad was out on the front porch with his son. Things had been softening between them, though they had never been particularly harsh. They simply lived in different worlds. But now, here, they were together, if only rocking quietly. They were each very aware that even this much counted for a lot.

It was just Dad and his boy, his Little Benito Burrito, out here sharing the peacefulness of a soft, drizzling day. That soothing sound of rain pattering gently on leaves, and brushing the shingles overhead. The kind of day life was meant for.

They'd been there enjoying the quiet together for quite a while by the time Frank got up, putting a bookmark in this moment, to head inside for fresh coffee and maybe sneak a cookie or two. He asked his son, "You want anything?" and Benjie responded with, "No, Dad, but thanks."

Calling him Dad. Frank liked that. That meant a great deal to him. Not that his son had ever called him anything else, he guessed, but out here it seemed to count for more somehow.

He'd grab a fistful of cookies for both of them.

Frank drew up though as he stepped through the kitchen. The air felt more dense than it had a bit earlier. Brittle from a tension lying thick over everything. He headed off to look for his wife, and found her watching TV news in the den.

"I just wish your President would just stop talking sometimes," Reenie told him. It landed like a slap against the softness of his own mood, and he cringed.

On the screen, America's leader was lost in another of his long, unhinged rants. Denying things he'd been taped saying. Claiming unprecedented successes where the world knew he'd failed. Accusing others of crimes and atrocities he was afraid someone was about to catch him at. And now his border guards had been videoed letting scruffy local militias take potshots at children in cages. The films had gone viral, so he was falling all over himself trying to explain them away. He hadn't heard about this, but would look into it. He had heard about it, but it was Fake News; no one was doing any such thing. These vigilantes were truly good people; fine, upstanding, patriotic citizens; to be honored for their service. It wasn't him; he had nothing to do with it. It was the President before him did that. This wasn't his fault. And on and on. He stood, waving his hands around, spewing nonsense. At rally after rally his massed followers cheered, taking every word as God's honest truth. Not really understanding much of what he was saying.

His bumbled words, meandering sentences, disordered tirades, and self-contradictory excuses had given Reenie a headache. The evil behind them had dug into her more deeply.

"Why don't you just turn that off?" her husband all but demanded.

"You can't, Frank. You don't dare. You can't just watch hatred and fear spreading everywhere and just turn your back on it. My dad's dad fought with the RAF against Hitler, we thought they had killed that all out, but now here it is, taking over again. If we just ignore it, one of these days it could be our own little Benjie in one of their cages. They've hidden him off somewhere, and they're starving him. Crammed in with thousands of other little boys and girls sleeping in filth. We can't just…"

She broke down and wept.

Frank felt his guts tighten when she said, "Because Benjie's skin is a little dark, he has a Jewish name, or because his mother was born overseas."

And then he knew how very personally she was taking this. If something terrible happened, it was their fault.

On that huge, widescreen, wall-mounted TV right in front of them; so gigantic and so glaring they could not turn away; heavily armed and bearded yokels were strutting for the cameras, talking about "Puttin' the fear o' God in them little caged bastards."

Frank wasn't even trying to console his wife after a while. It wasn't clear which one of them needed it more.

He headed back outside, but pulled up short in the doorway and just stood there, studying his son. His little boy. His precious, almost sacred Little Benito Burrito. They had only just now been getting to know each other. He had never spent enough time with his kid, and now it was suddenly too late. Rabid wolves were heaving themselves against even these doors. Starving for little boy flesh.

He studied his child, but said nothing. He spoke no words to Benjie, just as there had been none he could have offered to comfort his wife. He studied the boy like he had only this one last, single chance to memorize all his details. The color of his eyes. That crooked part in his hair. His favorite outfits.

Benjie felt his dad standing back there, studying him. It made him squirm, but then he too held his tongue.

That was the summer when everyone changed.

> *"Chance is a word void of sense;
> nothing can exist without a cause."*
> —Voltaire

Chapter Four

After his family's return to the more scrupulously polished estates of their gated community, Benjie started spending more time in the strips of wooded land scattered through them. Stretches of natural growth from earlier times, aesthetically interwoven with carefully pruned lawns, pools, and tennis courts. Little touches of Nature positioned and confined so as not to inconvenience the well-to-do. There, as much as anything, to remind the wealthy that they could own pretty much anything. Even Nature itself. Benjie now saw them from a deeper perspective though, and even here they called to him.

He'd come home with new thoughts and feelings playing around just a bit below the surface, and an unshakable urge to start writing about them. About how people had once been able to feel the balance of things. But how in such exclusive communities as his own, the world had been folded into tight little creases and stuffed behind rose arbors. Everything so tediously sterile, so carefully structured, and tightly controlled. Even as the world outside these gates seemed so terribly and frighteningly out of control.

His heart hurt for what had been lost. He pictured natives once growing their own food. Gathering their medicines from the plants. Chatting and murmuring together at night over campfires. Hunting deer, rabbits, and buffalo right here where he stood. But then he figured probably not buffalo. Not around here. But still, maybe there were still arrowheads in some of these tree trunks. Wouldn't that be cool?

What would their languages have sounded like, he wondered? What had they talked about before they'd had television? Could they actually communicate with wolves, ravens, and maybe even the winds? Had there still been giant mammoths around? Even somewhere here in New York State? Did we still have wolves here today? How had we forgotten so much of what we'd once known and loved about Nature? What we'd shared with it? Benjie mused over how maybe man had lost just about everything important once we'd started telling ourselves we held power over all living things. We'd started making demands, sucking things dry, but offering nothing back. We'd stopped listening.

Could we ever learn to again? In the park one day he tried really hard to listen for something thinner than air, and quieter than the quietest sound.

The thought came to him that if he heard anything, he should probably write it down.

But he didn't have a pen, or any paper. Who carries stuff like that around with them?

He listened until he thought (or at least hoped) he could maybe almost hear something. Maybe an Indian spirit was trying to get through to him.

But all he could think was, "This is a test." And it was only in English, so he must be talking to himself again. "This is a test. This is a test." Why would an ancient Indian be talking in English?

Maybe he should write about that anyway, because it was unusual. But what was he going to do? Find a stick and scratch it in the dirt?

"This is a test. This is a test. Write that down. This is important."

You know how little boys can be. Imagining all sorts of things; most of them really dramatic and adventurous. They are shiny knights on huge white steeds, itching to set off on some glorious quest. There are vampires, and dark twisted evils just outside the door, and only you can hold them back. You think you're from Mars or somewhere, sent here to learn things, then you'll wake up and be home again.

You know young boys.

He imagined all sorts of things that day, but in the end decided he'd been only pretending.

He walked home along the edge of the woods, thinking it had been fun anyway. He should do it again, but next time bring some paper.

This wasn't his usual way back. He was pretending like Indian spirits were guiding him, but he was only just zigging and zagging. It'd take him forever to get anywhere that way. He didn't mind though, cause then he wouldn't have to start washing his hands, and doing his chores, or whatever so soon.

He meandered like a stream through ancient sacred lands. Stopping to look around. He didn't know this area. He was an explorer on an adventure.

Strolling along, lost in his thoughts, sometimes he didn't even notice he'd stopped until he'd been standing somewhere for a while. And then, one time he started feeling someone was staring right at him.

He didn't notice that other boy at first. A kid about his own age, all red-faced, and panting. Standing at the bottom of what must have been his own driveway because why would he be hanging around like that all alone at the bottom of someone else's? He was looking straight at Benjie like they knew each other and he'd been waiting for him for a while. But then why would he be panting like that? Like he'd rushed out, scared he wouldn't make it in time?

He was staring at Benjie really hard. It was creepy. But he wasn't saying anything. Maybe he was waiting for Benjie to start. It was weird.

They made full eye contact and froze like that, just looking at each other. Benjie felt like he'd been captured. Like he'd been pulled in by some kind of a spaceship beam or something.

He couldn't think of what to do, so he just stood there.

This must be that odd kid everyone talked about. Said he was retarded. Couldn't talk. Didn't even know where he was half the time.

But that didn't seem right somehow now that he was looking at the guy. His eyes looked like he knew stuff. He just wasn't talking about it.

He was holding a handful of loose papers and a pen like he'd just run downstairs, grabbed them up along the way, and now wanted to give them to some stranger who just happened to be passing by.

No. He was looking at Benjie like he'd been waiting specifically for him. Thinking Benjie really, really needed these papers right now, and should know what to do with them. Just standing there, holding those papers out, acting like he was waiting for something.

Neither of them moved for a couple of minutes. The strange kid lifted his papers even higher, more insistently, shoving them out in Benjie's direction. His eyes seemed so eager and expectant. Benjie needed these, he should know that, why wasn't he taking them? He should know what to write. What was wrong?

The kid's eyes seemed to overflow with this eerie, unnerving sense of certainty.

Benjie got a flash for a moment that they were asking him, "Well? Did you see them? Did you hear them? Did you do what they asked?"

But that was probably just his imagination acting up again, he thought.

So, there they stood. This strange little neighbor kid he didn't know from Adam, the both of them just standing there, and Benjie didn't know what to do. Some weird little chubby kid who didn't even know enough to say Howdy, had just come running down the stairs, and now he kept shoving those papers in his face, and what was Benjie supposed to do about that?

Well, not right into his face exactly. There was still some distance between them, and Benjie planned to keep it that way.

He would have to walk past the kid to get home though. That could be a problem. He didn't want to be rude and just turn around and head back the way he'd come, because they'd both know he was only doing it to get away from this guy, and that would be rude. And it was too late to pretend he hadn't seen him. So, what should he do?

As always, he fell back on good manners. He finally said Hello, as his parents had taught him to do. In the process he realized he'd been holding his breath for a while. His shoulders had crept pretty far up toward his ears.

This was that challenged-learning kid; that autistic everyone talked about. Benjie hoped he wasn't dangerous, and didn't want to find out.

For some reason, he wasn't actually scared. This boy might be strange, but seemed harmless enough. Only reason he'd been thinking the kid might be bonkers in the first place was because that's what kids at school said about him. Said his parents didn't dare let him go to a regular school because he might flip out and kill somebody. He might tear somebody apart and then eat the pieces. But now sort of almost meeting him, that didn't seem right.

And so, they only stood there, studying each other.

That was pretty much all that happened between them that first time.

"Nice papers," Benjie told him after a while, but then realized how stupid that had sounded.

Of course the other kid didn't tell him so. The other kid still wasn't talking. He kept thrusting those papers out, pushing them through the air at him, like he really knew Benjie wanted them, and why was he acting so stupid?

Or at least that's how Benjie saw things anyway.

After a long moment of trying to figure things out but not getting anywhere, Benjie just kind of sidled past the boy, keeping that safe distance, a couple of yards between them, until he'd gotten past him far enough he could just say, "Well … bye… See ya."

He gave an awkward, hesitant salute, turned the rest of the way around, and continued on moving toward home.

Turning back a couple of times, he saw the kid still just standing there, studying him, holding out those papers. Now and then giving them a little rattle, to no avail.

As all of this was going on, they were both being watched.

Laurence Beaufort had been headed for the kitchen for a nice glass of iced tea and happened to glance out one of the windows along the way. He'd seen his son standing unattended at the bottom of their driveway. Which was odd enough in its own right, but then he also seemed to be holding out a thick wad of loose papers to a stranger.

"Who's that boy out there with Madison?" he asked his wife, who had noticed the same thing and now was standing beside him.

Danni turned to take a hard but loving look at her husband. "You can be very over-protective sometimes," she told him.

"But I soooo mean that in a nice way," she explained.

As she studied him though, she saw how troubled he actually was.

"Something happen at work you're not telling me?" she asked. "You seem awfully high strung lately."

Laurence couldn't tell her about that gang of government thugs at the office. How they could grab your kids anywhere; even out of your own home, at any time.

But then, he wasn't doing her any favors keeping that a secret from her either. Not telling her that boys like their son were in very real danger.

Ailana and Sylvie had ways of hearing what people tried not to say. Sylvie called that "hearing with their other ears" or "seeing with their other eyes." Living so far outside the hubbub of city life, folks are often more closely attuned to Nature, catching things most people don't, but this was more than just that.

Strangers came from far away to vent, seek advice, or lay their troubles down before Ailana, and she welcomed it. She was known to be a great listener.

Sylvie was not. This happy and spontaneous little child rarely let their visits upset her complete lack of routine. She had important playing to do, things to figure out, and had "no time or patience to just frivol away on big peoples who just like to complain, but don't do much to fix what's bothering them."

"Even if they have dogs," she had added once or twice, though how exactly that fit in probably only she knew.

Sylvie could buzz around in goofy circles right where a stranger was sharing something of dark importance with her Auntie, figuring they could just ignore each other if it came to that. But she also seemed to sense if one of them really needed to play more. If, as she saw it, they kept getting trapped inside their serious faces. When she came across someone like that, her whirling joy and goofiness could help to drain some of that oppressive seriousness out of them.

Or she sometimes just sat off in the distance to watch and really study them for a while. Hauling herself up onto a rock, or a low stone wall, or high up into one of the trees, they wouldn't keep distracting her by chattering all that nonsense about the kind of people *they* thought they were. Most people were usually wrong about that. And even if they did know themselves pretty well, they were not particularly honest telling someone else about it. So Sylvie just watched what she called their "Dancing Lights." How the air changed colors around them one way when they were angry, or some other way when they were sad. How it got all gray and gloomy and nothing was moving if they thought everything was hopeless and they weren't giving life much of a really good try. How she could see flashes of red, or sometimes even black, like little lightning bolts, popping out through all those other colors sometimes, and she could tell even from far away and up a tree that they were probably trying to tell Auntie Ailana that they were a really nice person thinking good and sweet things only, while in their hearts they really weren't. They were maybe even trying to convince themselves of that, but then their inner hearts were saying something different. They were mad about something and would not let that go.

Sylvie knew her Auntie probably saw this herself, but was probably over there listening, and being a great big sweetie by not mentioning it.

Sick people came to her auntie's gardens to have her lay her hands on them and make their sickness go away. She was really good at helping them feel better by just waving her hands around. Sometimes whole circles of nurses would come from all over, and drag their chairs out into circles on the lawn and have her tell them how she did that.

Mostly people came to just talk to her because they had something going on in them they didn't like. Or maybe they had to figure some stuff out and it helps to get things off their chests, they would tell her. A few of them came just to sit quietly and enjoy the peacefulness of the gardens for a while, and listen to the birds singing; which when that happened, Sylvie didn't want to get in their way. If they came here to love the peace, and how pretty things were, then most probably Sylvie would like them as people, and they didn't need her help. They had already figured things out.

Auntie had classes there for the nurses who wanted to learn how to use their hands to help people magically. Sometimes when Auntie wasn't around; and the nurses didn't know Sylvie was standing right there, listening to every word they were saying; they got all quiet in their voices like they were revealing some special secret that not everyone should know. They talked about how they had heard that these gardens were on magical ancient land, and on some kind of a line that connected them with churches and stuff. This of course made this place really, really special, they would say, like those great big gigantic rocks standing in circles on the other side of the ocean where nobody knew how they got there, and places like that. And then they would all nod and agree with each other and say these really strange and goofy names of other places they knew about, and it wouldn't even sound like they were talking English anymore.

People said a lot of odd things when they didn't stop to think that maybe Sylvie might not be ignoring them this time, and might be listening in on them if she actually wanted to.

Nurses murmured to each other that this was a "special center," built by the gods for special purposes and stuff like that. That life around here could never be normal.

Which was perfectly fine with little Sylvie. She didn't think she would like "normal" very much. She and "normal" would probably not get along.

"Life can be funny sometimes," her mom would say when she had run out of things to talk about, but wanted to keep talking anyway. Some folks are just not gifted with quiet.

"Indeed they can, Mother," Sylvie had responded a couple of those times. "Indeed they can." And then she had walked out the door, leaving her mom thinking she might have just spoken something really deep, when she had really just been making words that didn't mean anything. Showing her mom that Sylvie could talk like a big people by not saying very much.

Like when the nurses said her Auntie had always been there, in these gardens, since the beginnings of time. That no one had ever known where she'd come from, or when. Some people just didn't age, they said. And then their eyes would go all wide, and their mouths would go like, "Oooh!", but no words would come out.

To Sylvie's mind, that made no sense at all. Nobody just stood around waiting for monkeys to stop being monkeys and start being people, so they could finally have someone to chat with who wasn't too busy eating bananas. That made no sense. Nobody was there since forever.

But you know big peoples. They do like to talk.

However, she did recall now how she had once asked her auntie if she was Sylvie's mom's sister, or her dad's. Ailana had told her, "Oh, no. Your mom has been calling me Auntie since she was your age. I must be older than I look I guess, huh?"

Putting things together now, Sylvie found this all very mysterious.

She was thinking about this one afternoon as she was sticking her finger into things along that edge where the woods met the gardens and kind of danced in and out of each other. If she pushed into one of those holes that a woodpecker had made, it felt rough. But in a worm's hole it felt wet and smooth. These were important things to make note of, she decided.

Inside Ailana's Gardens it was springtime in the winter. Plants there didn't always seem to be paying as much attention to the weather as some of the visitors had apparently been expecting them to. Things being so green there caught a lot of folks by surprise. Some of those murmuring nurses had even suggested that maybe they were blooming for Ailana herself.

Sylvie was thinking about that one day when she came across a bird who was quite obviously dead; so apparently not everything could stay healthy forever just because it lived in Magicland. This bird was frozen hard, its eyes were mostly gone, and it was not gonna get up and start singing again. It couldn't, because it didn't have any glow left inside it at all, which meant it was really and truly dead and forever. Once the light had moved out of something, and you couldn't find it anywhere around the animal that was lying there, then you could pretty much know it was dead. Because when that glow left away from you, it took the life with it. Some said the trees died in winter, but that wasn't so. They just took their light more inside them for a while was all. She could see it was still in there; just hidden more, and moving more slowly.

But this bird was really, truly dead. She didn't try putting her finger into it to see what death felt like because she knew without experimenting that his would be about as much fun as getting snail goo all over her tongue.

And she knew this snail part from personal experience.

She'd seen people come by to visit with Auntie when they were dying, but could tell this was something they considered very personal, and so she did not stick around and get in the way. She could see their lights were fading, and they felt sad, or scared, or hopeless about it, and she figured this was none of her business, so she'd just left them alone.

Nobody had ever hung around so she could actually watch them die. Maybe they just didn't want her to go poking her nose into their private business, which Sylvie figured was understandable. She probably would do that, knowing herself. And anyway, when somebody was dying; or at least when animals did; they usually sorta liked being alone.

She had noticed though, that sometimes when somebody knew they were dying, even if they didn't want to talk about it, they might like having little Sylvie sit there quietly with them, and sometimes smile up at them, or touch their leg.

There had been a couple of times when even after they had died, their lights had come back to the gardens for little visits. But this didn't happen very often. Maybe once you are real and officially dead, you have better things to do.

But this bird was just dead. He had no light or song left inside him at all. He'd be making himself dirt pretty soon. This bird was dead.

"Dead as a door nail," she thought as she gave it a couple of pokes, but only very gently, and only with a stick.

But then she started wondering what the heck was a door nail, and so of course she had to wander off and go looking for one.

Her auntie walked up about then and told her, "You know, Sweetie, we all have to die some time. I hope you are ready for that. I feel pretty sure you'll be able to handle it when my time comes, but we can always talk about it if you want to."

The two of them could always be direct with each other, but this time the little girl sensed that Ailana must be telling her more than her words and mouth were saying.

"But not you," Sylvie told her. "You've been around since forever before time began."

Her quote hadn't been exactly perfect, but she had gotten the point across, but then her Auntie had had one of her really good laughs over that, and little Sylvie couldn't really figure out why. So, she just stood there, staring up at her like the woman had come unhinged. "Maybe even longer than that," Ailana said when it was finally time to take a breath. But then she just started laughing again.

As she calmed, she studied her tiny niece like she wanted to pick her up, settle her onto her lap, and cuddle her, and then they could laugh together for a while.

Except she couldn't do that, Sylvie saw, because you can't put somebody on your lap when you are the both of you standing up.

So, she moved in, and wrapped her arms around her mom's auntie's left leg.

Ailana looked down at her until Sylvie could feel the soft, soothing warmth of her smile running all through her. And then she maybe understood a little better why people came from so far away to have her Auntie Ailana touch them, and make their hurts go away.

Benjie felt unsettled. He didn't know by what, but thought he maybe knew by whom. It was that strange kid. The little chubby guy with the papers who'd kept shoving them in his face, staring at him. He could see why everybody felt so uncomfortable around the guy. It was more than just that he didn't use words. It was like he was from some other world.

That was one strange little dude. Sure, Benjie thought, he could have been a little more friendly. Probably should have been. Said more than just Hello anyway. And maybe taken a look at those papers that seemed so important to him. What harm would that have done? He really hadn't been very nice.

Benjie was great at guilt tripping himself once it was too late to change anything. He couldn't ever think of the right thing to do until it was too late. But he'd never had any real friends to practice on; so how was he supposed to learn how to talk to them? Or maybe this was *why* he didn't have any buddies. He wasn't good at talking.

Now this weird kid was making it all worse. People like him made you think about how you're not as nice as you thought you were. Benjie could see why that'd bother most folks.

Benjie had been outside much of that morning, which was unusual for him since this was Sunday, and he would normally be inside somewhere reading. But then again, nothing had seemed normal since they'd come back from vacation. Nothing was like how it used to be. Everything had been knocked on its side, and he was looking at it slanted. Some kind of a lid had been lifted, and light was getting into corners he hadn't noticed before.

Maybe this was what growing up was like.

He'd be starting fourth grade soon. He still felt like a kid, but did seem to be changing.

Walking the woods as he pondered, the more he wandered through his thoughts, the deeper he felt buried in their shadows.

He watched light shining down through treetops. Beams of strangely colored light pointing out secret pathways through the trees. But then everything would clump back together, and he would only have his shadows again.

More and more these days he kept almost seeing stuff, but not really.

Everything and everyone had changed since the mountains.

His dad had been goofing around more, but sometimes even then he looked stressed. His mom was like two different people. Like she knew she didn't have to keep fussing over all the tiny details anymore; it wasn't going to do any good anyway, so what was the point? But then other times she got all serious, and had to start fussing even harder, like that was all she knew how to do, and if she didn't do that, then she had nothing.

The whole world had been kicked all lopsided.

Listening to whispers and stirs through the forest, nothing seemed quite as it had been. He sat by a brook for a while. Its gurgles sounded like a little girl laughing far away.

He started feeling there was some special place he needed to be.

Lopsided.

The whole world had flipped over and now he was looking in at everything through some strange, hidden door in the side of it.

Things had "gone all skalla-woochy!" in little Sylvie's world. A world of Nature, and bugs, and things that may or may not feel like playing with you. Thinking someone you loved might be dying changed everything.

Sure, if a leaf died, then you just waited and sometimes watched as it decided to be dirt. But you couldn't watch for too long because that was just boring. Or if an animal was getting ready to leave us, it would wander off somewhere to do what it had to do without you getting in the way. But if this could even happen to Auntie Ailana, then that just changed everything.

Sylvie was going to have to give this matter some very serious thought.

Watching those lights that glow from inside people, she had seen that when the sick ones came to be touched by Ailana, they weren't glowing very brightly at the beginning, especially if someone had to help them get out of their cars.

She studied animals in the woods with her other eyes. They were a lot easier to figure out most times than people sometimes were. They didn't have as many emotions she guessed maybe, because their lights didn't have as many colors. She learned to tell when they were scared, so then she wouldn't try to feed them or pet them. And, truth be told, she also figured out that they were never really, really exactly overjoyed to see her in the first place, like she had always thought they had been. Maybe they were only just curious sometimes.

Or they thought maybe she might have food. Which she usually did.

But death was something else again. Nobody seemed to want to let her watch that.

Her Auntie wouldn't mind. Auntie always let her watch everything. Sylvie had been noticing lately how sometimes her lights faded a little, but for the most part they looked to be all the same colors. So, if she really was dying, then it sure didn't change her emotions much, if any.

So, maybe this wasn't what she'd meant. Maybe she wasn't dying after all.

But then again, Sylvie had been seeing something out of the ordinary happening with her. Sometimes it was like her auntie had two bodies. Like there was the one walking around with its clothes on; the one that anybody could see; and there was the other one made out of lights that looked like it was starting to slip off to the side of her a little more now. Like the two parts of her were sliding apart.

"To be truly human is to walk the path of compassion, to breathe with the rhythms of nature, and to recognize our kinship with all forms of life."
—Joy Mills

Chapter Five

Benjie had mysteries to solve.

Maybe they lay in the wild, chaotic attraction of unmanicured greenery; of Nature allowed to run free. Maybe they had to do with that strange boy who lived at its edge; himself seemingly untamed; not like most folks. Benjie couldn't stop thinking about that kid. There was so much going on in his eyes. Could he really be retarded like everyone said? Benjie didn't think so.

But he wasn't exactly normal either. There was definitely something off about him.

As Benjamin wended his way through the forest, he felt like Robin Hood. Except he wouldn't shoot any deer. This was a lot better than hanging out at his big, polished house where he never dared touch anything because he might get his fingerprints on something. He couldn't touch the banisters because they might've just been polished. His folks even had a room where the furniture cost so much you had to keep it covered; it was only for when visitors came. You weren't supposed to be on it unless you had special guests, and then you had to sit up straight and don't move so much.

And if you wanted strawberries, you had to finish your meat first.

There were too many rules on the inside, so being outside was a whole lot more fun.

His mum let him be out here. She knew he didn't like to climb things, so he wouldn't hurt himself doing something stupid like falling out of a tree. The weather had been getting "more crisp" lately, as she liked to say. So he'd been letting Clara dress him in thicker jackets, and sometimes had to wear a sweater at the same time. She liked to put gloves in his pockets "just in case."

Benjie didn't hang out with other kids. He'd never particularly felt like throwing balls around with the guys, though he did sometimes wonder what that would be like.

Not the ball part. He couldn't see what anybody thought he was accomplishing by knocking a toy around. There had to be things they could do that might actually accomplish something. "Time and energy are precious and functional, and not to be squandered." Had he read that somewhere? Then why did his memory hear it like a voice from long ago? "Thoughts, words, deeds, and emotions are forms of energy," this voice had told him. "They should be focused, and used wisely."

Something seemed off about his life. He didn't belong in a polished house with a manicured lawn. He should have been born someone else. He must've gotten dropped off here by mistake. Probably other kids felt the same way, but he was pretty sure of it.

Weaving his way through the trees, wondering if maybe there were spirits in there somewhere, he wished he could see them. Or a fairy. Or an angel, like his grandmother used to say she could see before they put her in a home and then she died there.

Had the angels come for her when she died, like she always said they were gonna?

He'd read all kinds of books about ESP, but still couldn't make things slide across the table, or send messages to people with his head. None of that worked for him. He kicked at a rock. Nothing was going like he wanted it to. Maybe he didn't even have a third eye. Maybe some people didn't.

He wandered along, poking through forest debris, and through thoughts he had never told anyone. He started getting that feeling again like he should be paying attention, not just talking to himself. So he started examining each step, and whatever he passed. He started noticing this kind of fuzziness, like those floaty things you see in your eyes sometimes, but then you can't find them because they keep sliding away. Wherever you look, they float off somewhere else. One of those. Well; something like that, but this one kept moving ahead of him. He'd been following it for a while.

It stopped for a moment. Like it was waiting for something. He tried harder to see it, but it still wasn't there. It was probably just one of those… Well, he didn't know what the heck it was.

He just imagined things sometimes.

As he stood there, he saw a house off in the distance through the underbrush, and figured he'd go check it out.

But when he got to their backyard, he didn't know what to do next. It was none of his business to go up to somebody he didn't know's house and just knock on their window like he had every reason to be there. And what did he care who lived there anyhow?

He felt like an idiot. What was he gonna say if they came out? He couldn't think of a reason he could tell them why he wanted to be there. "Sorry, I'm just a jerk who walks around all the time without knowing where he's going."

He should head back home before they caught him.

But he didn't do that. He stood around, arguing with himself instead. He did manage to move a few hesitant steps back into the woods, but that was all. He didn't really feel like going home.

He found a big rock, and sat down on it. He'd brought along some bread to tear off pieces for the animals, so he pulled that out of his bag, but then didn't do anything with it; he just sat there. He felt caught up in something he couldn't figure out.

Birds and squirrels came up to play, a few of them waited for the bread, but others just romped and ran around among the trees. Forest life didn't have to be entertained. Animals didn't need humans to put on a show for them.

Slowly, a few soft feathered flakes of snow began to drift down around him. One of the younger squirrels started chasing them like a dog might go after a ball, or a cat might chase a light someone was flashing up the wall. Benjie watched with such rapt fascination that when he heard a delighted giggle from somewhere behind him, he thought for a moment it might be one of the squirrels.

He turned to see a boy his own age.

It was that alien kid with the handful of papers. Except he didn't have them this time.

He knew the kid's name was Madison because he'd asked his mom one night when they were watching TV. Probably no one else bothered to find that out. Kids at school already had their own ugly nicknames for him. Adults probably insulted him more politely, pulling their punches because it wasn't nice to talk about… Well… You know. But nobody called him who he was.

This was "that learning challenged boy up the street", "the autistic", "just stares at the wall." "I've heard he screams if you try to touch him, or if anybody…" "Well, I heard…" "They say…"

All this hearing, but pretty much nobody actually knowing anything about him, Benjie thought.

And now here he was, standing behind him, watching that crazy dancing squirrel, and laughing.

Benjie nodded, and laughed along. No words were exchanged, but none were needed. They just quietly got along from the start.

After a little bit of a while, the neighbor boy moved closer, and sat down beside Benjie; each mildly acknowledging the other one's presence, but not making any really big deal out of it.

They'd been there a while before Madison's mom caught sight of them through that little window over the sink. At first she was stunned. Then she called her husband over, and they both of them just stood there, staring out at their son along the edge of the woods.

He wasn't alone.

Madison had never had anyone to sit with before. And this, just weeks after they'd seen him standing out in front of the house, holding a pile of papers out to a passing stranger. Was this a dangerous development they should be concerned about? Or a commendable and unprecedented urge to socialize? Should they call one of his therapists and ask their advice? Make an appointment? Was their son reaching out, wanting to communicate, or should they be putting more locks on the doors?

They stared. They worried. But the mom's eyes glistened a little as she watched this other boy being gentle, and knew he didn't want to hurt her son.

They watched as sometimes the two kids looked toward each other and smiled for a moment before turning back to watch the forest life. They seemed comfortable together. Their boy didn't appear to be in any real danger. He seemed happy. They didn't dare speculate beyond that, but their wonder in that moment tickled the vulnerable underbelly of a rare state of contentment. As though something they had long been waiting, but hadn't dared hope for, was finally falling into place.

To Benjamin's side, Madison was leaning forward, staring hard into the woods with such fixed intensity that Benjie was almost convinced he was counting those sparse and scattered snowflakes. He was sure watching something that only he could see.

Benjie tried to make out what the kid was looking at. Trees; now gray, and barren of leaves; stood out in all their stark complexity against the dimly shadowed air. Really, really looking hard at them, Benjie saw thousands of connections. He'd never paid much attention to them before, but now they seemed to be everywhere. Things branching away behind other things, roots from one tree coming up between those of another, until he couldn't tell what was reaching out from where. More connections than could ever be counted.

But Madison sure seemed to be counting them. Following out every turn and twist like he was reading something terribly important. His eyes were so locked on some deep inner purpose. Had nobody ever told him that was just how trees were? They stuck out in all directions, but it didn't mean anything? They were just trees.

Madison apparently saw more than that.

Benjie started wishing he could see it too.

Wisps of fog drifted, thickening and thinning. Trees were pressed flat inside passing sleeves of mystery, but then reached back out, just being full trees again. Just like they'd always been.

Benjie imagined some hidden wizard off behind them somewhere; casting his spell over the boys. Coaxing them in deeper. Illusions, and connections. The seen and the unseen.

Limbs and underbrush rustled, but then held still. Benjie listened in more closely, as though everything did indeed count. They whispered, but then slipped into secrecy again.

Blue tinges through the gray. Something ancient, and something fresh. Some hidden message being offered for just this one moment, then withdrawn. He felt a quiet space clearing through his chattering mind, an opening outward through his heart as he listened more softly. With more clarity, and focus.

To everything.

And all the while, this strange boy from some other world kept counting. Like everything depended on him knowing all those hidden details. Like it was those little special parts no one noticed that mattered most.

He didn't seem to mind when Benjie watched him. He just kept right on counting, or whatever that was he was doing.

Benjie told himself he had to start paying more attention. There must be a whole lot of stuff he'd been missing.

"What is it you're looking at, Madison?" he asked, though he knew after he'd said it that he had really only been talking to himself again. It's just that usually he didn't let other people hear him. "What do you see that I can't?"

He didn't really expect any kind of an answer. The kid couldn't talk. And who knew but what he might be deaf too, on top of everything else?

But there it was, and he'd said it. The words had just come out of him somehow.

This new kid probably wouldn't care that he was sitting there talking to himself like some goofball. Some kind of a nut job or something. Maybe it was okay to act a little weird around Madison.

He tried to tell himself that this was all of it just his imagination acting up again. That he was only watching snow drift, and fog through the trees.

But then again, even that was pretty cool. Drifting snow and fog did hold you in a kind of a magic.

A crow cawed, and he thought of ancient natives again.

Connections.

He studied this new oddball beside him. Was this the way he saw things all the time?

The boy turned toward him, but then he just there sat there. Like he was trying to figure out what was happening. But when Benjie studied him closer, the other boy's face looked like he might be thinking about something more important than just that someone was talking, and he didn't understand. Like he might be considering the cosmic significance of this moment or something.

Or maybe he was just staring, Benjie thought. That logical side of him trying to take back control.

"I like to be called Maddie," the boy said.

For some reason, all caught up in that very strange and otherworldly moment; as though even he himself had been knocked into some other dimension; it didn't surprise Benjie as much as it could have that this weird kid could talk after all. Maybe most times he just didn't feel he had any real need to. Or didn't figure other people would understand. Benjie knew what that was like.

"I'm Benjie," he responded.

And then they slipped back inside their comfortable silence together.

No stranger passing by would have guessed these kids hadn't long been good buddies. That they were essentially meeting each other for the first time. Their body language was so casual. They slouched, as little boys do, leaning in toward each other every now and again, seeming to anchor into each other as though it would now be them against the world. They looked to have been through so much together already that they had come to expect this other to always be there. As though this much at least had been established, and now the rest of this particular lifetime could be built on that foundation. Just as earlier lifetimes might have been.

As they sat together on their special boulder, Benjamin reached his hand down to rest it on the rock surface between them, the other boy lowering his at that very same moment. It was as if this had been a long-practiced ritual between them, and when they found their hands resting side-by-side, they just left them that way.

The temperature of the air around them dropped, but still the boys just sat there, and watched.

It was like the tundra of lifetimes was thawing. Seeds were awakening. Something inside them connected. Something unspoken that each almost recognized in the other.

Soft floating feathers of white drifted, like those thoughts and images in Benjie's mind that he could never quite grab hold of.

*The worst and the best are anticipated.
Special times and individuals foreseen long before
they arise. Seeds of guidance and rebuilding
are sown before dire necessity strikes.*

Chapter Six

Benjie was reading ghost stories in bed. He did that a lot, but was stuck at home today and had to stay inside, so he'd been reading a whole bunch of them, one right after another. They were the kind where furniture kept moving around, but nobody was doing it. The good guys were some place they shouldn't be, like in a creaking, scary house in the woods they'd never been to before, and the lights kept going out. Something was writing big, terrifying words on the wall in dark, dripping blood. Benjie was so scared he felt ghosts crawling out of his books and standing right there in the room with him. Writing in his mind. "That which stirs the heart can open doorways to other dimensions."

Not as scary as the blood-dripping wall words, but they'd come into his head out of nowhere, so that was definitely spooky.

They'd found him. No use trying to escape. It never did the guys in these books any good. They kept falling down, screaming, and then the spooks got them anyway.

He wanted to go try the doorknob. A ghost mighta locked him in. To finish him off. He was too scared to even sit up. His heart was pounding really, really hard. His muscles had gone tight. He thought maybe something was nailing him to the bed and tying all his sheets into knots.

He loved these books.

He grabbed another Kleenex and blew. His wastebasket was filling up like sands in an hourglass marking how long he'd been trapped in his room.

He tried to sit up, afraid he'd see grisly shadows slithering toward him. Like in one of those dreams where you *want* to wake up, and you *think* you woke up, but you really didn't, and you are still in your nightmare where the bad thing can get you, and you can't even move because you are petrified. He tried to drag his legs out from under the covers. He was like a zombie after his body parts had been cut off and all that was left of him was his head. He braced his arms behind him to winch his body up, up, up like a crane creaking an old coffin up out of its grave. He made the noises with his mouth, moving himself around like the chain was old and rusty and could bust at any moment and he'd fall back into bed and be stuck there forever under the power of an ancient curse.

There was someone watching him. He could feel it.

What if his room broke away into some other dimension or something and his mom couldn't get to him, or even find him? Like in those old TV shows where kids disappear under their beds, or into a closet or something, and you can still hear them in there, calling for help, and weeping, but you can't see them, and can't reach them? What if his mom couldn't reach her arms inside that other dimension and pull him out?

He tried calling for her, but his voice got stuck.

He should write about what happened in case they never found his body. He started with, "Mom said I have to stay inside today because I have a bug.

"And that is when it all began!!!!!" he wrote, darkening those exclamation points a whole lot of times.

"It was a sunny afternoon. I could have been outside doing something, but my mom wouldn't let me. She said it is because I have been running around without my hat on again and someday I will learn. And then she did that thing she always does with her eyes…" He knew she was only trying to protect him, but he didn't write about that part. Instead, he wrote, "And that is when the spirits came!!!!!"

He stopped to blow his nose again.

He started scribbling into his journal faster and faster until he couldn't even read what he was writing. It was getting even sloppier than usual. His penmanship had always been messy. His teacher kept telling him that. But this was worse.

He started feeling strange. Like someone was reaching inside his brain.

He tried walking it off, fiddling with things on his shelves. Someone was watching him! He poked through his video games but didn't pick one. He tried drawing horses just to think about something else, but kept messing them up. He tried drawing Indians, but they came out even worse than his horses.

He kinda liked the one Indian though. He had a strong face with long hair, and his eyes even looked like real eyes. Like he was looking right out of the paper at Benjamin.

These medicines were making his head go all funny. It kept thinking strange things he didn't ask it to.

He picked up a rock from beside his pirate's chest. A grayish one with a pointy top covered in some sort of stony white stuff. He'd found it beside a river once and carried it home. It reminded him of a snow-covered mountain. There was a little hole in one side that in his mind could have been a cave where some really tiny people lived. Probably monks. They had important work to do, but needed to do it where no one else could find them. The best stuff sometimes had to stay hidden.

Or maybe a bear lived in there. That'd be okay too, but he would rather it was monks.

He pictured himself in that cave, locked up in icy weather for a really, really long time. But now springtime was coming. Baby animals stirred in hidden spots all through the forest. Icecaps would be melting, vegetable gardens could be planted, and the world could start over.

"My favorite time of year," he thought, and felt others nodding and mumbling along.

"My mum says I was born here," he wrote in his journal. "But sometimes I think I've been other places too. I think about how things use to be. She says memory can be a funny thing (but not funny ha ha she meant). She says sometimes you only think you remember something but it was maybe only something I dreamed and only think I remembered it, but she is very nice when she says it."

"Ah, young wanderer; but which is truly the dream?" Benjie wrote without even knowing he was doing it. It came out much neater than his usual scribbling. It didn't even look like his writing. He couldn't write that neat no matter how hard he tried. Like for an important essay at school or something. And besides, all these letters were long, and slanted, and kind of fancy with little curls in them and stuff. Like he'd drawn them with one of those old feather pens from the old days.

Plus, he didn't know what the words meant. He thought about them for a while, but it didn't get him anywhere.

But then he thought, Hey! Maybe he was finally talking to a spirit! Maybe that was somebody else writing that.

He wrote, "Who are you?" in his own sloppy handwriting, and then the neat letters told him, "We met long ago, in times before those you can call back to memory."

"Are you a ghost?" Benjie wrote in his usual messy scribbles, but then his neater letters told him, "There are those who might think so."

"Are you my dead Uncle John Gordon?" After he'd written it though, he knew that couldn't be it. Uncle John Gordon had always been drunk, and sometimes you couldn't even understand him when he was talking to you, let alone when he was trying so hard to write something, but missing the paper, and almost falling over. Nobody could ever read what he wrote. It took him a while to even just figure out which end of the pen to hold sometimes.

So, Benjie asked into his journal, "Does my mom and dad know you?"

"We have never met."

"Then I must know you from school."

"In a manner of speaking."

"You talk like a big kid."

"I am rather large."

"How are you doing this? How are you writing with my hand?"

"Some day you will remember a great many lessons you had once studied but have for now set aside. There will come a time when you can make better use of these and they can therefore then again be awakened, but that time is not yet."

"Remember what? What do you mean?"

"That time is not yet."

"Is this like Edgar Cayce saying things when he was asleep? Are you like The Seth Material? I tried to read that a couple of times but it doesn't make a whole lot of sense to me so I just quit. That lady sure smokes a lot!!!"

"That she did; she did indeed."

Benjie wasn't getting any of the answers he wanted. But there was a part of him that seemed to think he should already know them anyway, and not have to ask. Like when he was taking a test in school, and almost had the answer, and knew he should know it, but was afraid his teacher would ring the bell before he was ready.

He had a vague picture of someone from somewhere a long time ago who, when you asked him a question, didn't do like Benjie's mom always did; say you were wrong but do it nicely and then give you a little kiss on the top of your head. He told you that you already knew but just weren't looking deep enough.

Benjie was scrawling the words out even faster now, picking up speed, the ink practically flying out of his pen until he didn't think he'd be able to read this later on. He never re-read his journal anyhow. That's not what it was for. He wrote in it to get things off his chest. The more he wrote, the more he saw how he felt about what was going on inside him.

The neat, slanted handwriting must've heard him thinking that. Because right away it told him, "Once one has set himself the task of looking deeper, he will at times receive communications from other parts of his being. Journaling can provide one of the means for that. Perhaps through cyphers and metaphors he will need to examine."

But then Benjie thought maybe it was changing the subject because it started telling him, "Once this journey has begun he might also in his <u>outer</u> life be brought in touch with someone or something he is convinced he has never seen before and yet still he might know them.

"However, it has often been the case with you, young wanderer, that even at key moments you don't always choose to take hold of what has been offered, and then that opportunity may be set aside. You are not always open to messages. Even to those hints which we ourselves might be placing before or within you."

Benjie was pretty sure he knew what a cypher was. It was kind of like a code, like in his spy books. But metaphor he wasn't too sure of. He decided to look up both of those words later.

This was pretty cool talking to a ghost. A ghost with very neat handwriting. Or, maybe Benjie was like Bridey Murphy, who remembered living in Ireland in an earlier lifetime, and could still talk and write in Irish when she was hypnotized. Wouldn't it be cool if he started talking in another language now?

The slanty-handed ghost told him, "Life is a journey, wherein our earlier steps might be hidden from us, and quite justifiably so. Otherwise, we might cut ourselves short of true understanding by dwelling on that which had once held us back, but which we have already surmounted, and need not revisit. The <u>essence</u> of what we have learned never abandons. We carry the seeds of what we <u>seek</u> always within us. And thus, we are favored in each new lifetime with outer forgetfulness of times and lessons passed, and yet still with connections to our deep inner truth."

Benjie didn't even try to figure that one out.

Instead, he wrote, "When did I know you?"

"When you could see more than you do now," came the neatly penned response.

"Are you a spirit? Are you one of my dreams? Am I sleeping?"

"Perhaps. In a manner of speaking."

"Which?" the boy asked. "When did I know you? Who are you? What…" he started to write, but then scribbled that last word out and tried again. He tried, "Did I used to…" but then that didn't sound right either, and he scribbled through those words as well. He was working on, "Can we meet somewhere?" when his handwriting suddenly changed back to that fancy type again.

"Windows open as you are ready to see. Not just the Who, or the When; but more importantly, the Why."

"But who are you? Are you alive or are you a ghost? Where do I know you from? How do you make me write to myself like this? What's going on? Am I being a psychic now? That would be sooooo cool!"

His hand wrote, "Sometimes the first steps toward seeing clearly lie through no longer desiring this for one's smaller self, and with such passion."

"But who are you?"

There came no answer. No slanted letters.

His room was just a room again.

You wanted to tell Ailana everything. Share all your secrets without her even asking you to. She was like that best buddy you hadn't seen in years and you had so much to catch her up on. Even if in the real world you had only just met. You felt like you had a kind of connection. Some folks are just that way. You instantly like them. You trust them. And then, once your mouth starts flapping, you can't seem to hold anything back. She had a presence about her.

Ailana stood out. She was not just somebody you'd run into at the mall and ignore.

She said what she meant, but said it kindly. She had no pretenses, and encouraged you to drop yours. To just be whomever and whatever you might really be deep inside. You knew you counted for something with her. You felt honored that she saw you as special enough, important enough, to spend her time with you. You wanted to be worthy of that. Not that she would ever think ill of you otherwise, but still, you wanted to try a little harder.

Ailana was simply good people. Like your mom, except this was a mom you'd let read your diaries. The ones you locked with a tiny key, and hid under your mattress.

She wasn't a tall woman, but she wasn't short either. She wasn't fat, but she wasn't skinny. She was quietly healthy, but not robust. She was like that softly hued sunset you could enjoy, but not gasp at. That sunset you stand and watch all by yourself. The one when Nature has wanted to put on her best display, but wasn't in the mood to get all show-offy about it.

The Gardens of Ailana were known to very few, but those who knew tended to be special individuals. They might travel in from surprisingly far away just to spend even a little bit of time there. Some considered it a sort of a pilgrimage. Something they did for themselves, but would only take on when they were ready. Or when they felt particularly needy. There were those who held Ailana on that delicate edge of reverence. Like how you feel about your mom after she's died. When she isn't there to chat with, you still think of her a lot and miss her deeply.

Ailana laughed heartily, but lived quietly. Her gardens seemed to be in bloom even in winter. In her heart, as in her gardens, there was no time when beauty ever faded, or when love was not fresh.

There was a certain magic about even these mountains themselves. Or at least a deep level of peacefulness where magical things could happen. Maybe some of that was because the area was so underpopulated and yet so beautiful. No honking thoroughfares or giant discount malls. No major office complexes or resort parks. People had to either be born here, or pretty much know what they were looking for, or they sure wouldn't have taken planes, trains, and long car rides through slow-trodging sheep country to get here.

Maybe the region seemed magical because it was so uncrowded and yet so beautiful. Or maybe it was uncrowded despite being beautiful because there were forces overseeing the planet that could keep certain areas pristine, and untrodden by the masses. They kept some places clear *because* they were magical.

Let us hope so anyway. The world could certainly use some of that.

Not so very far from the Gardens of Ailana, and not quite as deeply snugged in among the hills, there was a rustic retreat center called Green Man's Glen. You could only get within twenty or so miles of it by local, slow-moving, village-hopping train; but then someone would have to drive out along back country roads in a station wagon to fetch you. Which was of course part of its charm. You maybe took turns getting out along the way to open and shut the sheep gates as their car kept passing through them, one, after another, after another. It maybe said something peculiar about a visitor if, when a few of those critters baaaa-ed at him, he felt it in his heart to baaaa back. Particularly if the sheep then appeared to understand him.

William Rand Jeffers and Shirley Spears lived there at Green Man's Glen all year round; much of it alone, making sure the barn roof didn't collapse under heavy snows, that downed lines were reported, and nothing washed away by those flash floods that sometimes rushed through. In milder weather then, volunteers traveled in to help out for days, weekends, or whole months.

Through later spring, summer, and partway into autumn, this camp offered weekend or week-long retreats. Beginners came by to learn how to meditate, or hear talks about medicinal herbs they could find in their neighborhoods. There might be drum circles, or native chants. They held vegetarian workshops where guests could trade and experiment with each other's recipes. There were silent retreats for those who more or less just needed to get away from their own lives and cities for a while. Workshop leaders and the more experienced often stayed on a few days after class had ended and students gone home. Just hanging out in the peace, enjoying each other's company, and confabbing over the deeper layers of life and the universe.

Guests could stay over in screened cabins scattered among the trees, sleeping on lumpy cots that probably smelled of mildew and pine. With moody electrical connections that kicked on and off. This far from more proper civilization, there was no television, radio, or internet. If you traveled this far out into the boonies to get away from modernity, you had better be committed to roughing it. You would most probably be making some sacrifices.

Visitors could pitch tents or sleep in their own camper vans among the trees, maybe near a stream, or small chattering falls. They could take part in workshops if and when they felt like it; or sit them out. The Glen was just a nice quiet place to hang out for a while.

Vegetarian meals were served in the spacious dining area of the main farmhouse, taken at long wooden tables with dozens of strangers and perhaps a few friends. Scraps were later composted for the vegetable and herb gardens. You could help with that if you wanted to, but you would have to bat away some hard-biting horseflies, and deer flies, and maybe mule flies while you were doing it. Visiting the encampment, you could feel Nature coming alive, all around and within you. And occasionally taking a painful nip out of your flesh.

This was Green Man's Glen. Known to those who had been coming for a while as Green *Guy's* Glen, or 3-G.

Ailana had been scheduled as one of the featured presenters at a couple of their upcoming workshops, but then so many nurses and healers had responded that they'd needed to start turning them away. And still came the clamor of new applicants, and so now they were looking at maybe adding additional weeks.

On this particular day, Rand and Shirley had stopped by the gardens ostensibly to chat with Ailana about some of the details, but mainly they'd just wanted to share some time with everybody's dearest old friend. They'd driven in from the Glen, Shirley laden down with cookies she'd baked from scratch, and now they were staying in two of the guest rooms.

They had already mapped out key dates and times, and now were brewing herbal teas to just sit around outdoors with for a while. Little Sylvie had popped in, helped herself to a generous double mitt full of cookies, listened for a bit, but then wandered off again. Shirley had iced Sylvie's name onto several of the little girl's favorites. When these guys all got together, it was like a family reunion. But one without the drinking, political arguments, or shouting at games on TV.

As the child headed out the door with her treats, she was already breaking one of the "nutjob delights" into little pieces for the squirrels. Shirley beamed one of her radiant smiles as she watched; her soft, gentle eyes alive with the joy of her love for that sweet little girl.

The three adults carried their teas out into the gardens. Sworls of ferns through the woods reminded Rand of an ancient burial mound he'd hunched his way through in Ireland. William Rand Jeffers was a rather large modern man with broad shoulders. People back then had been much smaller, and his back ached a little even now as he thought back through its dark and confining hidden places. He looked around Ailana's at islets and rills of fern forming into clear, geometrical patterns exactly like those carved into its walls. Timeless symbols passed among shamans since men had first become men. Built into ceremonial structures from times long before Stonehenge.

Ailana sensed what he was mulling over and asked him, "How was the trip?"

He smiled. "You caught me again," he told her.

Shirley had already heard some disturbing stories from his most recent travels, but sensed he'd been holding something back. He'd climbed right up against the edge of something he'd really wanted to share, but then shut down. He hadn't been able to finish. Shirley would never want to push him. She made cookies, not demands. But she could tell he was hurting. And Ailana had something about her that drew out what people needed most to share. What they needed to take a hard and honest look at. Maybe she could help Rand with whatever this was, Shirley thought.

He gazed out among the ferns again. Thought about those very first temples. Those first efforts of primitive mankind to connect with their gods.

And how sometimes, their gods had struck back.

Ailana took a couple focused stirs of her tea. A quiet but insistent rustling started up through the forest Something shifted.

He held back for a very long and thoughtful moment but at last told them, "Something broke open in me over there."

He'd traveled a lot over the years, and seen some very strange things. But in all that time, very few had dug into him as much more than memories and colorful tales.

There had been moments, of course. Deeply piercing encounters that still echoed inside him. Shadows he carried years, even decades later. Haunted old monasteries. Certain key churches infused with something powerful that had changed him.

Ancient burial grounds still troubled by spirits unseen. Dark, haunted, terrifying shadows. Wandering, and reaching. Sometimes leaving little bite marks, and burns. Edinburgh seemed to be churning with those.

He wondered now if this had been much more than a game for him at times. Exploring, and hoping, but not expecting very much. Staying in haunted houses, and maybe hearing a rattle or two, but never quite sure. Touring magnificent cathedrals or the ruins of monasteries and maybe feeling a little inspired. Before now, these feelings had always been vague. Mere hints and maybe's that could have been part imagination. They'd never dragged him inside them, so hard and so personally before. Like they'd been waiting eons just for him. For him in particular. They would not let him turn away. It was time.

A part of him had never left Edinburgh.

"Places like that can tear off a chunk of your innocence," he said, with no further clarification at first.

Ailana only sat there and listened.

He was hurting. He felt broken.

"You mean that castle?" Shirley asked. "That tiny, cramped room where you felt those soldiers who'd died a long time ago; starving and freezing all around you? I couldn't have taken it. That must have been horrible. Those poor, dying, suffering men."

His friends read the anguish twisting his face as he climbed back in among the dying. "All those months," he said, trembling. Part of him wanted to shut those doors again, but he knew he really needed to share it. "Not even knowing why they were there. What they were fighting for. It tore me apart.

"Feeling their misery creeping out of the walls."

He told them, "It was like I was starving right in the middle of them. All of us all locked in a tight, stinking huddle of our friends dying slowly in agony. Watching them fade and drop all around me. Couldn't help but think we might have to start eating each other. Not knowing why we couldn't just go home to our families; just let the other guys have the castle.

"And nobody; not me or anybody else; we wouldn't dare say any of that out loud. We must've all been thinking some of this stuff, but we just couldn't… What horrible things would they do to us if we tried to leave?

" 'I should be out there taking care of my family,' we were thinking. We wanted to go home so badly."

His eyes looked strained by the grieving of centuries.

"And the rats. And the filth. We could feel them eating at us. All around us. Everywhere.

"But sometimes it was just too much to chase them. We just wanted to die and get it over with.

"I felt their torment. Those poor soldiers. Slow. Terrifying. Weakening and dying beside the bodies of our neighbors and friends. There was no hope. There was only the waiting.

"I just can't shake that out of me," he told Shirley and Ailana.

Watching him, they could tell how awfully hard he was trying to.

He looked off into the gardens, watched a sweet little child breaking off pieces of her favorite cookies for a chipmunk.

He told them, "And now Sylvie reminds me of that little girl's ghost in a buried street just a few blocks away. She'd had to live and die in squalor, and stench, the Black Death creeping through every shadow and crack.

"Watching Sylvie out there so innocent and trusting. Like that poor little girl's ghost, how she had trusted, but everyone had turned away, and she didn't understand, and how terribly lonely she was. She couldn't understand. She couldn't understand why nobody talked to her anymore. Why everyone kept turning away. Why nobody cared.

"Why can't a child keep her innocence? Why do such horrible things have to tear them apart? Why must they hurt that way?"

"What little girl?" Ailana asked.

"Tell her about that little girl's ghost," Shirley said.

He took a long and careful breath.

"There was this street there, from back in… I don't know. Whenever the plague was. The Black Death.

"Mary King's Close, they called it."

"In Edinburgh?" Ailana asked. "In Scotland?"

"Right. Edinburgh. In Scotland," he told her. "There was this street.

"It had been a poor people's neighborhood. And then, when the rich folks got richer, they just built the town over it. This whole neighborhood was just basically buried underground with everybody still living in it. Like this underground tunnel of filth. People pissing and taking dumps in the river, but then they had to drink it and bathe in it too, because that's all they had."

Shirley had heard this much before, but he looked more intense in the telling of it this time. Her face mirrored his pain.

Ailana simply listened.

No. Purely. She listened purely. Neither feeding his hurt nor wanting to take any of it from him. She just listened.

He dug deeper.

"We went down some stairs in this old building until… Well, I don't remember how we got there; it doesn't matter.

"But that street; all those lost rooms… how they'd had to live. It tore something open in me."

Ailana said nothing. Something almost unbearable had just slammed home inside him. He was visibly shaken, his face deeply sorrowed. He needed this.

He had to take a couple of deep, quivering breaths. He told them, "We got to this one room. Maybe just about as big as a good-sized bathroom maybe. There was a fireplace in the wall at one end and it was piled over with toys.

"Modern toys though. That part stood out. It jarred a little against everything else."

He had to stop again.

Then he told them, "I… I felt a small child pulling on my pant leg." He reached down toward that area, but his hand stopped short of connecting.

"Somehow I knew it was a girl before I even looked. But then I looked and…

"And she wasn't there! Just my legs, and the floor, and nobody was standing there!

"I was… I was overcome by something. It was… I…

"She was so very, very sad. So deeply, terribly hurt, and… Such deep, agonizing, desperate loneliness. It just tore me apart. I felt it all through her! God help me, I felt all of her pain…"

His words paused as his friends watched these horrors shredding him. They held back from interfering.

He tried opening even deeper into the worst of what he'd been carrying around, unable to voice. "She felt so terribly abandoned," he told them. "For so awfully, awfully long. Since forever. For years, and years, and years. Nobody ever stops to talk with her. What happened to her parents? Why couldn't she play with her little sister anymore? Why wouldn't they at least come and talk with her? She was so terribly alone, and she didn't understand. It hurt so awfully badly."

He was himself on the edge of crying now.

"Why?" he asked, nearly weeping. "Why, of all the people on that tour, why did she pull on *my* pant leg? Why mine?"

The guts of what had happened to him back in that room were yanking, and twisting, draining everything out of him. He looked stricken.

It was not unusual for people to look like that when they were opening up to Ailana. As they were setting loose what had been troubling them so long.

"I knew she was standing there; I just knew it," he said. "She was a dark, streaky blonde. Her hair was all matted and stringy. I think I almost heard her voice a couple of times.

"I was sure of it.

"The tour guide was watching me. He must've seen I was going through something. He told us the legend had been that someone had died in that room. No one knew for sure if it had been a child, or one of the parents. Someone had gotten the plague and been abandoned there to die so she wouldn't infect the others. It might have been the mom, the guide said. But one of them had needed to be cut off, locked away from the rest of the family, so they wouldn't all of them catch it. They didn't know which one of them, he said.

"They didn't know.

"They didn't know.

"But I knew. She was standing right there. I could feel her. I might have only been imagining what she could've looked like, but I was not imagining she was there.

"I could feel her."

He drew a deep, racking breath.

"And she could tell that I could.

"That was the horrible part of it. She knew that I knew she was there.

"All those years, and all those tour groups being rushed through, one right after another, and she kept crying to them, but they kept brushing her off, and she didn't understand. How could she know they couldn't even see her?

"They just kept walking away. Nobody loved her, she was thinking. And how terribly that hurt.

"Why did everybody keep abandoning her? she was thinking. Why did they keep walking away?

"And so, I wanted to stay behind, and be with her for a while. I… I tried to tell her in my heart that I cared. I really did.

"I wanted to stay with her for at least maybe half an hour, or an hour or so. I don't know. For just a little while anyway. Let her know somebody heard her. Someone did care.

"But by this time the guide was getting really antsy. Kept telling me to keep up. The rest of my group had already moved on into the adjoining room. I could still look back *toward* where she was, but I couldn't go *to* her. And she couldn't get out of that room. He said another group would be rushing in right after ours, but they had to know we were out of there first. They were on a tight schedule.

"I moved just a little bit closer to the rest of them, but didn't squeeze back into that tight knot of people. I held behind. I only moved up very slowly, and didn't really join in. I was… I was still looking back. Trying to comfort that poor little darling. Even though now she could see *I* was walking away, too. I was just like the others, she thought. She was holding out her hands to me, but she had already given up. I was just like the others, and they were all walking away.

"How else could she see it?

"But we had to move on."

He stopped, lost in the wretchedness.

"I have hurt for that poor child ever since."

He told them, "I did some research when I got back to my B & B. Found out what I could on the internet. Apparently some psychic had gone through there back in the 1920's or some time, and said she'd heard the little girl asking what had happened to her dolly. 'Have you seen my dolly?' she was asking. 'What happened to my dolly? Where did my dolly go?'

"And ever since then, people have been coming back, and bringing her toys. It's why that fireplace had been so piled over with all sorts of modern toys."

Rand sat there, lost. Buried in his grief. "A lot of me wants to go back," he told them. "Try to spend some time with her. Maybe talk with her a while. But it wouldn't do any good," he said. "They'd just rush me right out again like they did the first time.

"I can't help her."

He stared at his own hands for a while.

Then he added, "But I can't let go of her either. I just… I can't just abandon her.

"We have connected."

Ailana gave him a moment.

"And now since then, I've been feeling so many other hurting people out there. Something busted open inside me and I am feeling them everywhere now."

Ailana suggested, "You were ready to move on to your next stage. They were helping you see you had untapped gifts the world will be needing."

"I don't know," he told her. "It's like I'm more sensitive to everything now. I hear things; I notice things I've never paid attention to before. Very subtle breezes against the little hairs on my arms. Whispers. Different ways of seeing things. I feel emotions that don't make any sense."

Her tones were exquisitely gentle. "The world is moving us through great and troubling changes," she told him. "Those who have seen this coming have been inviting special people to help out. We will need those with very specially developed sensitivities to help us get through it, help prepare for some kind of recovery on the other side. Some are being called to ready themselves in service to some deeper purpose they can't always see. We're going to need to find new ways of seeing, and connecting."

People were spending more time on the internet these days, reporting all the tiny details of their lives, sharing what they'd heard and read that may or may not have been true. Folks were learning more about people from what had once been distant, hidden corners of the planet.

More and more they heard tales of children with bizarre talents appearing pretty much everywhere. Some folks used the word "miraculous." At a time when so many felt so awfully weary; worn down to the point of exhaustion by seemingly insurmountable issues of politics, poverty, and man-against-man; even then, new life and spirit was being seeded among them.

Children born as though from some other era. Standing out as Newton must have from neighbor kids in his own very long ago days in England. As da Vinci or Ben Franklin probably had in Italy, or the pre-USA; just before those worlds had begun changing so dramatically. Startling individuals. Not like most from the crop of more everyday humans, but maybe fitting perfectly into something much greater. Forerunners of revolutions unforeseen by the general populace of their times. Seeds perhaps of preordained renaissance.

We watched videos of youngsters playing Mozart or Paganini flawlessly. While still so small that they could barely spread their hands across their keyboards and strings. Awards programs had to keep adjusting their age requirements downward to allow for ever younger children playing Tchaikovsky, or painting masterful portraits.

A little girl was completing Beethoven's unfinished masterpieces beautifully; spilling out lines of music faster than most of us could write sentences. But she had never been trained in any form of music, and couldn't read what she'd written once she'd written it.

One young man could be flown in a helicopter over any city, and only one time, but then come home to draw every street sign, window, and mailbox; draw the entire metropolis on gigantic stretches of paper, and from any angle.

There were those who called such almost supernatural youngsters child savants. Others called them indigo children because of a particularly rich shade of blue some psychics said they could see in their "auric fields." A blue also seen around exceptionally compassionate and selfless adults. Goodhearted, charitable people bearing gifts of beauty and new ways of seeing.

Sure, there were those who could do amazing tricks with Rubik's Cubes, or Hula Hoops, or who could spell any word backwards while simultaneously translating it into Latin. But there were also those like Frederic Lee Benton, who set out one day to demonstrate how Einstein had erred in several of his computations, and was teaching at a university before he was old enough to drive himself there, or take a bus or cab without adult supervision.

Many young folks were being drawn to medicine. Working independently and together to study viruses, crippling illnesses, the diseases of small isolated villages, and pandemics they feared would soon cripple much of the world.

Was time bending? Were these kids gathering in from somewhere in the past, or the future, or both? Perhaps from some other dimension entirely? Was a new era being seeded? Was this how each renaissance in history had always been sparked? Or was it merely that in these times of mass communication and the internet, we compared notes and told each other stories more than we had been? We saw them out there as we passed these fun videos around.

Had such children always been here, but we had just never noticed? Or if not; then why now?

Dictators had been murdering their own citizens in private prisons, secret poisonings, and public beheadings. American political leaders were legalizing the slaughter of pretty much anything and anyone anywhere. You could open fire on humans of "lesser" races, religions, or political agendas. Every day, innocents were gunned down by unhinged white guys blasting through crowds on the streets, in offices, concerts, or churches. At national borders, infants were torn from their moms, shoved into cages and sold. You could hunt and kill baby bears asleep in their caves for the winter, club baby seals, wipe out endangered species. Science, the arts, news media, investigative reporters, and even historical facts were openly censored.

But while all of this was sullying and draining the spirits of humans; while man was being stirred up to turn against man; there was that cute film of the goose handing bits of fish food to large koi at the edge of a pond. The dramatic video of an orca rescuing a diver it must have thought had been drowning. Elephants gathering to pull trapped mammals from other species out from under fallen trees, or out of muddy pits they'd been unable to scale free of on their own. Some ape rescuing a child, or a kitten, or small bird.

It was as though Nature itself was evolving, even as the darkest hearted of humans fought to stop it.

And then, there were these children.

There were also special adults, reawakening to the purity of that child spirit within them.

> *"Watch children playing.*
> *They seem so wise."*
> —The Moody Blues (Days of Future Passed)

Chapter Seven

We can sometimes see more through a cool morning fog or a deep starry night than we could otherwise. We slip through dimensions that lift up our hearts, and spring our imaginations wide open. We can lose ourselves completely. Even while feeling, for this one instant, we've touched home.

Ailana treasured the softness, the essence of beauty filtering through her. A peacefulness so vast, and yet so intimate. Reaching out beyond her as she sat on her bench with her eyes closed. Bits of her hair tossing in slight breezes. Three tiny wrens playing nearby drew in closer to rest around her, where they too grew quiet. A deer settled into the shadow of a nearby tree. Nestling in among the ferns, he laid his head down, and closed his eyes.

Sometimes it feels like something vast, and wondrous, is watching the world through us. Times when even time steps aside.

From within such a pure state of bliss, if we hold a warm thought for someone else, they might sense it. As though they were being drawn into some sweet, calming loveliness, and all things have suddenly gone right.

In The Gardens of Ailana, such magic feels at home. Her gentleness exuded through the air and the land all around her. The beauty of her kindness glowed from the flowers. Perfused richer shades of green through the trees. Humans who had visited here and left again drenched in its magic, now gave a little sigh from wherever they were as she rested and sent them good wishes. They maybe felt a smile forming, though they might not have understood why.

Ailana sat with the birds; with the deer, the flowers, and the greens; with that glow of the forest all around and within her. Before this new day had long been unwrapped, before the ribbons of sunrise had quite fallen away, Ailana saw all things more clearly, and held the world in her heart.

She'd learned to follow any visions or insights she found in such deep states of clarity and contentment. When a thought or picture appeared, she'd learned to trust it. As she sat with that deeper life this morning, she was shown an image of little Sylvie as a young teen, maybe ten years or so from today. After Ailana herself would have passed away. In this vision, Sylvie was still a very happy child. Her auntie's heart glowed as she watched the small-sized young lady playing in these same fields and forests. Watching what she thought of as a herd of ants dying by the hundreds trying to weave a net of their own bodies across a tiny pond they could have walked around. She didn't interfere. Nature had her ways, she knew.

Ailana listened in as the child considered how for humans, struggling with life's problems could be a good thing. Through suffering and sacrifice they could grow into something much better than they had been. But were these ants really learning anything? Was this courageous self-sacrifice, or just acting on autopilot?

But then she thought about how even humans could follow blindly. She looked back over some great devastation that had by that time torn through much of mankind. Clusters of ant-like humans dying needlessly. Making choices that killed off their own families, communities, and church groups. Choosing politics over good sense. Laying their lives on the line trusting in people the whole world knew could never be trusted.

Ailana sensed horrors and isolation that had eaten through much of the world. What had happened? Some great war? Something people had been offered some kind of choice with. To die from, or beat back. What could this be? What was coming?

She heard Sylvie considering how some were learning to care more about others even as their own pain was unbearable. Growing more sensitive, a lot of them would be drawn to these gardens. They'd have new issues to deal with. Whatever this was would have left trails of death, grief, and destruction Excruciatingly sensitive folks; newly minted special ones; would be needing special help. Consulting with her Auntie might not always be quite enough. Sylvie wanted to help out, but how was her silliness ever going to help anyone?

She would just have to trust the teachers knew what they were doing. It kept coming back to that. Maybe everything was just as it needed to be, and even she might have her own strange ways of helping. We're probably all of us just where we need to be, and there will be those who are ready for what we have to offer, she thought.

By accepting who we are and what we can give, we can each be that magic the world has been waiting so long for.

Ailana's vision cut off here, and she was back watching fog with her animal friends.

All this from the mind of a teenager, she marveled, and couldn't help but feel a glow of pride, along with that gratitude she always felt flooding her.

She broke into a quiet laugh, picturing her goofy little cohort playing with an adult who had long suffered the plight of being way too serious. There had been enough suffering, and now Sylvie was helping lighten that load. Having a fun time helping some poor fellow play with bugs, and walk more tenderly with Nature.

Ailana had been offered many such glimpses in preparation for her coming demise.

Suddenly it was like someone had slapped her very fondly on the back of her head. She saw something she hadn't noticed in this vision at first.

Sylvie had suggested that seekers would still be coming to consult with Ailana.

How could that be? She was dying. She'd been shown that quite clearly.

Sylvie might never actually think those exact thoughts. It was likely, but not an absolute given, that she would develop along these lines. Nothing in life was ever truly guaranteed. The future is never locked down. But in those thoughts she *might* think, Sylvie had suggested that people would still be coming to consult with Ailana.

That didn't make sense. She'd be no more than ashes in the soil by then.

How could this be?

Another image came to her. A strange idea. But not impossible.

It would have only been her body that had died after all.

Benjie had figured out that when Maddie watched you talk, he was probably doing more than just listening. He was maybe studying the little flecks of color in your eyes you probably didn't know that you had. How the hairs in your eyebrows headed off in different directions; or your nose made a funny whistling sound. One ear was at a different angle than the other. Maddie seemed to be counting the universe, atom by atom. But he was also listening. He was definitely listening.

He came alive in the silence. And now, as they sat together in Maddie's backyard, Benjie saw him lean forward; eager, and alert; peering into unmoving fog like he almost expected it to say something. Maddie was a strange sort of duck, as Benjie's mum might say. It was that eerie, unnatural quiet of his. It caught hold of you if you were with him for long, like it was maybe contagious somehow. You had to be so still around him that you started looking around, too. Noticing things in more detail. Even your own thoughts. Benjie had always been a thinker, but now he was sure he was getting better at it.

Maddie had an almost bizarre depth of peacefulness about him. A true sense of presence Benjie hadn't noticed at first, and most people never would. He was sensitive to things most folks had learned to ignore. He moved slowly, as though each little increment came only after careful deliberation. To Benjie, his friend was a mystery. He took calm to whole other levels.

In the quiet around Maddie, Benjamin started noticing a kind of balanced perfection in the world he'd always lived in, but never maybe paid much attention to before. He saw and heard things more clearly. Like in the blending of animal sounds, the smells, and the breezes. If you looked at things hard enough—actually, maybe it was more like you had to look at them *softly* enough—you could see a kind of sensibleness and order.

Sure, he could still just look out into the woods and say, "Yup, there's a whole lotta trees out there," and let it go at that. But when he really looked now, he saw whole networks of roots, branchings, and connections reaching in and out from everywhere. Weaving together like maybe the whole world was a vast, gigantic teeming of connections. Animals and plants all working together. He could see and understand a whole lot more about all kinds of things when he slowed down to take a good look and a real careful listen.

And you pretty much had to slow down around Maddie. He didn't leave you much other choice.

He was somebody you were never going to figure out if you kept thinking you already knew him. Some folks were maybe there to unsettle us. Show us we don't know as much as we'd thought we did. Knock us loose from how we used to see things. Maddie was never quite what you'd expected.

Maybe none of us were.

Maybe life never was.

"Are you here to see my Auntie Ailana?" Sylvie wasn't usually all that eager to greet strangers, but this one was different. She didn't think he was staying in any of the guest rooms, and she hadn't seen his car anywhere. He was suddenly just there, standing in the path, smiling at her; and she loved how strange it felt when somebody was *POOF!* suddenly just there like that. A robin hopped and poked through the grass right in front of her, looking for wrigglers, but she just ignored it.

"And to see you," he said. "If you like."

He had a funny way of talking, which she thought was probably just as it should be since he looked a little funny as well.

He or she. With some folks you couldn't really tell.

Sylvie had been poking around through some stuff at the edge of that special dark part of the forest most people didn't know about and that she didn't usually go into. She wasn't too sure if he'd maybe already been there awhile and she'd just caught up to him, or if he'd just flashed in like a fairy. She hadn't really been paying much attention, so he could have been there the whole time. She'd been thinking some things in that picturing part of her head. She did that a lot. Her mom called her a real space case. And then *POOF!* She had seen him in her brain, and looked up, and there he was. Walking along right beside her. Even her mom would probably be able to see him, even with her regular eyes, if she was there, which she wasn't, and it was just as well because some of her best and strangest stuff happened when her mom wasn't around.

The stranger didn't say hello, but then neither did she. They just started talking. She didn't ask his name, and he didn't ask hers, but most times that wasn't important. And anyway, who cares what your mom and dad wanted to call you before you were even born and they didn't know you yet? She would probably find something she wanted to call this person eventually. But like everything else she named, he would have to earn it first.

She already liked this guy, and he was smiling great big at her like he meant it. He asked if it was okay if he hung out with her for a while, and she told him, "That would be just swell!" but then she thought, "That was really strange!" Because that was something her daddy said when he was just being goofy. She herself never said "Swell!" She never used that word. But then she thought, point of fact, she actually just did.

And then she wondered, why was she chattering at herself in her own head?

The stranger laughed as he watched her.

"I had considered bringing you some flowers," he told her. "But you 'don't like them to be cut off and forced to die just so a person can hand them to somebody else'."

"My exact words exactly," she told him. "That's true. I don't. They are gonna turn to dust some time, but they should just be allowed to live the way they want to until then. They shouldn't be hurt by somebody just so I can look at them somewhere other than where Mama Nature put them."

"I understand," he told her.

"And anyway, I have all this," she said, waving her hand everywhere around her.

"You are a wise child," he observed.

"I am," she agreed.

"Which is part of why I'm here," he told her. "And also 'that dying thing'."

"You mean my auntie?" she asked, although she sort of knew already.

"I'm here to help her," he said.

The two of them apparently weren't going to need a whole lot of words to understand each other, she thought. They said things like they really were, without pretending, like most people usually did. She could tell that about him right away.

He was not a tall man, but he was confident, so he looked big, she observed. He was sure about himself, but not mean, or pushy about it. As they strolled together he told her, "Everything dies, Honey. You know that, don't you?"

"I know that. I've been finding a lot of dead things around here lately. I think Mama Nature has been trying to show me them on purpose. She's been trying to tell me something."

"Sometimes we find things for a reason," he agreed.

"Even my auntie though?" she asked him, but this time her voice hurt a little. "Even she has to die? I thought she had been here forever."

"Even all of us," he said. They had slowed to a pause in their walking. She turned a little bit toward facing him. He turned all the way toward facing her. He reached to rest his hand very softly on her shoulder and it was like the busy part of the world quieted down for a minute. Although maybe the birds started singing a little prettier.

"Even your auntie," he said. And then somehow she felt better about that, hearing it from him. It was like they'd known each other for a very long time. Since before she'd been born maybe even, she thought, and he smiled as she thought it.

A bear wandered by, stopped to look at them, but then just moved on. Sylvie named him Mr. Paddy Paw because of how softly he stepped. She didn't think she had ever seen a bear quite this close before. He looked big, soft, and pretty. All shiny and black. She wanted to pet him and scratch around on his great big head, but not everybody likes to be scratched on their heads like that. And anyhow, some people you only get to know for a moment, but then they have to move on.

"I guess my auntie has other places to go now?" Sylvie asked. "She has worked her purpose and done what she can around here?"

He laughed a soft and knowing laugh. "Quite an insightful way to phrase that," he told her. "And that's a part of what your auntie and I will be talking over. She still has options."

"She will do whatever is right," she told him. "That's why I like her. She always does."

"And yet, even within what is right there may still be choices," he said.

"This is true," she told him, but she knew she would have to be thinking about that one for a while.

They wandered along. He didn't seem to have any more *Hurry up!* in him than she did.

He looked kind of oriental, she thought, but knew she wasn't very good at sorting things like that out just yet. She was after all only about six or so years old. She wasn't very good with numbers yet either. His eyes were kind of like deer eyes, but not really. They were big, brown, and shiny like a deer's, but without all the flies. So, she wouldn't call him Deer Eyes. But anyhow, they didn't look like most people's eyes.

He asked her, "Why do you suppose people come here to visit your aunt? You said she had a purpose. What do you suppose that purpose might be?"

"Other than you?" she asked. "People visiting her other than you? Cause you came to visit her too."

"Other than me." This fellow always seemed to be smiling. It was the kind of smile that felt like it was giving you a hug.

She didn't answer him right away. He wasn't the kind to just ask questions to be talking. He said things to make you think about stuff, and so she did.

She told him, "It isn't just Auntie Ailana they come to visit. It is also this place."

"Ahhh," he said. "Perfect. I was hoping you had noticed that."

"I notice lots of stuff," she told him.

She found one of those seeds with long wings that whirl as they fall down out of the trees. She picked it up out of the leaves and tried to throw it a few times but couldn't seem to get it to go very far.

"And so you do," he told her as he watched. He was having a good time because she was. "You are quite the little noticer."

This fellow really seemed to be happy.

Then she asked him one. She asked, "Can I learn to do that thing she does with her hands that makes people feel better?"

"I would not be at all surprised," he told her. "You would like to?"

"Uh-huh."

"Well then maybe, when you're a bit older we might see what we can do about that."

"So, you'll be sticking around for a while?" she asked, her eyes bright in eager expectation. "You'll be around when I'm older maybe?"

"You are already older than you were when we first met," he said.

"This is true," she admitted, but then seemed to think that what he'd said must have been terribly funny because it set her off in the giggles.

"But I wouldn't be at all surprised," he told her again. "I might keep visiting if I'm welcome, and if the need is here. If you decide you are ready to learn certain things, I may be able to help you with them."

Sylvie thought about how her aunt wasn't going to be around forever. This still made her sad. Auntie had told her it shouldn't, but it did.

She didn't say any of that out loud.

"Some things take a while," he told her, and there was great comforting in his voice.

He seemed to have all the time in the world to just hang around with a little girl, and that surprised her kind of. So she asked him, "Does Auntie Ailana know you're here?"

"I suspect she always has some idea of where I am," he told her. "I think she probably knows."

He paused for only a moment, looking back in the general direction of Ailana's house, although they really couldn't see it through all those bushes and trees from where they were. "Yes," he told her then. "She is aware."

They talked for a long time, but then he went away. They'd talked about everything she'd wanted to by that time anyway, and now she had some playing to do. She didn't watch him go, because she was busy with something else at the time.

But then, she hadn't really seen him come in the first place.

In a fog this thick, when you can't see twenty feet in, you lose details you had counted on. Things disappear into it like they had never really been there. But Benjie felt like these particular clouds rolling past him today were actually hinting at things that *were* there; he just wasn't seeing them. Suggesting greater depths. Offering peeks into the subtle nature of strangeness. It was as though some mystical deeper life was slipping forward, reaching for him from somewhere unseen within the trees. Calling him into its mysteries.

He tried walking into the thick, slithering mist, even as stones shifted beneath him, and he couldn't see where to place his next step. Cool wet breezes brushed at his neck. Like cold cloths pressed against a feverish brow, they at once shocked, but also soothed him. His hands were numbing from the iciness even as he shoved them deep inside his pockets. Even when he pulled them out to tug at his clothes and re-layer them a bit, he wasn't able to snug his jacket in closely enough. This shivering cold still reached through.

Part of him wanted to head back indoors where everything would be warm, cozy and familiar. But he stayed. His grip on reality morphing and oozing with the fog banks. Drawing him right up to the edge of some crossover point where he'd need to choose which reality he wanted to sink into. It might be only his over-active imagination, but that morning, the world came alive with *what if*'s. He keep telling himself this was only fog. There was nothing here but wandering lumps of humidity. Shifting their shapes, but not actually meaning anything. And yet he loved this sense of deep and unsettling eeriness creeping everywhere through him.

He stayed. Watching dragons and dreams sliding by. Other worlds forming, then fading back into secrecy. Peeking out from behind curtains that had opened too briefly, but then slid closed into silence again. Actors in some mystery drama dimly lighted, but then disappearing backstage.

Soft whispers of promise.

Mere suggestions. Nothing solid. Some familiar presence, like murmurs of his past.

Somewhere a bird cawed. Unanswered. Drying leaves sighed, falling free from all that had sustained them through more comfortable seasons. From security they'd come to rely on. Benjie heard their grinding moans as they brushed against bark in their tumble. Even his bones were shivering now, but he stayed.

That everywhere wetness gathered into one single drop hanging on, just below the tip of his nose. When he wiped at it, another one formed in its place. This would be a fine day for hot cider, or cocoa with marshmallows later, but for now it was out here, in this frigid, unsettling dankness, that he wanted to stay for as long as it appeared to be welcoming him.

He wiped at his nose again.

But then let that next drop just linger.

He'd brought a little notebook along, tucked into one of the leg pockets of his gray cargo pants. He worked it out and held it open, hoping to capture what he could of this fog and its dreams.

From time to time he'd been whipping out his pen and paper, scribbling something quickly, then shoving them back into his pocket again. He wrote even when he could barely see his own hand. He wrote when he was scribbling in such rapid fire bursts he wouldn't be able to read it back later. Still he wrote.

And then, everything shifted.

It started with a settling of calm. Like a soft, slowing breeze sifting through him. As though all the world had slipped into a pure form of knowing, and stillness.

He turned to a fresh page in his notebook. Establishing a clear separation between this morning's pileup of scribbles, and whatever might be coming.

Then he waited.

He gathered himself together for a long moment.

He stood there, and waited, and listened.

With great care, and focused clarity then, he slowly inked out two letters.

He wrote, "*Bj.*"

Then he paused.

In that moment, those two letters felt like some kind of incantation. Drawing him outside of himself. He stood listening for what couldn't be heard. It was as if they were calling to him from somewhere deep in passing mists.

Bj.

The slow, focused, inking of those two letters; drawn as though carving them into some sacred ancient stele; were like taking a step into magic. An invitation he didn't know how to follow up on. The very act of writing *Bj* drew him aside from himself, and he waited.

When nothing came for a while he tried drawing them again, retracing over them again and again. He kept scratching at them, making them darker and darker; just kept writing *Bj*. Tapping hard at the paper with his pen. Trying to wake himself up.

He stopped to stare at them for a long time, not knowing what to expect, or to hope for.

He left a big space underneath then, and moved his pen lower. If those two letters were supposed to be some sort of a statement all by themselves, he probably shouldn't write too close to them.

Farther down the paper, he started scribbling out words again, just to be writing something; even though he couldn't think of anything to say. He was really just moving the pen around and stuff was coming out.

And then; those dear, strange, slanting letters started to form.

He was more or less just basically watching as he wrote, "The time is nearing. Energies are joined. Upheaval is unavoidable. Many will suffer. Hearts will be rent asunder, and will be in need of comforting.

"Stand ready.

"Keep listening.

"<u>Care</u>."

The next he remembered, he was back in his house again. In the living room, watching TV. His winter outdoors gear was off and probably tucked neatly away in a closet. His notes from the fog were nowhere to be seen, and he was wearing different pants.

His mom was sitting beside him, chatting warmly, and he had apparently been holding up his own end of the conversation, but now it took him a moment to anchor into any of that. He had to stop and refocus before he could call to mind what they'd been talking about.

Outside the window, the last traces of mist were clearing away.

A sudden burst of wind through the calm startled both of them, and they turned for a moment to watch. Leaves arching through the air like flying munitions.

And then, all was settled back into how things had always been.

In his bedroom alone that night, Benjie opened his laptop, hoping to find some good internet sources on calligraphy where he could research that funny handwriting style.

Instead, as he waited for his computer to warm up, he watched a pretty flower in a pond blooming outward from the center of his screen. A dark hand holding a white feather quill wrote words in that same slanted handwriting across the still water. Slowly and neatly it spelled out, *The Buddhi Connection*.

Then it wrote, "We welcome your return, young Bj."

Even in these hurting times there were those trying to build toward something better.

But there were also those serving something much darker. American leadership had been trying to turn its people against science, history, and even their own best interests. Throwing everything they had into forcing the whole world backwards.

It seemed most people had gotten snagged in the middle. Paralyzed by their own gathering dread, they couldn't or wouldn't push back. Mired in such deep feelings of hopelessness they felt afraid to even draw their next breath.

As the minds and hearts of many slowed to a standstill, clotted, and scabbed over, others were just coming alive. Some deeper life was spreading ever outward through a vital, growing fascia of compassion, connecting all parts together, and strengthening the whole.

New life was sparked.

Soon to be followed by death and devastation.

*I wanted to be comforted. To be told, and to believe,
that I could someday reach for kindness and truth again.
For purity and hope.
But Darkness lay everywhere, and needed to be fed.*

Chapter Eight

Even as scattered individuals appeared to be awakening in odd ways, whole cults and communities dug themselves deeper into the comforting familiarity of their ignorance. It was an age of separation, as when Renaissance had grown out of the suffering and depravity of Dark Ages. Or when strangely evolving sea creatures had first climbed onto land. These struggling early amphibians had left masses of sea life behind, but there come times when a rare few are meant to step forward out of the pack.

Scientists in Oswego, in Minnesota, and in La Plata, Argentina were developing ways of detecting ever more subtle energies. Not intentionally working together, they often hit on strikingly compatible ideas simultaneously. Almost like their work was being choreographed. Astronomers could then probe farther out into the heavens, where they found pulses suggesting that someone might be watching back. Researchers exploring how thoughts and emotions interacted with others far away suggested a sort of parapsychological entanglement. People all around the globe were waking up with new ideas for projects they really wanted to take on.

In state and national capitols; in boardrooms, and on the streets; powerful, clear seeing, soul driven women and miraculous children moved as a solid, cohesive force against overpowering tyranny.

And yet, all the while, darkness still encumbered many hearts. The world was evolving even as many fought to shove time backwards to more stagnant eras when their own race, their own kind had reigned smugly and often abusively uber alles. An onrush of idealistic and highly ethical young citizens; many of them ladies of color; had been voted into the United States Congress, but there were still plenty of entrenched, rich white males in the Senate and White House to block them from doing any real good. The President told them to go back to the "crap hole countries" their people had come from. Leave America in the hands of violent white extremists where it belonged. How dared they get themselves educated, his media echo team demanded? "We don't need *your* color in *our* country!" *White and Right* leaders fired up their base to grab guns and take these uppities out. Anti-lynching laws; laws against hate crimes and discrimination; laws protecting women, children, gays, and Native Americans; laws that had been in place for decades; were revoked.

Pressure kept building. Both sides hit the streets.

The keynote speaker from Families for Peaceful Tomorrows, Andrea Corman, was climbing to her conclusion at the Columbus gathering of Women Waging Peace. Cameras, mikes, sound trucks carried her words, commitment, and passion to the world. "Even here in the very heartland of America, our children are far from safe. They *can* never be; they *will* never be truly safe until children everywhere are protected not just from violence, but from the greed and corruption that create it.

"We must help them grow into adults who can work together. Not one against another, but as an international, intracultural family. If they don't, there can be no hope for any of us." Over rousing applause she told the world, "America must learn that its true strength lies not in its missiles, but in its compassion."

From her makeshift stage beside a multicolored bus painted with flowers, rainbows, and the names of lost loved ones, she told them, "International relations dare not be about which bully is bigger, whose weapons are louder, and who punches first. We must learn to listen, and to care."

Off in the back, a news commentator told Marta Henry they should all just go home. The world wasn't interested. He told more than asked her, "What could any of you know about negotiations? Men work the deals. Women clean their houses. Nobody cares what you think."

"Which is why the world is in such a mess," she told him." It had damned well better start being about what we can build together, not just what you bullies can tear down. About the families who actually live in those ravaged lands; not just how many missiles we can lob over there to rip their poor bodies and lives apart so we can grab their oil. If we don't start turning things around, and I mean right now, this planet is not going to survive."

A rush of pickups and 4WD's stormed in, spraying their old bus with bullets. Men piled out. They started dragging women off the platform, or knocking them down where they stood. Women as old as eighty, their children and grandchildren, were thrown to the dirt by raging males shouting vulgarity.

One cracked Andrea's mouth open with a rifle butt.

They called women "breeders." Told them to know their places, stay in their kitchens or laundry rooms. Women had no rights, and children were worth less than nothing. They were there only to work for the pleasure and profit of men. New laws gave rapists power over children they'd seeded through their heinous assaults, but put women in jail for fighting back.

Around the world, journalists trying to show any other side than their government's, were dismembered, slowly, and screaming. Or beheaded, imprisoned, or found dead. Publicly ridiculed as purveyors of "fake news" by those who almost never spoke truth or allowed it to be spoken by others.

But as all of this was tearing communities apart, drowning the spirit and last hopes of adults, young people were taking on causes abandoned by their elders. Mad men blasted through schools, killing thousands of children with mass-murder weaponry, and young survivors fought back against the system that allowed it. Kids took to the streets, to the media, and to Congress; fighting for gun control, compassion, and truth.

A tiny girl sat alone with a hand-lettered sign on a sidewalk in Sweden, warning locals of dire threats to the climate. Millions soon followed her lead, massing streets everywhere, fighting to save the planet their own leaders had turned so hard against.

Greta Thunberg told the world, "Since our leaders are behaving as children, we will have to take the responsibility you should have taken long ago."

The heart of humanity was still beating.

She'd been assigned to dig into rumors. But it wasn't her reporter's nose she was following; it was her heart. She wanted to get inside and hug some of those children. Children torn from their moms and dads so long ago they'd probably cried themselves dry by now. Hundreds if not thousands of them packed together, sleeping on concrete, and probably not one of them had been hugged for as far back as they dared remember.

Would they trust her even if she could get inside? If she reached her arms out, would they flinch? Would they cower away from her, whimpering? Expecting the worst? Would they stand stoic, all feeling drained out of them?

Shondra Bevins wept a little herself at the thought of maybe sitting among them a few minutes. Could they believe even then that an adult could feel compassion? They'd see her as only an American. Their time in these cages had proven that Americans were born without souls.

Sleeping crowded together on thin foil sheets over concrete. Maybe piled on top of each other, even in this horrendous desert heat, she imagined. Eating God knows what, relieving themselves wherever they could. Some things she didn't even want to think about.

She had to try to show them somebody still cared. Would some at least remember how to smile?

Her network had arranged a ride for her on a bus with doctors, inspectors, and medical aides from the U. N., Red Cross, and Doctors without Borders. They were bouncing along roads torn through fragile ecosystems. From his window seat her cameraman was filming ranch houses reminding her of her own childhood. Lying on thick, soft carpet with her brothers, watching Bonanza reruns with the folks, or Little House on the Prairie. Stories where good guys spoke true, treated people fairly, and bad guys always met their comeuppance. Now beautiful homes like Ben and the boys had lived in on the Ponderosa were being stolen by government bandits. Rich guys growing fatter off their prison and export system. She'd heard about some of their parties. Pretty children cleaned up and brought in to "entertain."

"God, I hate these guys," she heard, though it took a moment to register.

She turned toward her cameraman but didn't reply. He was filming a lovely old log home a little ways in from the road. He had buzz cut red hair, scattershot freckles, and the deeply creased leather skin of someone who'd spent his childhood in saddles.

"I knew a lot of families like these," he told her, still filming. "I knew their histories. I knew that pride. How they'd never give up, no matter what. If they got hard bit by a rattler, they'd just bite it right back.

"To see this all stolen from them like the government done…" He didn't want to ride that thought any further.

"I had kinfolk around here," he said.

"Eminent domain," she said.

"Whatever," he said. "Pure, black heart thievery's what it is. Pennies on the dollar.

"And anyway, that part don't matter," he told her. "These folks don't want no government handouts. Just don't take their land if they've got no mind to sell it. That's their family. Their pride. Don't ever try to take a man's pride. Not out here, you don't."

They were quiet then. He shut off his equipment, dropped it to his lap, but didn't turn toward her. His eyes may have been aimed out the window, but his heart was looking back through his past.

"Really pisses me off how they keep fuckin' so many good people over. Stealin' from all of us so's they can hand juicy contracts to their rich buddies, makin' roads where there shouldn't oughta be any. Like none of us ever counted in the first place. Just them gettin' richer's all't matters.

"Damned border walls and kiddie prisons," he said, then went quiet again.

She'd never known much about this man she'd learned to rely on. He'd never been much of a talker. Must be the private sort, she thought. Or just been raised out here in land so vast there would rarely have been anyone to chat with.

Everyone called him Scratch. It was what he went by. Said it had something to do with the quality of his beard when he was young. His real name on the paperwork was much less interesting. Hank Carley. Said it never had been Henry. They'd written Hank on his birth papers. But Scratch was what he'd always gone by since he was little. Claimed he'd grown his beard, saddled up and started riding when he'd hardly made it out of his cradle. A cradle probably handmade and passed down from his ancestors. Men like that did tend to come with stories, she thought. Stories and tall tales.

"Folks like us, we don't go down easy," he told her, breaking silence again.

What was she doing in the middle of this, she asked herself? She'd never worked the heavy stories. All that hard-driving, investigative digging into political cover ups, pastor pedophiles, or institutionalized debauchery. The stuff that made people's careers, but cost them privately. That wasn't her. She did puff pieces. People around her on this bus, with all they'd been through; all those wars overseas, and disease, and starvation; the kind of ugliness they'd faced down; these guys were true heroes. War-hardened medical professionals who'd watched children die by the hundreds. Held their little bodies as they were being eaten away by some horrible, flesh-eating diseases, or torn to tiny, weeping shreds by landmines near their homes. These caring but tough men and women had held them knowing they'd just have to let this one go and move on to the next dying innocent.

How could they keep going back in? How could anyone witness that kind of uncalled for suffering, and keep going? Just move along to that next infant, that next war, that next outbreak of pestilence? How could they keep putting themselves out there like that? How did they get out of bed in the morning?

She didn't deserve to be among heroes. She had no right sitting anywhere near them.

She'd just written happy stories about adopted kids finding their moms, or someone donating computers to schools. When a blind child's lost dog came home. Not this kind of madness. She only wrote about the sick and the dying if she knew there'd be an uplifting twist at the end. In her world, people held each other's hands after a love spanning decades, and then died together; having made this a better world for those who'd known them.

Not this. Where had the idea come from that she should ask for this assignment? What had made her think she could handle it? And why had the network said yes? They should have handed it off to some seasoned investigator who could bite through steel. Why her?

She didn't even want to make eye contact with the doctors around her, let alone interview them. They must be hurting and scared themselves. Why go digging around in fresh, seeping wounds and make it all worse for them?

What had she gotten herself into? Children disappearing by the hundreds from cage cities inside *American* borders. Records conveniently lost, or wiped clean. Attractive "young exotics" tattooed and branded for resale. International child sex cartels getting so cocky these days since their kind had taken over the government. Russian mobs, Middle Eastern mobs, cinema moguls, Senators with tastes for exotic flesh. The President's buddies with their private islands. All so arrogant in their untouchability.

Less marketable kids left to die in their cages. Dysentery, contagious lung diseases. Even rumors of the plague coming back. Their corpses left lying where they'd fallen in crowded pens.

These doctors had been everywhere, and seen the worst. Starving villages in faraway lands. Pestilence and filth. Had they ever imagined America deteriorating to no more than a blight-ridden third world nation? She should ask how that made them feel. But she couldn't. She couldn't move. She could only sit there, and watch them, through tears.

Still miles from the prison's defensive perimeters, big ugly signs were rising up outside their windows. Dire threats of dismemberment, torture, or worse if they came any closer.

Or at least that's how she read them, anyway.

Warning!
This is a restricted United States Government Area.
It is unlawful to make any photograph, film, map, sketch, picture, drawing, graphic representation, three-dimensional representation, or word description of this area or facility now, or at any time in the future.
Long distance photography from surrounding area or flying overhead is strictly prohibited.

Several signs warned them the:

Use of deadly force has been authorized.

If anyone so much as sneezed, they'd all be snuffed out by heavily armed troops.

"See those white, weatherproof things on poles?" Scratch asked, pointing a couple of them out.

"Sure," she said. "They're everywhere."

"Motion detectors," he told her. "Security forces could be camouflaged pretty much anywhere. You'd never see 'em."

They passed more of those signs.

"Hey, Scratch," she said. "This is getting serious. They mean business. Think you better put your cameras away?"

He told her, "Fuck them!

"What're they gonna outlaw next? Our memories?"

He told her, "They been watching us for miles. You think they don't know we been coming, who we are, and who our folks were? They know our grandkid's names, and where we buried our pets, for Christ's sake. We ain't hidin' nothin'.

"You can't just give in to that shit and let 'em stampede us."

This is a U. S. federal government facility, she thought. American citizens are not welcome here. Turn around before we set the dogs loose on you!

Beware! Be very-fucking-aware, she told herself.

She wondered if the driver was as terrified as she was. This wasn't bulletproof glass. Just a normal rental bus; not some armored tank with cannons. Despite it's aggressive cooling system, she could see beads of sweat breaking on those sitting near her as they passed denser massings of those signs. They'd been caught inside civil wars, and tribal conflicts. But it had always been somewhere overseas. Now they could be facing down the might of the American military under absolute dictatorship of a man with no heart. These folks had been through Hell; faced down the worst that life and this world could throw at them; but she felt the tension, anxiety, the shared and private terror building.

Maybe you could never completely deaden your heart to the worst of the danger, cruelty, and ugliness out there.

Scratch was still looking outside. He hadn't moved for a while, but had been watching intensely.

And then his face grew even harder.

Nodding toward the window he told her, "We're probably little more than a half a mile out or so, looks like."

Leaning in, she asked, "How can you tell?"

"Them damned vultures. They feast on the dead. On body parts. No decent scraps left for them to survive on this far out in the fuckin' desert, less someone's been feeding 'em somethin'.

"What you suppose them fuckin' guards been feedin' these damned scavengers 't draws 'em in so close? Tearin' off chunks of little Pedro, or Jose, you suppose?

"I wouldn't put it past 'em. The fuckers."

The scavenger population tightened in, gathering in larger numbers.

As they drove on they started seeing dozens of the birds blown apart. Feathers, blood, and innards splattered. Like someone had been using them for target practice.

They started hearing gunshots. Then that horrid, subhuman, back country howling. The barking, hooting, and baying of alpha male triumph and testosterone. Their vehicle slowed as they passed pickups and camper homes. A loose gathering of men with huge beards and bellies, waving their weapons in the air; pointing some of them at the bus, firing over and around it, until the driver was forced to a stop.

"What are you doing?" Shondra cried out to him in panic, but Scratch laid a firm, settling hand on her arm. He silenced her with a look before she could draw any more attention to herself. He shook his head. No!

They waited.

All was silent inside the bus while outside the mania exploded. The medical pros had learned to back away from warlords. They'd learned to back down to tribal leaders and savage revolutionaries. They'd learned to hold quiet until bidden. All that mattered was offering whatever help they could to however many victims they could reach under the circumstances. If they had to pack up and flee this time, they could maybe find a way back in later. A lot of locals would have died by that time, but there would always be new batches of suffering innocents.

Cruelty was a disease they could never find a cure for.

The private militia outside thrilled to their own primitive racket. A few proudly sported bright orange MAGA hats. Most were dressed more like Rambo in the Sahara, but with beer kegs. Walking around all sides of the bus, banging it with hands, clubs, or rifle butts. Jumping up to make faces through windows. Some kept firing shots into the air, or pointing weapons at the faces of passengers watching them. They were cannibals who'd just captured their enemies; hooting and stomping as they piled more logs on the fire.

This was going to get ugly, and they wanted their fresh prey to know it. All flesh on that bus now belonged to these tribesmen, and no one was going to die quickly.

They let that terror build for a while. Like natives drumming and dancing around the flames well into the night as their captives, tied to trees, could only strain at their ropes.

Shondra watched her partner ease a small knife out of his pocket. One of those all-purpose gadgets with a thousand hidden tools folded into each other. The kind you'd expect a man like him to carry.

As everyone else was distracted, he loosened screws, positioned a small transmitter up inside the overhead panel, and closed it up again. He wedged a tiny camera into an overhead rack.

A few of the larger two-legged bulls gathered to the sides of the bus and started rocking it, grunting, and jeering.

Shondra was gripping her own mouth, her nails digging into her thigh, stifling any sounds of her panic.

Scratch knew what she was thinking. He told her, "We can't just turn tail and run. Wouldn't last long in this desert once they've shot out our tires and put some holes in the gas tank."

She could smell the gathering sweat. Almost hear people's teeth grinding. And these were seasoned professionals who'd have a much better idea than she could of what was coming.

The driver had been staring out through the closed door to his side. Now he slowly put his hands up like he was being robbed. It was clear from the look on his face that someone had a gun on him.

He held off for a moment but then had to give in. He reached slowly for the lever, and they all heard the rubbery grind of that door opening.

The first head poked through, looking back over its captives.

It grinned.

Someone shoved him from behind and then climbed on behind him. One by one they came aboard. Taking their time. Milking it. Letting it all build. Fanning the coals of anxiety.

They gave a jab here and a pop there, quick punches through the air toward people's faces, really getting off on it when they could make someone flinch. They hooted and jeered. Poking each other for bragging rights when they got a rise out of someone. Making sure everyone knew who was in charge. They were like cats playing with a mouse, in no hurry to finish it off because then the game would be over.

Shondra couldn't tell if they'd actually reached the prison walls, or been cut off short by marauders along the way. These couldn't be standard issue prison guards, but feds must certainly know they were out here. Their little encampment seemed so dug in, with all the pleasures and comforts of modern illiterate guerrillas. Would real government agents come riding out like cavalry to the rescue? Probably not. Prison guards can't go trooping outside the walls every time there's a little ruckus.

But there had been all those warning signs, and these guys were obviously trespassing on government property.

No, this White House had been calling for private militias since they'd first taken over. If these braying jackasses tortured and killed a few people who might otherwise have embarrassed the President, he'd probably give them all medals.

Thugs bobbed and strutted their ways up the aisle, throwing air punches and darting near-blows.

Strangely, Shondra found herself growing calmer. Some new clarity settling through her. Greater strength taking root. Like everything in her life up to this moment was moving into position.

Some inner voice told her this was no time to over-react. She firmed up inside, and readied herself. Fear got her reflexes twitching and ready. It wasn't that brittle, desperate, explosive fragility of panic she'd grown used to. This was preparation. She would move with each step as it showed itself. She was still terrified, but something was telling her she could handle it.

Shondra chose the weakest, most nervous of the intruders and looked him full in the eye.

He could see she had intentionally snagged his attention, and that unsettled him. Her air of confidence shook his flimsy grasp on his own. His childhood memories weren't as happy as hers. No innocent TV moments with a loving mom and dad. His dad had beat his mom bloody, then come after him. Standing up to the guy had meant broken bones, but whimpering and hiding had pissed him off worse. "Come here, ya little bastard! Stand up and take it like a man!"

He tried to tell himself this wasn't his pa; just some damn woman. And he was armed this time.

So was she, probably. Everybody was these days. She must be drawing him into some kind of trap. Like them Rambo movies. Spikes coming out of the walls and shit. He tried looking for trip-wires, but she locked onto him with her eyes. Some kind of a witch. Had him in her spell. Couldn't break free.

Wake up, he told himself. Rambo never walked into nobody's trap.

But he wasn't Rambo.

There ain't no trap, he tried to tell himself. You're on a damn bus! What the fuck is wrong with your head? Guys been messing with your drugs again? Put somethin' in your beer? Get their fuckin' rocks off makin' them scary noises at me when it's really, really dark. Watching me run from things ain't even there. What the fuck is wrong with you? That is just a damned woman.

He stumbled, caught his sleeve, not watching where he was going. Grumbled, cussed, yanked himself free, snagged on something else. Banged his bad knee a couple times. Blundered all over himself in a mad dash of internal babble. Pa smashed him when he done that. Told him, Pay attention! "Never did have the good sense God give ya." Beat him real bad. Told him his head was fulla gibberish. Stop walkin' into shit, he'd say.

But this she devil had him in some kinda spell. Some kinda giant witch spider; drawing him in, and drawing him in. Everything he kept catching on was one of her sticky ropes she kept spinning out to snag him. Hadda be the drugs. But what if it weren't?

His gun caught on something; feet tangled in something else. She's wrappin' him up. Gotta cut himself loose. Giant spider in a swamp. Fumbled for his gun, but dropped it. Or something grabbed it right out of his hand, and she kept drawing him closer. Mad doctors with great big needles everywhere. All around him. He hated needles. Couldn't hear nothin', but his own heart thumpin' in his ears. Take his eyes off her for a second and she'd gobble him right up. Wrap him away for later, for her kid spiders. Hunnerds of 'em. He wouldn't fall for it. What'd she think he was; some kinda fool?

Something was clear wrong. Something sure as Hell was big time, terrible wrong. T'other guys'd gone all quiet. Docs probably shot 'em all up with some kinda Chinaman bird flu or some shit. Gonna stick 'em in cages; turn 'em into some kinda animals half wild monkeys or wolves or some shit. He'd seen them movies. How they did t'ya when they got ya.

Couldn't recall why they was on that damn bus in the first place. Everything's all in a muddle. Now it's just him all alone with all them mad doctors, and they's took all his guns. He seen them damn movies. Fuckin' apes tore ever'body to shit.

Panic can make nonsense of a man. Scramble him till he can't see what's in front of him.

He kept his eyes locked on that giant she-spider. Her drawing him in closer.

Scratch slammed a hard right to the man's skull.

He would have followed with a face-buckling left, but his legs wedged between the seats, with Shondra sitting smack in his way. He swung from too close in, only knocking the guy's nose sideways.

It started bleeding a real mess. Till his huge, bushy beard couldn't hold any more. Something had come outa nowheres, he thought. Never seen what hit him. Started looking around all crazy and wild. Chattering and mumbling all sorts of gibberish about mad scientists with needles. How they'd all wake up in a cage; howling like mad she-dogs under the moon, and them cutting their body parts off.

This guy's on something, Scratch figured.

The bloodied man started flopping his fat bulk around, getting caught up in ammo belts, and them tight quarters on that damn bus just like the clumsy, scared walrus he basically was. Trying his best to watch out for danger coming at him all directions at once. Not back into one of their damn needles. Slamming into his buddies, knocking 'em every whichaways, not even seeing 'em there. Managed to get himself off the bus, but it sure did take him a while.

"What's his fuckin' problem?" his buddies kept asking, trying their hardest to look cool, collected, and tough after he'd just sent them staggering. Knocked a couple of them sailing flat on their asses across the floor.

"Asshole," they called him.

"Fuckin' shithead."

"What's his fuckin' problem?"

"It's them fuckin' drugs o' his. Been messin' with his head agin."

"Fuckin' asshole."

They swore like they always did, trying their best to play hard guy; but the sight of him bashing and flailing in blind terror at something they hadn't seen, but might be coming at them next, set them off a little crazy inside. What'd bloodied him up that way? What's he saying about mad doctors with needles? Jab without you even knowing it. Giant spiders somewheres.

Backing themselves out, they heard feds driving in. They looked relieved scrambling back to solid ground again.

Speakers on the incoming cars were blaring for all the world to hear. "Attention, you on the bus. This is a United States Government facility. You are not welcome here. We know who you are. We have not requested medical assistance. There is no need for your services.

"I repeat…"

They pulled in and parked. Nondescript, all the same, black vans with heavily tinted windows. Men climbed out. Big men in gray uniforms with shoulder patches in red, white, and blue. They stood for a moment, establishing their fearsome presence. Looking like they wanted someone to start bowing.

They moved in toward the gathering of thugs, holding themselves tall and straight. They slapped a few backs, though only half-heartedly. Shook only a few of the hands, reaching for cleaner ones. They chatted a few minutes, letting tensions build inside the bus.

After letting the passengers stew a while, the lead cop climbed aboard. Followed by mean-looking deputies. He didn't introduce himself, just opened with, "We seem to have ourselves a real problem here."

The medics knew not to speak until invited. Like the thugs who'd just left, these guys carried themselves as tribal chieftains and you had trespassed on their hunting grounds.

The lead officer told them, "This here is Federal Government property and you have not been invited. I am sure you saw the signs. We couldn't o' put it much more plainer than that."

He locked eyes on a couple of doctors who seemed to have a sense of authority about them. He let them see he was in charge.

"So now we get to decide what we want to do t'ya. This here is a serious breach o' government security. Y'all'd best hope we don't find no cameras, 'cause that there'd be espionage.

He nodded to other officers. They started grabbing things off shelves, and out of people's hands. They dumped medical bags, smashed supplies under their boots, grinding them dramatically to heighten the effect. When they found anything that looked remotely like a camera, they'd stare the owner hard in the eye. Grow extra serious and even more threatening. Turn around to show it to their buddies, who would nod; looking grave and somber as though this was clearly a hanging offense. Spies had been tortured and shot blindfolded for less.

With great fanfare, they worked their ways back. Scratch had made no attempt to hide the equipment splayed around him.

"We're with the press," he told them, though in these days of "Thug in the White House versus all honest media," he had to know it wouldn't do him much good.

It didn't. "Fake news," the boss told him.

Scratch held his cool as they started tossing his cameras back and forth, threatening to drop them.

"Hold on, boys," the boss told his team when he saw this wasn't getting them anywhere. "I could use me some nice thousand dollar cameras like these here ones. What say we confiscate the whole lot, 'n' shoot us some kiddie porn?"

He looked disappointed when Scratch and Shondra didn't react.

Scratch calmly suggested, "I am pretty sure none of this is legal. You might want to check the Constitution."

The agent drew himself up to full height and power. He looked Scratch over like he'd come across some strange kinda bug and had to decide how to stomp him.

He told Scratch, "Ain't but one man can decide what's the law and what ain't. Don't need no damn Constitution. Don't in no ways matter if'n there's a law agin somethin', or there ain't. He decides."

But then he told the whole bus, "And anyways, this never happened. Any o' y'all says elsewise, we'll just find us some room for yore own young'uns in there.

"Need to do some figgerin' on what we wanna to do to ya. Maybe rewrite yore priors a bit. Might just black bag the whole lot o' ya, we decide ya done somethin' unmerican.

He paused, then added, "We might just have us some fun strip searchin' a couple of ya. Drag you inside on your knees for a bit of *unfriendly* interrogation.

"Meantime, y'all just stay put. Our buddies out there'll let us know if'n any o' y'all misbehave."

His grin could not have been more cocky. He turned slowly so everyone could see it.

They didn't leave right away. They were having too much fun. They took their time. More verbal jabs at some of the women. One told Shondra, "Might could be we just drag a couple o' these here women inside fer some o' that *unfriendly* interrogation he spoke of." He dragged the word out for repulsive, lascivious effect, leering down at her, grinning crudely; licking his lips so close he could almost lick hers.

He told her, "Too bad you ain't jist a bit narrower in the legs, like how ah like 'em. Coulda had us a nice tumble afore I pass you around to my friends here, know what ah mean?"

His buddies laughed behind him.

He told her, "Coulda jist drug you right inside on your knees, and you beggin' fer mercy!

"Mussied you up a bit doin' it."

More laughter.

He started to turn away, but then twisted back toward her again. He asked her, "But don't you think a womern o' yore obvious *fuller* proportions…" he paused here to admire them. Then he finished off with, "Should maybe have her some much bigger tits?"

He acted like she'd profoundly and intentionally offended him. Then he was done with her.

One of his buddies leaned in past his shoulder to tell her, "You're lucky you're a little too fat for my tastes. I could cuff you and drag you in, but where's the fun when we get you there?"

One told a lady doctor, "You look about as dark as some of them Mex's we got. I might be able to find me a cage just your size." He told her, "Why, I might just have me a couple of my own in my basement t'home, come to think on it. And some chains fer the hanging.

"Quiet neighborhood. Nobody'll hear nothin'. Nobody never hears nothin'."

The men did eventually leave. Each strode out slowly, making a big show of it.

Leaving behind only quivering silence.

They drove away intending to be gone for the rest of that day and maybe well through the next one. They wanted these poor folks coming apart over what the government could do to them with no repercussions.

But things started going wrong for them. Things they hadn't made allowances for. Scratch's hidden camera had been feeding it all back to his studio, where managers were panning it live to the rest of the world, and all over the internet.

Recent impeachment trials had found the President innocent just exactly as planned, but blown wide holes through his popularity and sanity. His moods and meanness were out of control. Every day he sank lower, did something even more egregious and petty. Groveling Senators trying to explain away each atrocity got trapped in the crossfire. Voters were riled, and looking for blood. Hungry for anything they could pin on his administration. And now this video struck right to the heart of that. They had the bastards dead to rights. Sets tuned in from all over the planet.

The guards hadn't been giving any thought to modern technology as that technology had been fanning the flames. Their minds were stuck in the 50's. By the time these haughty soldiers for indecency had driven back to their offices, their mugs were all over the airwaves. Angry citizens across the U. S. and around the world were watching aghast as they terrorized innocent peacekeepers and healers. Smashed vital medical supplies. Debased women. Vile degenerates claiming they were acting on orders from their American fuehrer.

The world was watching it all. Sitting right in the middle of it. Taking it all very personally.

"Get me that kid who does local political trashing," news director Matt Pennington told an aide. "That mouthy kid, Q. Parker. This should be right up his alley."

"You mean the kid does all those rants about mayors with their hands in the till? The one they all hate?"

"That's the guy," Pennington told him. "This should give him something to rant about."

"You think he's ready for National?"

"A funny voice just whispered in my ear that he will be," Pennington said. "If he isn't, we'll hand it off. But we need someone *now*! I am not letting this one fade away to just another short-lived shocker we lose track of when he says something moronic. Has us all chasing our asses like dogs after his balls, and all is forgotten. Not this time.

"Something's telling me this is the one, and Parker is ready.

"Get him."

"Right away, Chief."

"Haul him off the air if you have to."

"Will do."

"And while you're down there in local?"

"Yeah?"

"Grab me a couple of those homemade brownies somebody keeps bringing in."

"You want them with nuts?"

"Just grab the fuckin' brownies and haul Parker's ass up here yesterday!"

But Quaid was already headed down their hall. Something had given him that exact same idea.

Even doing small stories, Quaid Parker had been growing a reputation. He was one of those old time reporters with more in-your-face ballsyness for speaking truth to power than any real sense of self preservation. Like Edward R. Murrow, or Marie Colvin in their own times. Or Murrey Marder with the McCarthy hearings. This was the one he'd been building towards. He hauled back and let it all fly.

He told the world, "We are being crushed, our nation torn apart, by a cruel and abusive dictator with no regard for our lives, our safety, or our laws. We stand helpless as his cowardly Senators and sham Justice Department turn against everything decent, truthful, and fair. Caring only to hide this man's evils, and punish his foes, they feed his darkest desires, and help set his worst ugliness free. These videos are but a tiny, disturbing taste of what they have turned loose." As Quaid Parker spoke, common folks everywhere heard one of their own go international. A mensch who knew their pain and wasn't going to take anymore.

The agents had carried off most of their equipment. They hadn't found the transmitter, but Shondra didn't know what good that was doing. She might not survive this, but something inside her refused to give up. She'd go out a voice for sanity and truth even if no one ever heard it. She had Scratch fish down one of his hidden minicams for her.

At first she only held it.

Then she started telling her own story. How being nice, and just getting along, had always been enough for her. But you reach a point where you need to stand for something. Something more than just what you feel comfortable with. When you see everything you ever were before as just steps along the way.

She felt a spark. Deeper connection. In that moment, a new Shondra Bevins was born.

In that same moment, the whole world was listening.

Quaid Parker told huge and building numbers that, "Their nationwide army of oppressors has been institutionalizing our tragedy; our poverty, suffering, and disease. Making it the law of the land. That craven greed of the heartlessly wealthy crushes down on us. In what had once been celebrated around the world as the land of opportunity we work too many jobs, only to drag ourselves home too weary to properly care for our loved ones.

"They spend our tax dollars caging other people's children, then tell us they've none left to help ours. Heap them up on the absurdly wealthy, buying them luxurious yachts and vast estates. We pay for reelection junkets and campaign rallies where they insist we must fear and blame the very weakest among us, rather than these oppressors themselves."

Citizens and voters tuned in, and listened hard. This Quaid Parker walks the same streets we do, they thought. He's one of our own. He doesn't pull punches. He's putting himself in great danger—for us.

"They need us weak and subservient," he told them. "Numb to the worst they can do. If these videos don't shock us, then they have won. We've let them deaden our spirits. Blind us to all that was once strong, good, and caring inside us. We've let them steal even our own hearts from us, while we have just turned away.

"The vain and immoral run roughshod over women. The lowest, the loudest, the most belligerent scumbags are given Presidential honors while true heroes are ridiculed, scorned, or ignored. Our leaders command us to attack our most vulnerable. To trample even our own kindheartedness and highest intentions, that the wealthiest and most heartless can thrive.

"And we let them."

Quaid kept stabbing one rampant sore point after another. International media watched that building outrage, and fed it. Hard-slamming attacks against fascist dictators made headlines. His passionate cries rode the airwaves. Clips went viral across the internet. Protesters wanted his face on their t-shirts. A man of the people. A hero for our troubling times. You could almost hear citizens grabbing torches.

He told them, "Hunger and homelessness ruin more lives than we could count. But they pass laws to take food from our children. They deny us health care as disease and pestilence ravage our streets. Selfless, deeply concerned medical doctors fly in from other nations because our own government will do nothing to help. In these films we watch helplessly as they are attacked by slimy, bottom-feeding, government-issue thugs.

"These poor children; caged, dying of untreated diseases, perhaps sold into sexual slavery; these poor young innocents have done us no harm. Nor did the women on this bus deserve to be treated as sexual pawns worthy only of feeding the lust of these uncivilized representatives of our own government. A government feeding at the trough of our degradation and hopelessness.

"We must look at these things, and look hard.

"Because this world has to change."

In an air conditioned office at the kiddie prison, the rage from DC tore at everyone. They could only listen helpless through their phone. "Polls already dropping precipitously, and now this? You think we need this now? Our guy's been in the Senate for twenty-eight years.

"Twenty-eight fucking years!

"You hear me? You know what that means? It means he knows just who to grease, and who greases him. If he has to lick a little White House butt for now; kiss the balls of some nut job with all the humanity of a ghetto rat; then we can make that work for us too. Voters have forgotten that shit with him and his lady pals because we keep them distracted. It's what we do.

"So now you fuckin' idiots and your backwoods hooligans want to go out there and stir it all up again? That's your plan, is it? We get it good and buried, so now you want to go out there with your little hillbilly shovels and dig it back up? Get everyone talking about your damned cages and lucrative overseas transactions just when we were finally managing to get that quieted down? That's how you want to run with this? Think that's going to play really well with the voters, do you? Even if we get the mad fuckin' emperor's fuckin' private A. G. to claim it's all legal, this is still going to be tough to spin with elections coming up, isn't it?

"And let me let you in on a little secret:

"Elections are *always* coming up!"

The lead agent started to explain, but was cut off. "Don't you say a fuckin' word!" the man yelled. "*I* am talking.

"You had better get your asses out there and…"

Outside the bus, a single van slowed to a stop. No one got out. It took a long moment for whoever was in it to gather his resolve. Finally a voice came through the car's mounted speaker. It told the bus driver and passengers, "Y'all best just turn around and head back where you come from before I change my mind and haul you all in."

He had been commanded to make nice.

This was the best he could do.

"We need to stand up for our values, defend our institutions, participate in civil society... even when the odds seem against us, even when wrongdoers seem to be rewarded, because it is the right thing to do."
—Former U S Ambassador Marie L Yovanovitch

Chapter Nine

Benjie's parents were watching news reports from that bus at the kiddie prison. As terrifying as it looked anyway on their big screen TV, Quaid Parker was making it worse. Disgusting creeps bullying women. Who knew what they might be doing to the children? Reenie sat stunned. Frank fidgeted in his chair. He'd get up, turn away, stand a moment, turn back and freeze there, staring hard at the TV. Walk back around, sit down again, start fidgeting, get back up... He hoped they wouldn't show anything inside the prison. Weak, suffering children in cages. Tiny kids trying to calm sobbing babies when they too had been torn from their moms.

He was starting to wonder if his subsidiaries might have made some of those cages. He didn't know it for a fact, but had suspicions. It wouldn't be his fault, he tried to tell himself. He was a big picture guy. Bottom lines, not particulars. It wasn't up to him to tell every little shop what they should or shouldn't build.

But he had seen things in some of their papers he'd wished he hadn't. Peeked a little deeper than maybe he should have. He'd put the rest together in his mind. A mind that had been troubling him ever since. He'd started figuring things out months ago, but hadn't told anyone. What good would it do? If they stopped making them, Feds would buy from someone else. He'd only put his own people out of work. How would that be helping?

He should have tried at least.

He studied his wife as she sat there aghast. Did she suspect his part in this?

He told her, "Let's just turn that off, Hon. You don't want to be watching this."

"I can decide for myself what I do or do not want to watch, thank you very much," she told him.

He held his tongue after that. He had meant well.

He'd meant well about a lot of things.

He felt one of his seizures coming on. He hadn't told her about the dizziness and body aches. That he'd fallen a couple of times. Probably stress. Things had gotten so out of control.

He'd only been doing it for his family. It put food on their table. Business was business.

No, he'd thrilled to those corporate battles early on. Taken pride from leaving others squirming in his dust. Modern day blood lust, pure and simple. He'd shut his eyes and heart to things that should really have bothered him. Things he'd been allowing, even feeding with that winner-take-all bravado of his.

It wasn't just the cages. Guards couldn't give those poor kids even just a tiny sip of water without Frank and his team turning a profit. Lawmakers from his political party pushed bills to take free school lunches away from poor children. Make them clean toilets if they wanted to eat. Earn their food the hard and dirty way, or go hungry. His subsidiaries were putting food machines in school lunch rooms for kids wealthy enough to carry credit cards, as poorer children standing right beside them were starved. This is how we raise tomorrow's leaders, he thought. Teach them to stomp down hard on the oppressed. Destroy the innocent for being weak. Power through conquest and domination.

Frank felt dirtied. He couldn't turn the channel on his own life. On what he knew. Had maybe played some part in. Things he'd kept to himself. Everything for those almighty profits.

The whole world was rotting. There would soon be no innocence left. It had all gone so horribly, sickeningly, terribly wrong.

Little Benjie walked in and tried to catch his dad's attention, but his father wouldn't even look up at him.

Shondra Bevins had made short, filler documentaries for local stations that had run out of better things to talk about. She'd seen herself as a mild-mannered champion of sorts, standing up for innocence. People had thought of her as softhearted and sweet. Her films had merely been lightly hued butterflies flitting past, and wasn't that nice, what a breath of fresh air, and then you got on with your life. She'd built her career out of finding and sharing the goodness around us, and had taken satisfaction from that. Pretty feelings counted for something.

But now she'd tasted stomach-turning darkness, and come away with grit in her soul. It was like she'd only been skipping through sunny fields barefoot, singing ditties with children, but now Nazi's were stomping those same fields flat, and molesting our little ones.

Some realizations slam in hard, stopping us dead in our tracks, making damned sure we pay attention. Shondra took time off to calm her nerves. But her nerves wanted nothing to do with calming. They were just getting fired up. They were on a mission.

She tried going back to making gentle, uplifting little videos, but she'd grown out of it. She tried to focus back in on just the pretty posies and pink ribbons of life, but they kept warping into something much darker.

Longtime fans had changed with her. They'd sat with her on that woman trashing, baby caging bus trip into savagery. Suffered waves of their own terror and revulsion. That day had changed everyone. The world would be needing a lot more out of Shondra Bevins from now on than just making sweet talk about tiny spoons of metaphorical sugar at the ends of passing rainbows. Even sweetness had to pack a punch these days. Nice folks shouldn't walk around blind. We had to stand strong.

Quaid Parker called this the rising, throbbing *Heart of the New America*. Crying out to its leaders, "Talk true, or we'll find someone who does. We won't turn our backs any longer. We are fighting for our souls."

Shondra tried making a film about a working mom with two jobs who'd been adopting special needs orphans. It hurt her so badly that this poor woman had to work so hard to scrape up so little money. Free lunch programs we'd depended on for generations had been cut. That one meal might have been all some kids got to eat on those days. Food stamps and unemployment help got slashed so rich jerks could get tax breaks on their third or fourth yachts, and the rest of us have to watch our children starve? She simmered at the thought of it.

She tried writing a script about a marine stationed in a war zone who had finally come home to meet his two year old daughter for the first time. She started worrying about all those vets stuck overseas while their families were being thrown out of their homes by a government that just didn't care. Epidemics of post-traumatic suffering left untended as they closed VA hospitals, and shut down counseling programs. Underfunded and sliced from the budget because the wealthy needed more. She wept as she thought of the growing numbers of veteran suicides, until she had to fight hard against herself not to make that the real story.

Soldiers who'd fought America's wars overseas, been wounded, suffered for their nation, watched their buddies die, were being kicked out of the country for the crime of having Latin ancestry. Shipped off like heaps of refuse to foreign lands they'd never been to. Without so much as a "Thank you for your service", their homes and possessions stripped from them. Handed over to wealthy banker and real estate buddies of the President and his family

Shondra gave a little talk for a local women's service group one weekend, but wasn't prepared for the kinds of hard-hitting questions they kept pummeling her with.

"What would you have done if they'd dragged you inside?"

"Are you going to sue the government?"

"What message do you want mothers of small children to take away from your experience?"

"Have any of those men been fired? Have you taken them to court? They should be in prison. What are you doing about it?"

"What did you secretly want to do to them while you were sitting there?"

They asked harsh, deeply stinging kinds of questions that just in the hearing of them started tearing her apart from herself. The kinds one has to ask even when they know there are no comfortable answers. Questions like, "Have they let any of those poor children go? Has it really made any difference?"

She started feeling maybe she had built her career, and been put on that bus for a reason. She couldn't just throw all that away. She would rally these women. Bare her soul to them. They had work to do, and it would take all of them. She'd spent years building a platform. She would make the world listen. These women had something to say.

It was time to speak out. Hit the streets. Run for office. She still believed in living a life of compassion, but compassion needed an edge to it these days. For caring folks to stand a chance in a world turned so hard against them; their soft hearts were going to be needing steel spines.

The White House trashed anyone making the President look bad. "His" Justice Department filed lawsuits against career diplomats, military officers, FBI and intelligence agents who dared testify about matters he wanted to keep hidden. They went after prosecutors looking into his crimes. They claimed vast new expanses of executive privilege until nothing he and his friends had ever done could be challenged. They spread lies about heroes, threatened to shut down whole networks for leaking his atrocities. He proclaimed himself Commander-in-Chief of the airwaves, with absolute control over every form of media.

But he was starting to lose an occasional battle in courts. Foreign leaders weren't playing along with his ever devolving fantasies by pretending to find dirt on his foes. Some of them openly mocked him, and then those videos went viral. Many in the general populace were awakening. Shaking their heads in disbelief. Wrenching themselves loose from blind submission. It became fashionable to belittle him for his lies; his twisted ego; and for his crimes against humanity, the American Constitution, and pretty much all life on this planet.

Quaid Parker took special delight in prodding his sore spots. The President hated him for it, so he had his propaganda channel call Parker a pedophile. Almost miraculously, men of low character started finding Quaid's laptops all over the country, every one of them loaded with child porn. They claimed he'd left them behind in shops and hotels in places he'd never been. But for the most part, the public wasn't buying it. Quaid called the President, "An oversexed preadolescent who hires hookers and has to pay them to not tell his mom", and this they believed.

Right wing networks called this treason. Cried out for Parker to be hanged as a traitor. Hate spewing radio mouths stirred that raging to full boil. Senators announced his home address, telling angry mobs to take things into their own hands. That a grateful nation would honor them as heroes.

Parker's own supporters massed behind him.

The President's notoriously fragile ego couldn't handle that. But he couldn't seem to do anything about it. He called Quaid crude, childish names, but Quaid was a street brawler, and kept hitting back. He knew how to punch where it hurt most. He smashed Tweet for Tweet and jab for jab, throwing out unsettling details of things the White House had been hoping we'd forgotten. Trying to play the bully, it was the President who kept getting bloodied. But even then, he couldn't keep his mouth shut.

He threatened to sue pretty much everyone, but his lawyers kept quitting on him. He ordered Parker's network to fire him, but that only fed Quaid's status as cult hero, and martyr for the common good. When POTUS called Parker a nobody whose ratings were fading, Quaid's popularity soared. The President called him a pussy, said he fought like a girl, but then that got the whole world talking about his disrespect for women.

Government agents were sent everywhere to demean Quaid in any ways they could. Egos like this President's had no self control. He needed to believe he was a winner; that everyone loved and respected him. That history would honor him like no other leader before him. He and his ego had to always get in the last word.

But he was up against Quaid Parker. People everywhere were championing this smart-mouthed young rebel out of nowhere.

A new spirit that would not be backed down was rising.

One-by-one, Senators from the President's own party fell silent. Hiding from reporters when he wanted them out there, defending and praising him.

So the President turned against them too. One, and then another, and another, and another. His ever-growing hate list of those he considered traitors; enemies of his own private nation; reached incalculable numbers. He attacked people on all sides of every issue. But then they started finding camaraderie in that. Former rivals gathered in common cause.

His appointees kept resigning or being fired. It was getting harder to find replacements willing to feed themselves into that madness. Offer themselves up to thankless slaughter at the mercy of his rabidly changing whims. His teams of defense attorneys couldn't hold their own lines. Armed only with rumors and fanciful twists of legal misdirection, they tried to push back against an in-rushing tsunami of lawsuits, only to fall at the hands of judges and juries. The President started firing and replacing the judges.

Finding dirt on jury members. Filling the courts with the friendly but often inexperienced and inept.

And still he felt his feet sliding. He squandered his days and nights insulting pretty much everyone. Couldn't understand why things were turning against him. It had to be someone else's fault. People who couldn't see his historic greatness were coming at him from every angle until his mind could no longer juggle his own deceptions, defenses, and counter-accusations. He started coming apart. He babbled for hours at rallies. Crashed weddings and funerals just to find someone who'd still listen. Insisting on things even the most ignorant knew differently. Spewing long streams of gibberish peppered with details he kept getting horribly, embarrassingly wrong.

The world everywhere watched as this lonely American President lost his mind.

And they watched as the people found their hearts.

"If we dare to speak up, he sends our police and armed forces against us," Randy Cuttering told the grumbling crowd below him. "Makes them bow to his savage lust for cruelty. Take up arms against their own families.

"He sets us against each other. Sees us as his to do with as he wills."

Ericka Tassell stepped out from behind him. She cried out over the noise of hundreds of protesters, "We have had enough!"

Randy told those massed on the steps and street, "We feel that relentless, unconscionable evil draining our spirit. Until we can find nothing left in our hearts but the relentless misery of our lives. We let them keep dragging us down, and dragging us down, until we're just emptied shadows of what we once were, or could have become.

"They station our own troops to keep us from *our* voting booths. Shut precincts down by the hundreds in poor neighborhoods, or in black or Hispanic areas. They change our laws to make damn well sure that only *their* friends can pick *our* leaders. They steal away everything we care about, and everything that ever made this nation great. Sell our military secrets to our worst enemies. Hand *our* taxes over to only the most ridiculously wealthy, while the rest of us can just go hungry for all they care.

"Knowing millions could die because of them, they don't care.

"They keep piling it on, and piling it on, until a part of us simply gives up.

"They are too strong, we tell ourselves. They make the laws. And we are so hungry. So weak. There is nothing we can do.

"They have robbed us of our health.

"They have robbed us of our dreams.

"They have stolen our democracy.

"They want to break us. Suck those last trickling dreams out of our hearts. Destroy what is left of our souls.

"Don't let them!

"Wake up! Snap out of it!

"We will not give up. We will not abandon our families.

"We will rally! We stand strong!

"Power to the hearts of the people!" He started repeating that again and again. Hundreds pumped their protest signs and fists in the air, chanting along.

"Power to the hearts of the people!

"Power to the hearts of the people!

"Power to the hearts of the people!"

Ericka yelled over the uproar, "Non Corporatis Carborundum! Don't let corporate bastards grind you down!

"Non Corpor-Rat's Ass Carborundum!" she shouted, pumping her fists in sync with theirs. She wanted to grab a flag and start waving it overhead like that child in Les Mis. "Non Corpor-Rat's Ass Carborundum!" she shouted. "Show them their ass is *yours*!"

"We will not take their shit anymore!" she shouted.

Across the street in the business center, Frank Squirrelmann looked down over a cheering crowd standing strong against all things immoral, uncaring, and unfair. From high above them in more ways than one, he watched jeering protesters and wished he could join in.

Or at least warn them.

"Those poor, helpless, well-meaning fools," he thought. "Just like lambs to the slaughter."

He ached to head down there and tell them to go home. D.C. had advised business leaders that there was a deadly virus spreading on our streets, but not to tell commoners. This was investment advice; keep it to yourself. Everyone was in grave danger, but keep your mouth shut.

Those poor fools down there were probably killing themselves packing together like that. But he couldn't warn them. He wasn't even allowed to let his own companies know. What could he tell these poor jerks? He knew something they didn't, couldn't say what it was, but just trust him? Go home, and don't shake hands on the way out? What sense would that make?

And why trust him? He'd already hurt them in so many ways; why trust him now?

But he *did* know things they didn't. *Because* he was one of those rich guys who mattered so much to the party.

To his precious, greedy, self-serving, literally and figuratively sickening "Family Values Party."

They'd told him this new plague could kill millions, but don't scare the stockholders. Don't rattle your subsidiaries. Don't slow anything down. The President is running for re-election on a thriving economy. Don't embarrass him.

Those lives down there don't count.

*"I have learned that you are never
too small to make a difference."*
—Greta Thunberg

Chapter Ten

Kids still in high school picked up banners; marching for causes their grandparents had set aside. They pushed back against evils that had been crushing the spirit out of the world they'd been born to. Children everywhere stood bold in their brilliance and compassion, crying out for a better world. Setting examples and leading the way. Old souls, some folks called them. Corporations bought up water rights, power grids, and stripped forests for profit. Youngsters found ways to help communities produce their own power and clean water. They farmed and gave their produce to the hungry. Planted trees. Took to airwaves and lecture circuits to fight for the environment.

They marched for saner gun laws. Politicians fought back, calling them vile names, launching unfounded accusations. Claiming that all those mass shootings in so many schools; tragedies that had killed thousands of innocents; had been faked. They spoke in Congress, saying these kids were just spoiled brats looking for attention. That all those broken families; that deep suffering and grief; that was all of it just play-acting. And through it all, these children stood. Inspired, and unyielding. Where much of humanity had lost its grips on their very last hopes, these children marched. As America's leaders censored or destroyed reports on the dangerous effects of profitable pharmaceuticals, and of impending environmental doom, kids still in their teens found safer cures, and did battle against those larger cancers eating away at the planet itself.

Once universally admired for its generosity, courage, and promise, America had in recent years been setting loose its most festering resentments, paranoia, raging hatred, and ignorance. Its darkest elements had come storming into power so swiftly, dramatically, and with such venom that it had stunned even its own citizens. People everywhere had been caught unprepared; crippled by intentional and diabolical confusion. Taking advantage of the chaos, fascist dictators trampled and crushed their own countries with such relentless, irresistible power it seemed common decency may have been killed out forever.

But then, all across small town America, more and more citizens started showing up at town hall meetings knowing too many of each politician's darker secrets. Setting them off on a mad rush of shredding records, hiding transcripts, redacting reports, and calling everything they touched a government secret. They stopped holding public meetings. They didn't want to hear from their constituents. They ran from reporters, hid in elevators and cloak rooms.

As funds were withdrawn from the arts, mere toddlers appeared who could play the classics flawlessly, and the world could not look away. As network programs got axed, everyday citizens filmed talented kids on their phones, sharing them all over the internet. Every land, nation, and culture seemed to be producing children who could paint and sculpt on a par with elder masters. Who could write powerful and eloquent poetry and prose.

At first they were seen as bizarre phenomena, quirks of Nature, just a few and special wunderkinds. Tiny, cuddly, brilliant miracles of wonder showing up just when mankind was being robbed of its truth and its beauties. But some claimed this was more than coincidence. That it all seemed too coordinated.

Adults gathered into small societies to speak of legendary beings long revered as "Elder Brothers" to the rest of us. Tales of these mahatmas, or masters, were often fantastical; beyond the belief or comprehension of most. It was claimed they could influence events by drawing others together in seemingly chance meetings. Set off complex chains of synchronicities often seen as miraculous. They planted seeds of inspiration. They helped people drum up the best in themselves, never knowing these brothers had even been there. They passed through lives, leaving no footprints.

Or at least so their legends went. Ancient myths about very special beings; compared to whom, most of humanity were as children.

These "Elder Brothers" if you will; for they had been known by many names through many eras and cultures; were now said to be gathering those purest of heart for the challenges ahead.

In an earlier century, the British Museum had archived a few letters among their guarded rare manuscripts that some said had been written by these great teachers to key students. Students who had gone on to change the ways of mankind.

Philosophers had long told tales of miraculous interventions in times of great need. But for most of us, our only hints that such beings even existed came in moments when everything in our lives seemed to suddenly and completely snap into place. When in that next instant we saw as though in a vision how both the good and the bad had always been leading us toward this one, crucial, and pivotal instant. How every one of our greatest challenges, failures, and blessings had been weaving together from the very beginning, and every bit of it suddenly made perfect sense. Moments like these were more than just rising hairs on our arms, or a strange and slight tingling in our neck. We had for a moment seen through their eyes. Inhaled that vast beauty of the universe. Touched incredible new levels of caring. And we knew we could impact other lives, offering healing and hope.

Or maybe this had only been a rush of adrenaline, we tell ourselves after a while. Mankind has always looked for magic, gods, and miracles. These Elder Brothers may have been no more than primal mythology.

And where some spoke of greatly advanced humans with special powers and influence, others suggested more abstract and objective forces. If the universe is a connected field of living energies always rebalancing and moving forward; why couldn't this process itself sometimes call out our better natures? In a world where beauty and truth are eternal, but ugliness and ignorance can be grown out of, why couldn't living, healing energies express themselves through goodhearted children? Helping us reach toward what is best in us?

Some said these two worked together. Evolved teachers acting from compassion, empowered and guided by the vast, overriding unity of all things everywhere. Sympathetic even to the greed and darkness that might at times sour the hearts of our weakest, while helping stronger hearts to reach beyond it.

But whatever they were, or were imagined to be; however they might have come to be born; special children were now stepping forward, and hearts were coming alive in response.

A scattered but gathering few thought they understood what was going on at deeper metaphysical levels. They could find others like them at an internet chatroom called *The Buddhi Connection*. They could talk out their theories there without feeling like fools. Ask deeper questions and suggest stranger possibilities than they'd expect even their own families to take seriously. From isolated villages and huge throbbing cities, they drew, or were drawn, together. Many of them wanted to believe that this very special site was somehow kept hidden from all but the few. That if you weren't ready, you wouldn't be able to find it through web searches. It was invisible to all but these special ones. You couldn't go looking for it; but it could find you.

Or so they said.

Maddie loved his PC. He could dim its lights and colors, soften the sounds, organize or hide all that clutter that would otherwise be begging for his attention. He could take time to study the sequencing of words. It was a world of neatness and order.

He had a special place he liked to sit when he "went in," as he liked to think of it. A special study (his parents called it a playroom) adjoining his bedroom. The walls were a bland and neutral shade of gray with no brushstrokes. There were no clocks, radio, TV, or anything that could flash at him. In one corner sat a plain wooden desk with a simple chair, and a curtain he could pull closed around him. He always gave his full attention to everything, so keeping the curtain closed just helped to soothe him sometimes.

He especially liked tapping into *The Buddhi Connection*, where they knew that everything was important, and you had to really pay attention. Most people in the hubbub world seemed to just walk past things without seeing them, but these people knew it all counted. Even what was going on inside them. Madison knew the word *Buddhi* meant your deeper intuition, so he figured *Buddhi Connection* must mean to make contact with special parts of your mind. Or to chat with other people who could. Those who truly knew the quietness, and the hidden voices. How sometimes you could see someone that other people thought wasn't actually there, and you were just stupidly staring at nothing. His friends on *The Buddhi Connection* understood.

"My friend Benjamin wants to see hidden people but he can't," Maddie typed to one of them one afternoon.

"He has in the past and shall again," came the response. "You could both of you see and hear long ago. We are each of us blind at certain stages of our development, albeit each in his own different ways, and for his own reasons. Everyone draws his own curtains around him. But while young Benjamin has been pulling his heavy draperies in tighter, himself blocking what he has been wanting so badly to see, the purity of your own caring has been opening you to that which most are not yet prepared to understand."

Madison told him, "I am not always sure if I can really see you or not. And I can not hear you if you are telling me something. But I want to. I just can't."

"We are aware of this. It is well."

Maddie typed, "I think maybe Benjamin can almost hear you sometimes. But he can not see you."

"He cannot hear us quite yet either. He must first learn to trust again. In himself, as in us. He is still in training. We are all still in training.

"He is beginning to understand at times at least the basics of what we would have him write down, if not clearly our exact words themselves. And sometimes he is open to letting us write it down for him, albeit through his own hand. But this all takes time and effort. It takes great added effort on our parts, great expenditure of what we might call psychic, or spiritual energies. And it will take time on his part to learn to listen clearly. To set his smaller self aside completely for others, and for others alone. To honor these capabilities as more than mere games, little more to him than intriguing inconsequentials. He has not yet learned to offer them as acts of selfless service, solely for the benefit of others, and until he has learned this, they might be hinted at, but must for now remain closed to him. We must each of us learn to desire only that which we can offer to help all, or be set back for yet another cycle. It will take time for your friend to develop those requisite sensitivities required of each of us if we are to truly hear, and to truly learn. This is why we are each of us given an eternity through which to unfold.

"All of life is a process. He is learning," this other person wrote.

Madison said nothing, but in his own way he did understand. In fact, a whole lot of things were becoming much more clear to him now.

"At your own pace, you yourself have been readied. We may now speak of how you can open yourself in service again, if you choose to. Call upon sensitivities you had once developed quite remarkably in an earlier time. But it cost you dearly then, and so, out of higher mercy, such memories have been inhibited, and you have thus been enabled to rest. Your special skills had in those times been exemplary, and should you so choose, could be again.

"Is this beginning to make a little sense to you? Paying not so much heed to my rather cumbersome words in themselves as to the visions I send into your mind to accompany them. Do you SEE what I have been saying? Look with your inner eyes."

"I do," Maddie told him. "I see your pictures, and I do think I know what they mean.

"Some of them are from other times," Maddie noted. "Are they memories? Are they my own memories?"

"They are. Do I have your permission to lift a little more of that clouding veil which has been blocking you from seeing what has brought you this far? Memories of your earlier training?"

"Up in the snowy mountains?" Madison asked.

"Up in the snowy mountains, yes," came the response. "Very high up in those sacred snowy mountains.

"From our own lofty perspective you are ready. You may, if you choose, take these gifts upon you again.

"You will not be alone. The world is now on the edge of such dire crises as might force many to see in new ways. To choose what they hold most dear: Their inner light, or their allegiance to shadows. More will be awakening. Many will be those who learn to care more fully and to know more truly.

"For a time now much of humanity has been separating one group from another. Soon, individuals will be forced into isolation, where they must give long thought to what they consider most important. Those like yourself will likely call upon the highest within, seeking only to ready <u>self</u> to help <u>The All</u>. Much is hidden within these words to be unraveled at each step as you become ready.

"We do not ourselves plan such global confrontations and yet we know they must be, and we can help to prepare for them. We get no vote on the inevitable. Ours is to assist those who are ready to move forward in service to others.

"I must make clear to you that such decisions must always be thine own. You shall suffer no consequence should you wish to back away. Nothing will have been lost to you.

"Do you understand this much?" That question did need to be asked.

Looking back over the pictures in his mind, Madison asked, "You mean when I used to hurt because others were?" he asked. "I can do that again?"

For he was beginning to remember.

Benjie had been journaling. Hoping those fancy slanted letters would start writing him secret messages again. That would really be cool. When nothing came, he tried faking it. He tried writing in that same sort of antique-looking way, but it only came out looking sloppy. He tried writing philosophically, but it just sounded goofy. He half wanted to get a bad cold again because that's what got it started the first time. Or maybe the medicine had. Maybe he should just take more of that until his head went all swirly again; maybe that would help. Like when angels show up when you're dying.

His mom had moved the flu and cold stuff out of his own bathroom cabinet, but he thought he knew where she'd have put it. He could reach it if he stood on the toilet.

Would that work? When his parents drank wine, or took their own medicines, did they write strange messages too? Maybe he should take *two* spoonfuls this time.

Except he didn't want to take *too* much, and maybe end up like his Uncle John Gordon who'd always carried vodka around with him, Probably even in the shower. Kept driving into trees and stuff until it killed him.

Or maybe be like Maddie, who couldn't think of anything to say.

That was mean! Why did he even think that? Maddie was a nice guy. He didn't hurt anybody. He just didn't talk much. But he had stuff going on in his head. You could see it! Sometimes he'd sit up really, really straight, and his eyes'd go all soft; so even if he was looking at something, he probably wasn't seeing it. He might even close them for a while, and it'd be like he wasn't even there. Sometimes it was like he was trying to listen for something with the back of his head. Like Beethoven probably heard music even though he was deaf.

Just sitting near him when he did that, Benjie sometimes started feeling softer inside himself somehow. Like something sweet was dripping through him. It was weird. But feeling weird like that was cool. He might not even be watching Maddie at all, but he'd start feeling strange, and he'd look over, and sure enough, Maddie was listening with the back of his skull again.

Benjie wondered if maybe Beethoven had done that when he was writing some really great piece of music. Closing his eyes and listening like that.

He probably did.

Maddie was strange, but it could be a pretty cool kind of strange.

He decided to pay his buddy a visit since he'd been thinking about him anyway. He'd bring his notebook along in case something strange happened, which it could around him. You never knew with that guy; he lived in like this whole other world of oddness. That, and Benjie was more likely to think of interesting stuff when they were together. Knowing Maddie was changing everything.

But as Benjie was reaching for his notebook, Maddie was walking in through the Squirrelmann kitchen. He'd never done that before, so it sure caught Benjie's mom by surprise. She was down there, making herself a cup of tea when the outside door opened, and this very strange little friend of her son's just walked in, and right past her without saying a word.

She couldn't think of anything to say either, but at least she smiled at him as he went past. The odd little boy heading through her own kitchen just ignored her and kept right on walking.

But then he didn't know where Benjie's room was. He got only as far as the library, then just stood there in the middle of it and waited. He closed his eyes, maybe thinking that could help him find Benjie somehow, or help Benjie find him.

Benjie came downstairs with a book about Edgar Cayce, one about Indians that had pictures in it, and his notebook. He wanted to tell his mom he was leaving, but didn't know where she was, and it was a big house. He figured wherever she was though, there would probably be tea involved, since she was English, and so he tried the kitchen first, and sure enough.

"I think he's in the library," she told her son.

"Who is?"

"Who do you think?"

"Oh."

He thought a minute.

Well now, that seemed very peculiar.

"Really?" he asked.

She nodded. Then she took another swallow of her tea, watching him over the edge of her cup.

What he and Madison might have done the rest of that day really didn't matter all that much, or at least it didn't stick in Benjie's memory. It was that first part of the day he found interesting.

The two boys were out on "a little shopping expedition" with Benjie's mum. She figured she'd need to move very slowly, guide him gently, and not say anything unless she really had to. Like when you walk a dog who wants to stop and smell everything, and doesn't listen to anything you say. Madison always acted like everything in the world was brand new to him, and he had to keep stopping to gawk at it. That poor child seemed so lost.

She had wanted to hire a special nurse to bring along in case he needed something but didn't know how to ask for it. Benjie had talked her out of it. "He's not a basket case, Mum," he'd told her, "He doesn't like being treated like one."

On the drive over, she'd kept peeking back at them in her mirror, looking worried. Benjie thought she might be scared Maddie would fall out of the car and not even know he'd done it. Just go bouncin' along the street, bumping into stuff, and keep smiling because he didn't realize he wasn't in the car anymore.

People sure treated the poor kid like some kind of a goofball, Benjie thought. What was it like, everyone always staring at you like most of you was missing? Did they think he didn't notice? Maddie saw everything! He was super sensitive. He noticed alright.

Maybe most people just didn't care.

When they finally got to the mall, his mum was almost *too* careful searching around and around for the exact perfect parking spot. Like if she drove too near the wrong color pole, or pulled into an odd-numbered space, Madison'd throw a fit. Some people just liked to worry.

But as she was acting all neurotic; kept circling around and around, searching for heck only knew what; Madison seemed to be making a real effort to act even more calm than he usually did. If that was even possible. He relaxed back into his seat, smiling, as though trying to assure her that everything was going to be okay. He started watching out his window at birds Benjie couldn't even see. Maybe he was only putting on a show to make his mum feel better.

Good ol' Maddie, Benjie thought.

They finally parked, but it seemed to take them like a week. And even then his mum was taking way too much time undoing her belt. If they'd been in a flooding submarine, she'd be dead already. Then she started checking everything in her purse. Sat there for a way long time, fidgeting with stuff, checking the mirror, making sure she had everything she might be needing; that she had all her credit cards and whatever. She did eventually decide she couldn't put it off any longer and she had to get out, but Benjie could just about have grown a beard by then.

Then she just stood outside her door for a while with this concerned look on her face, taking deep breaths and bracing for whatever. Like Maddie might have pooped on himself or something.

She opened his door very slowly, so she could help him out of his seat. Her son, she must've figured, would know how to undo his own belt, but Madison might need her to explain it to him, and then have to do it for him anyway. She didn't look especially relieved to see he hadn't made a mess in her backseat. She just moved on to her next thing to worry about. She didn't know what to do with her hands, for example. So they just kept fluttering around, or sometimes just sitting still in the air like they had frozen or something, Should she reach in and turn him, or was he liable to scream if she touched him? Could he maybe figure out how to turn on his own? If she left him alone, how long would it take him to see it wasn't doing him any good to just sit there? Should she give him some time to think about it? Or should she place her hands slowly and gently behind his back maybe? To help lift him? Or would that throw him into a panic?

"He knows how to stand up, Mum," Benjie told her. "He got into the car, didn't he?"

They managed to all three of them get out, and they did make it inside the mall, but it took them like three days, Benjie thought. And even then his mum kept looking around, looking all worried like she was afraid one of the boys was probably about to fall over.

But at least she didn't break down and start crying or something, so he had to give her that much credit anyhow.

They stopped at the food court first. Benjie had a gigantic, sloppy chili dog with everything, but didn't eat it with quite as much gusto as he wanted to, because his mum was there, and she had all these rules about proper etiquette and how he had "at least started out the day wearing a clean shirt." He ordered french fries for Madison because everybody loved french fries. He didn't try to pinch any of them, but just let Maddie eat them all. Very, very slowly. One at a time. Like it was really important he had to chew with every bit of his attention. Benjie started wondering if he was maybe counting how many nibbles it took to get through each one. He could sure be an oddball.

And then Maddie did something really, really strange. Even for him.

He stopped to study Mrs. Squirrelmann for a long couple of minutes it seemed, as though it was *her* he was counting this time. Then he reached his hand over and patted her arm. "I'm okay," he told her. "I am fine." Which really surprised the heck out of Benjie because Maddie hardly ever talked. He must be just doing it this time because now it was the sweet thing to do, and somebody had to put his mum out of her misery. Benjie liked his friend even more after that.

Especially when Madison pulled his hand back, and Benjie saw he'd left a big goop of ketchup on his mum's arm.

She of course tried really hard not to stare at it, acting like she hadn't even noticed. But she was a proper British lady and would most certainly have noticed, and she just did not go around with condiments on her arm for all the world to see. She did not know what she was going to do about this. He knew his mum and knew she was getting more and more stressed over it, but keeping it all inside her.

Neither boy said anything. They just watched.

After they'd both had their fun for a while, Madison told her, "It's okay. You can wipe it off. I was only playing."

The boys had fun at the mall that day. They got to know each other and Benjie's mum a little better. One store had a whole lot of mirrors. The kids kept standing side-by-side with Madison always on the right. They'd noticed that when skinny Benjie stood beside round-bodied Maddie, they looked like the number ten. So they'd just stand there like that and keep laughing.

They had a great time. Well, other than when Mum thought they'd like the cute bunnies and things in the pet store, but Maddie wouldn't go in, but wouldn't say why. He'd gone back to being Maddie the Mute again. Benjie and his mum kinda figured it might be because he didn't like seeing living things in cages.

After that, Benjie started noticing even some of the humans acting like they were in their own kinds of cages somehow. A lot of the ones working in the shops looked so achingly weary, like they just wanted to get outa there and run free for a while. Like they hated even needing a job, but most especially hated the one they had. They kept repeating the same exact words over and over again; the ones they'd had to memorize, greeting everyone the same way. Saying they were glad to see them, though they really weren't acting much like it. Telling them about the sales, and acting all cheery, while their eyes and smiles cramped up from even just the saying of those words again!

Outside the stores, some very old men, sagging under hats from their military units, clustered together in small seated lumps. They snarled through their miseries; spouting cliches at each other about weathermen, and Jesus, and how all politicians were alike. Detailing every pain, every treatment, and every medication. Verbally dumping everyone and everything they had ever lost, on each other. Resigned to sitting out the rest of their lives sharing cheap coffee the mall gave them for free, and telling the same stories over and over again. A fading clump of dried up old men who thought they had only this little bit of them left.

Young mothers dragged turbulent whirlpools of kids along the lanes between stores featuring pretty much all the same items. Loose swarms of loud, bratty tykes heading off in all directions at once. Everywhere but where their mothers wanted them to.

Visitors and employees, dragging themselves through what was expected of them. What their sorry lives had forced on them. Drenched in the sodden grays of those last dregs of spirit, so few seemed to be particularly enjoying what they'd gotten themselves caught up in.

Benjie watched until he too started aching. Hurting for all of them. Feeling in his heart what they were feeling in their feet. Pulled under by all those miseries they were drowning in.

Maddie stopped from time to time, lifting his palms toward the worst of them like he wanted to pet them all and help them feel better. Benjie smiled, knowing his friend's good intentions. Hoping maybe a couple of them could maybe feel just a little bit better now, if only from the purity of his friend's wanting them to.

At times, Madison would slow to a halt and just stare for a while. He might be looking directly at something, or there might be nothing there, but he'd just stop. He could be walking down the promenade between stores, or might be inside one. At a display, or walking past a mannequin, or wherever, he'd just stop. It was as if he was brand new to this strange, exotic planet and had to figure everything out. There were some things he didn't want to get near. Like bright lights, chattering voices, and hubbub. He liked things uncluttered.

As the day went on, the boys figured out all kinds of ways to play without talking, and even Benjie's mum learned to appreciate her son's friend's delightful quirkiness.

And as for Benjie; he began seeing things in new ways. More fully realizing how much he'd been learning from just watching and trying to understand his buddy. Madison. Strange, oddball Madison. With all his quiet, mysterious depths.

If there really was any such thing as an indigo child, or an indigo personality type—someone who shines out from the crowd as though they were radiating actual kindness; someone with rare brilliance in some special field of human endeavor that most of us by comparison may only be twiddling around along the edges of—then there sure seemed to be a lot of them showing up these days. Taking birth in different lands and cultures. Enlivening the arts *and* the sciences. Anything that could at its peak express the highest levels of human development.

Even as still tiny children they were amazing. Some called them freaks, while others saw them as miracles. They were painters, musicians, mathematicians, environmentalists, or charismatic leaders. As toddlers or just beyond, they hunched over tables, sometimes at major universities, spewing out theories and mathematical formulae using pens much too big for their hands. They marched in the streets, protesting gun violence. They painted and sculpted at home, or played in grand concert halls with major orchestras.

Indigos were everywhere, showing what it was to come from our hearts. Sharing what was deepest, most real and true. They lived their passions, reminding us of what was both important, and beautiful.

Indigos offered to lead us toward our own most caring centers. Through them we could see why these hold our true power. When we needed them most, these brilliant beings were there, reminding us of our source, our possibilities, and perhaps; with great work on our own parts; some purposeful and shared destination.

Ordinary people could only shake their heads in disbelief at first as amazing children showed up with unbelievable talents. Adults could often do little more than just stand back, gaping in awe.

But they listened. And they saw. And then some started getting the message. They lined up alongside them, and marched. They funded the arts, and/or stood against tyranny. They chose science over politics. Selflessness over greed.

The world, and humanity, and all life on this planet in general, appeared to be taking a major leap forward in its evolution.

As had preceded earlier eras of renaissance, the most brilliant among us were awakening. Taking birth seemingly in tandem and yet widely scattered. Reaching into all matters of deep relevance, and opening doors for the rest of us.

"The important thing is this:
To be able at any moment
To sacrifice what we are
For what we could become."
—Charles Debos

Chapter Eleven

What was wrong with Benjie's dad these days? He'd thrown a giant-sized fit when he'd found out that Mum had taken the boys to the mall. If he could have grounded her he probably would have.

He said it was because there'd been so many shootings, and crazy men with bombs, but you could tell that wasn't his real reason. He was hiding something. But he sure was steamed. It wasn't like he was about to start punching somebody; more like he was scared. Mum couldn't figure out why he was acting like that and he wouldn't tell her. She told him they had always been open and honest with each other, but he told her, "Maybe not." But then he left it at that. You could just tell he wanted to say more, but he didn't.

She didn't know how to take that, but she didn't take it well. He said it was just some things at work had been getting to him, but you could see she was still kind of hurt. She didn't really understand.

Benjie had been growing more sensitive, but also more troubled. He'd been feeling waves of anxiety and sadness like it was just pouring through the walls at him. Must be those crazy emotions they'd been telling the kids about in health class. How, getting closer to being teens, they'd be having strange feelings they wouldn't understand. They were changing, and it was liable to get awkward. He thought maybe Maddie felt that way sometimes too. Especially when he got lost in one of his states.

Sometimes Maddie got so quiet for so long that his parents came up to check on him because they hadn't heard him moving around for a while. They knew not to knock. They'd developed a way of easing his door open very quietly and respectfully. Benjie knew to look up at them, offer them a sort of a knowing but uncertain smile, and shrug his shoulders. They'd smile back, but still look kind of worried. They'd back out again, knowing their boy was in good hands, that Benjamin was keeping a caring eye on their son, and they'd shut the door quietly behind them and head back downstairs.

Maddie really had started acting even quieter lately. Looking off into the distance more, like he was expecting one of his precious spooky buddies to show up at any moment. He wasn't doing it to show off. Maddie wouldn't do that. But it was still hard to take. Benjie almost never had psychic experiences; why did Madison get to?

That intensifying envy started coming between them after a while. Benjie stewing over why it seemed like his buddy could see things Benjie had always wanted to. He'd worked really hard at becoming psychic since forever, but it had only happened that once because he was sick. And even then he might've only been pretending; maybe only writing to himself. He could sit and stare really hard all he wanted to, and not see any spirits. He could hold a pen over his paper till his hand cramped up, but he still couldn't force any spooks to show up if they didn't want to. And they never seemed to want to much with him.

It just wasn't fair, he kept thinking. What made Maddie so special?

Benjie started spending less time with his friend. There were whole days when he didn't even want to like him. Not how he used to, anyway. Especially when he got that look, like he was telling Benjie, "Come on, Man, don't you see them? Can't you hear what they're telling you? Why are you just standing there? What's wrong?"

What *was* wrong with him, he wondered. He worked hard, but it never did him any good. He read almost rabidly, everything he could get his hands on. If there really were special beings out there, on some other plane or something, how could they see him doing all that and just ignore him? It wasn't fair. How do I keep screwing this up? Even the retarded boy gets more than I do.

Stop it! he told himself. That's cruel! Don't call him that. Why do you keep getting all mad that way? Stop it!

Benjie sometimes got so frustrated, so bitter and resentful, that he almost started to hate Madison. His insides growled and he said mean things to him in his mind. But then he got mad at himself for being so cruel. Maddie was a good kid. He didn't deserve that. If there was ever anybody in this whole world that nobody should ever talk to like that, it was Maddie.

But slowly his mean-spirited envy, and that growing frustration with himself, drove a wedge between them.

Benjie felt like everything was coming apart.

Madison stayed calm and sweet-natured. It might not have been possible to offend him. He never took anything personally. He even asked his guide on *The Buddhi Connection* if he and Benjamin would always be friends.

He was told, "Most likely your reunion will be brief. Much of this lies in <u>his</u> hands, but at present this does not appear likely. He still has much to work on. Since each meets their challenges moment by moment in their individual ways, no future can be guaranteed. Oft our paths may only parallel another's across but a brief span of time.

"Your own future may lie elsewhere, should you accept each stage as it is offered."

Ever since Benjie had gotten all screwy-headed that time, and started writing cryptic messages in someone else's handwriting, he'd been walking around thinking he wanted to do that again.

Sure, maybe it had only been the meds making his head go all flukey and he'd only been writing to himself, but what if that had been real? What if it had opened some kind of a door? Like with Ram Das. And all those shamans who chewed on cactus buttons and shit. He had to find out. Would they come back if he took those drugs again? Could he do it without his parents finding out?

He kept talking himself out of it. He'd probably get caught. And anyway he didn't want to get like his drunken Uncle John Gordon; everyone acting all sorry about the way he was, even after he was dead.

The idea kept eating at him though. He couldn't chase it away for very long. He really wanted to talk to that spooky messages guy again, and didn't know any other way to do it.

Well, that plus he was really, really curious about why his uncle had kept drinking all the time even after he'd started driving into bridges maybe two or three times until that last time he did, it finally killed him. What could make you want anything that much? It wasn't like Benjie was merely curious about it; he really had to know!

His mum was away at teas and ladies' circles with her friends a lot of the time; and his dad was always at work, and even when he wasn't, he'd started hiding like he didn't want to be with anybody anymore. And Benjie could always slip away from the help. That part was easy. He did it all the time. They'd always trusted him to be a good boy and he'd never given them any reason not to.

Problem was, the cold stuff came in such small bottles they would know if he started taking big gulps of it. But his folks had more booze than anybody could measure. Their liquor cabinet took up practically a whole wall behind the bar in their special room for guests only. Maybe that'd work. They'd never know. He could probably slip in and out without anybody noticing.

By the time Benjie's age had reached double digits, he was having trouble holding back. Sometimes he snuck in and poked around a little. You can't just think about something all the time, but not do anything about it. His curiosity wouldn't leave him alone until he at least tried the stuff.

He slipped in one day while his folks were out and when he knew where all the staff were. His heart was pounding really hard. If somebody asked why he was in there, he could tell them, "Oh, no reason"; but even if he said it with a great big innocent smile, they'd probably figure out he was doing something wrong. They could see that from how he was acting. How he was being all nervous and stuff. He would make a really lousy criminal, he thought.

But he did eventually start sampling their liquors.

At first it was only little sips out of a couple of bottles, trying to decide which he liked best. Turned out he didn't really like any of them. They might have looked really pretty, with all those colors and fancy labels, but this stuff didn't exactly taste like soda. Maybe a couple of the red boozes weren't so bad. One of them even tasted a little like cinnamon, but burned his throat afterwards, so he guessed he didn't like it after all. Maybe if he watered it down with root beer or something it'd be better.

He didn't go in very often. He was a very self-disciplined kid. But he started thinking it was kind of cool he kept getting away with it. He knew he could get caught; he just hadn't been so far; so that gave him a thrill. And it wasn't exactly like he was killing anybody.

He refined his technique as he went along. Started bringing his own glass in with him. If he used one of their fancy crystal ones, he'd have to sneak it out, wash it, and sneak it back in again. What if it was somebody's job to count the glasses and he had one in his room at the time? His mom was really into counting and organizing stuff; she coulda told 'em to do that. And anyway, he couldn't get the glass near as clean, and all polished up and shiny like the help did. And what if he dropped one and broke it? The thought scared the heck out of him. So he just started bringing his own.

Was he turning into his uncle? Did he have his uncle's "sneaky drunk" genes? Sometimes that'd start to worry him, and he'd stop for a while.

Which Uncle John Gordon had never been able to. Everyone said that about him. That otherwise he'd had good sense, but when it came to his liquor he just couldn't help himself.

At least Benjie could stop when he wanted to. Which meant he wasn't an alcoholic after all, he thought.

So he'd start sneaking in again.

He started mixing only a tiny bit of this with just a little bit of that from different bottles, always careful he didn't take too much out of any one of them so they might notice. Then he oh-so-carefully positioned each bottle back just exactly like it had been. He got really good at that.

He didn't know what was supposed to blend with what, so just started sloshing things together. Sometimes it tasted godawful and he'd make all kinds of horrible faces, and stomp his legs; but have to do it very quietly. Other times it maybe wasn't so bad. But it never tasted really great, like it was probably supposed to, or else why would adults keep drinking it?

If he lost track of time, it got a lot harder to walk back up to his room looking all casual like there was absolutely nothing wrong. Even if his legs were holding up okay he might get all paranoid, and have to keep checking to make sure he hadn't done something stupid; like maybe left his glass down there, or brought one of theirs up by mistake.

He started doing strange things and then forgetting. Like leave his computer on, and then the next day someone would be thanking him for something wise and important and wonderful he'd told her, how he'd probably saved her life, and it had come just exactly at the perfect moment when she'd needed to hear it; but Benjie didn't know what the heck she was talking about.

One time he even found that slanted handwriting again, but this time it was a note on some kind of odd, lumpy paper, folded very elaborately into a triangle and propped up neatly against his pillow. It asked him, "Must this be the way we rejoin our connection? Can you find no other means or manner?"

Which was still no real proof he hadn't written it himself, since he couldn't remember.

He got up one morning, rubbing his aching head, and saw his hair was even messier than usual. He was starting to think it got drunker than he did. His hair still looked wasted the next day while the rest of him was trying so hard to act like everything was cool. He half expected his follicles to start belching. One of these days he was going to look out the window and catch his hair staggering home at four in the morning; lurching into stuff, and singing stupid songs way too loudly. That next day after one of his binges, no matter what he did to smash it down, keep soaking it, and taking a hard brush to it, he was still afraid his hair was gonna give him away.

He was slapping and grouching at it over his sink this one morning; swearing at it under his breath, but kept hearing the "Ping!" "Poong!" "Bunng!" of his laptop going crazy in his bedroom. He tried to ignore it.

Until he couldn't any longer. Someone was bound to come in and ask what the heck was all that racket? They'd see what a mess his hair was in, and know he'd been drinking because his scalp obviously hadn't sobered up yet.

He had to go in there and do something.

Smashing a particularly unruly patch of insubordinate curls hard against his skull with both hands, he headed in to find out what all that Pinging and Poonging was about. People weren't usually all that eager to get a hold of him.

He'd been trying really hard to not keep leaving his computer on when he was three sheets to the wind. He didn't want to start doing stupid stuff, not covering his tracks, making a lot of noise and drawing attention. But he'd apparently passed out and done it again, because it was flashing and booping all over the place. Or maybe it was just the headache made it seem that way. He must've been looking at that site Maddie liked so much; that *Buddhi Connection*; because that's what it was opened to now.

"You were right," someone was telling him. "I should just think of this as a lesson and figure out what I'm supposed to learn from it. Stop just grumbling and quitting all the time. Thank you. I really needed to hear that."

I probably just got that out of one of my books, Benjie thought.

But maybe not. Edgar Cayce was always passed out on the couch when those spirits talked through him. This could be really cool, or he could be just faking it.

Someone else told him, "You said I should respect my own truth when I think someone is attacking me because I'm not good enough. That feels right to me. That helps a lot."

Benjie tried to remember what all he'd put in his glass the night before, and how exactly he'd mixed it together, because it must've been like one of those magical elixirs in an old Disney wizards and sorcerers movie. Like when somebody pours a lot of weird stuff, and lizard eyes, and bat tails together in a steaming beaker during a lightning storm and then he drinks it and turns into a big shaggy dog. What the heck had he drunk, he wondered?

This was pretty cool of course, and put a real buzz in his morning, but didn't stop him from sinking back into one of his funks after he'd convinced himself he'd just been quoting someone else.

That night he dreamed he was in Florence, Italy at the time of the High Renaissance. Every day he toiled at grinding pigments for the master. The great one then took what he'd worked on, and turned it into magnificent works of art. He, as an apprentice, could test his mixtures with a lower quality brush, but was not yet allowed to paint figures on canvas. He couldn't even begin to understand how the great one worked his magic. The student could lose himself in the power and beauty of his teacher's creations. With all his heart, he ached to pour his own passions out for the world. He could feel that magic in his soul, but when he tried to sketch in charcoals, this other-worldly beauty never quite reached out through his hand.

Out on the streets he watched common men toiling and dying in their filth. At least he now and again had a few coins. He had enough to nibble on, and a fire on cold nights. A great plague was raging, littering streets with the dying, while he so far was at least healthy.

But he wanted so much more for himself. He could see there was so much he would need to learn first, but he sometimes lost all patience.

He watched his master focus in on each creation until you felt the fire, the glory, the truth in every brushstroke. He brought the very gods themselves alive on huge canvases, on the ceilings of great cathedrals, on walls everywhere throughout this, the world's most beautiful city. Benjamin wanted so badly to learn how to do that himself. He could see the beauty, he could touch it, but he could not call it out from within him.

Out on the foul-smelling streets, so many of the common folk never even looked up, to appreciate the beauty all around and above them. They had never let themselves feel uplifted by his master's magnificent creations, though they were everywhere for anyone to see. He had painted them even on the sides of these very buildings. Commoners struggled only within their dark hopelessness. Until that became all they could see. They did not lift their eyes and hearts to the beauty. They just kept moving along through their filth. Looking ever downward. Plodding the streets as they always had. Weary and broken. Caring only to step through the excrement. So few pausing to see anything higher. Great frescoes surging with epic tales of mighty adventures. Deathly battles, defeats, and inspired victories. Heroes raising glorious, shining hope high when all else had been lost. The student watched as common people trudged through their own stench and shadows, not even bothering to see.

God spoke through even the labors of this mere boy whenever the master turned his soul toward working miracles with his colors. There were times he felt blessed by even being there to witness. He felt honored by an occasional nod of recognition as his brilliant maestro passed near. There were times he felt gratitude as he watched his own lesser efforts turned to great service on the brush of another. Just to know he had been chosen, taken off of these streets and placed in this studio where he could watch. And he could learn. He watched his master toil mightily through long hours to create that which would appear to others to have flowed effortlessly from his hand. The apprentice watched, and felt humbled.

And yet, throughout his own long hours of toiling in the studio each day, he often felt only his aching hands, and the misery of knowing he was so far from such greatness himself. Was this truly any kind of a blessing? Or were the gods merely taunting him? Every hour another cruel reminder of how slowly he was progressing, if at all.

Did the master ever feel he himself was being wasted? A failure because so few looked up to admire what he had wrought?

Or must the work itself be enough?

*The world keeps grinding away at us
until we don't want to wake up here anymore.
Not like this.
Not the way things are.*

Chapter Twelve

In even these darkest of times there were those trying to sow healing. To start work on building something much better.

But there were also those driven by an almost desperate need to shove the world back to a time when things could still be squeezed into what they'd rather believe.

And there were many deeply mired in their dread and paralyzed by hopelessness.

As it had always been before, and must ever be, when the world tries to change for the better, not everyone wants to step forward. People who didn't want to see beyond their own ways fought loud and dirty to keep things as they had been for them and their kind. Heaving chains of stubborn ignorance ever more rigidly around themselves, their families, their communities, and their lives. They launched belligerent and often armed attacks against anything unfamiliar. Change was the work of the devil. Their own ways must never be challenged.

At times of widespread catastrophe, people tend to either step forward, help others, and grow stronger; or to shrivel up inside themselves and die a little.

It was like those early rocket launches when we had first begun to explore what was out there beyond our own world. Each stage had been built slowly, laboriously, piece by piece from raw materials.

Now it lifts skyward. Rising, rising, now reaching rarefied air. There were bright new worlds to discover, but not until it had jettisoned anything cumbersome that could still hold it back. Lower stages were released, bursting into flames as they fell.

Father Clark clenched the dying child to his heart and wept in Latin.

Buffeted and drowning in spirit, tossed about through a sea of wailing souls, the empathetic priest had long been besieging his beloved Heaven, his God, and his redeemer, with a perpetual stream of prayers for fortitude and guidance, but recently had also been begging forgiveness. He found it so hard these days to feel Christian charity toward those who willingly brought on this kind of hardship, these levels of anguish. He beseeched God's forgiveness for how he felt about these people sometimes. He sought guidance because he felt so overwhelmed. Could he truly lift the burdens of these wretched and brutalized masses? Was there any hope left on the planet?

The child spasmed and groaned. He had only minutes left. It never got any easier for this sorrow-burdened priest, even after attending thousands of deaths through his long and wrenching years in some of the world's poorest communities. He gave his life over to helping the suffering, but saw no proof he was doing much good. In their final moments he might be offering more support, comfort, and maybe even companionship than some may have known in their misery-infested lives; and yet still he felt he had failed them. His training and his faith helped him smooth their return to the Father, helped ease open doors to their paradise; but still he carried inside him the gnashing shards of every one of their dying moments.

Maybe because so much of this seemed so unnecessary and senseless. Throughout a long and wearying life that seemed built around the dying, Father Clark took every death personally.

God couldn't want things to stay this way.

Carlton Mosely was a school bus driver who dearly loved children. He loved their aliveness. Their pure and honest faith in life. The ways they could see hope and possibilities even as their worlds tried to steal it from them. And for those having a little trouble finding the good side, he could maybe sometimes nudge them a little.

He greeted each individually, often by name, offering words of encouragement about how much they were going to learn, and what exciting worlds they'd be discovering. They always smiled as they saw him. Sometimes they brought him little gifts they may have made themselves. A few did little dances of excitement as they watched his bus drawing closer.

Carlton had never been able to get much of an education himself. His dad had left the family, his mom had tried her best but had suffered addiction issues, and so Carlton had had to drop out of school early, taking any little nickle and dime jobs he could find to help feed, tend to, and care deeply for his siblings. A tale of abandonment and struggle not uncommon in his impoverished neighborhood. Perhaps in his own heart, he'd never stopped raising those siblings. Everyone was his little brother or sister these days, and he wanted to see them fed well, dressed warmly, doing their studies, and sleeping peacefully at the end of their day.

Everyone loved Carlton Mosely. If a child looked like she hadn't been eating well he might show her a magic trick, pulling a dollar or two out of her ear. He really couldn't afford very much. He had his own wife and children to help as best he could. But it was always more than enough. He had not only bought that child lunch for that day; maybe even an extra milk, or a treat; but had filled her with wonder in the process. Carlton was truly one of the good guys.

This was very early days for the virus in America. Most folks had probably heard about it, and maybe cared about those poor Asians and Italians, or whoever it was, coming down sick with it somewhere overseas. But the President had assured us he'd never let it reach our own borders. America was still a magical place, and we at least were all safe. In reality, he knew it was already here.

That things were bad and getting terribly worse. He just wouldn't let anyone tell us. There weren't any mask or quarantine policies yet, and as far as he was concerned, never would be. Schools and businesses would stay open. Period.

So at first, Carlton thought he maybe only had a little touch of the flu, and felt a little achy. He didn't want to cough it all over the kids, so he called in sick and went to the doctor.

And that was when his whole world went crazy. He fell through the walls of reality. Kept seeing people wearing masks all around him before he passed out again. One held his hand through the night and into the next morning one time. But if she said anything, he couldn't hear her. A priest saying prayers over him. None of it made sense. And always he kept disappearing into some kind of void. He knew nothing but terror for days, maybe weeks. Maybe years had passed; he had no grip on reality. He lost all connections to time and sound reasoning. He was strapped to a cot with a tube down his throat. Where was his wife? Where were his kids? Why had they abandoned him? Was he dead? Was this Hell? He was always so groggy. His lungs hurt so badly. Why were they doing this to him? Who were these people? But then they would all disappear again and he saw only grays. And then nothing. And more days probably passed.

Where was his wife? Where was Cindy? Had they captured her too? Were they hurting her?

There were moments when bits and flashes of memories came back to him, but even those didn't make a whole lot of sense.

He was in a hospital. He'd caught that Covid thing. Kept forgetting what exactly that was. Why couldn't he think? Why couldn't he remember anything? Why did it hurt so badly? Why couldn't he feel his hands? Why was he strapped to this bed? Who were these people?

In early days of the pandemic, they knew it could ruin your lungs and maybe wreak havoc with your mind, but didn't yet realize all the ways it could mutate, the parts and systems all through you it could invade and destroy. When he was finally able to grasp his situation, that didn't make it any less terrifying. He had the virus, he could die, he was highly contagious, his family could not be allowed to visit, and so if he did die, he would have to die alone.

His loved ones were probably worried sick about him, but all he got out of the staff who did visit him sometimes in his isolation room was that his wife and kids were still testing negative.

He'd slipped into a coma a couple of times, a priest had been called in, but then somehow, miraculously, he'd pulled through. He didn't recall walking down any tunnels toward the light, or being visited by dead family and friends, but then everything had been such a head spinning fog of hallucinatory chaos since he'd been checked in here. How would something like that even stand out?

He slowly got better. The whole hospital was jam-packed and they needed every room for only the most dangerously sick. Now that he was merely borderline, he no longer qualified. They needed to send him home. He had to give up his room for someone in more desperate straits. His hands were both bandaged from where they'd had to remove three of his fingers and one of his thumbs. They would have to keep an eye on a couple of the others and one of his feet, but for now they had hope that he might yet be able to save those. They would also be monitoring his kidneys. They might have to take one of them too, or he may have to be on a dialysis machine for the rest of his life. But the whole building was stuffed full with the bleak and terribly sickened and dying. Makeshift tents were being set up outside, on several levels of the parking garage to triage and care for those who maybe didn't absolutely need to be on ventilators just yet. He hadn't heard about the fleet of refrigeration trucks they'd been using as spillover morgues.

They wheeled Carlton out on a chair, down a hallway where nurses, doctors, and aides lined the sides to salute him as he passed. A few held their hands over their hearts in sheer joy and gratitude that this one at least hadn't died. They hadn't lost this one. They hadn't failed this time. Each survivor was taken as a special gift to those who had worked so hard and so long for so many.

He tried to smile back at them as he was rolled by, knowing they couldn't see it under his mask, or know the terror and utter misery in his heart.

Carlton knew he would never drive a bus again. It hurt him terribly to think about how children would probably be scared of him now because of all of his surgical deformities.

But at least he was still among the living. Barely living. His medical bills would bury them and they'd lose their home, but at least his family could still get to worry about him a while longer.

Was this really any kind of a blessing?

"To that nasty disease!" Ryan called out, lifting his drink high before a room packed with maybe a hundred friends and celebrants. "Long may it move and breed among us!"

He looked to be standing guard at the end of one of the buffet tables the catering service had set up in the main ballroom. Like he was keeping an eye on the lobster dip. He'd see that heads rolled if that bowl ever ran low. He liked being the big man in charge. The one they'd all want to know. BMOC. Throwing this kind of money around for digs this grand, he figured there'd be plenty of kids here from established families at *his* party. He'd be the star among stars.

They had a game of Fuck the Heiress going on in the lounge. Snotty rich brats bored with all that money and celebrity, trying to trash their family names up a little. Grabbing each other's parts; licking and stuffing anything they could find into any body opening no one else was using at the moment.

Throwing a party when the whole planet was so terrified of Covid stirred a little thrill through their long stultifying ennui. Added an element of danger. And politics. And dangerous politics. Anyone there having tested positive, or showing symptoms, was treated like a star. Harrison Benson had just tested positive twice! So he stood with Ryan by the food display, occasionally coughing over everything but Ryan's treasured lobster dip. For the rich and the pampered, this was adventure. As near as any of them was likely to come to real peril. It was a way of telling everyone, "Fuck you! I do whatever I damned well feel like!"

"Lift high your glasses," he called out. Celebrants did as they were told. "To our great President; may he live long, and lead us all to Hell!"

"Here, here," a few called back.

Their state governor had banned massing together in such numbers, but any fines he threw at these kids would be chump change. So there they stood, rebels with no cause. Free to do whatever, and no one could stop them. Their money, their names, and their lawyers had gotten them out of worse jams. They always came out unscathed, making life even more boring. Danger with no consequences. Only old folks got sick, and the poor, and the coloreds, so why should they care? The world, life, other people, even Covid were there for their entertainment, and when they got bored they could always find new games. And so they toasted, and they partied, and they cheered; but if you could look inside their actual hearts, you'd see their reactions were decidedly mixed.

Some were just college kids with hardly a penny. Deeply in debt for the rest of their lives for classes they really weren't taking very seriously. But what did any of that matter to them? They felt young and invulnerable. All the world was their party. Kids their age weren't dying, so fuck it.

A few of them were actually worried, but trying to hide it. They maybe had parents who were doctors and/or hospital administrators and these kids had been warned. They knew how bad this pandemic truly was, what it did to people, and they'd catch Hell if their folks ever found out they'd gone to one of those infamous "Covid Parties."

For some, it was just about politics. They hated those namby pamby liberals with all their do-gooder attitudes. Always trying to find homes for the homeless, and food for the hungry, but then crying about overpopulation. So, let some of those lazy damned losers die off! And why should we talk to our enemies if we could just launch a nuke up their asses? Fuck negotiating! Nothing's ever good enough for those damned libs. Keep talking shit about the President. Like White Power is such a bad thing. It's how this nation was built! Buncha damned fuckin' snowflakes!

But some of them wanted to weep. For America. For humanity. For all the death and the pain, and the grieving. In a world of big industry and no regulations, even tap water could be toxic. The air in some cities could raise welts. The power grid was only for profit. Summer blackouts were often intentional. Poor people died from the heat; old folks froze to death in the winter. Children were starving. Anywhere you looked, if people were dying, and dying horribly, investors would be turning a nice profit from it. As one of the Senators had recently been caught saying, "Only the dead need a conscience." And so some of these kids hurt even being there. But they were kids. They needed to socialize, and follow along, and keep their contrary opinions to themselves. So they too held their drinks high, dipped their crackers, chatted, and laughed. They stood tall when they wanted to cower, or weep, or to beg for forgiveness.

The parents of children who had loved Carlton Mosely drove them by his house to wave as they passed slowly, sending their love to him from a few yards away on the street. Sometimes one car at a time, and sometimes in small organized parades of affection, they came by. Some stopped long enough to drop off presents they'd made, or written tributes and drawings. They left him and his family gifts of food, or maybe toys or books for his own kids. They and their parents waved if they saw anyone watching them through a window, or sitting out on the porch.

Carlton started popping in to make guest appearances in their online classes, where he became somewhat of a local celebrity, soon growing national. Some folks have a gift for lifting spirits and bringing out the best in those around them.

With so much time on what was left of his hands he began writing up his favorite moments with the kids. People found them inspirational, entertaining, endearing, and uplifting. He gathered them into little books the children themselves illustrated. Through their sale, and matching contributions from corporations and individuals, millions were raised for children's charities. Especially for kids whose families were having trouble feeding them.

After the pandemic had struck, citizens in some areas were told to stay home; not go wandering around catching and spreading the disease. They called this "self-quarantining."

Many took advantage of this period of quiet, eating healthier, fixing their homes up, and beautifying their gardens. They planted flowers and food crops, cleaned and painted their cabinets, fixed their own plumbing. Spent quality time with their children. They read more, and spent time in contemplation. Examined and fought their personal demons. They started seeing themselves and the world more clearly, touching deeper levels of truth. They made better choices, and dreamed brighter dreams. Dreams often including the empowerment of others.

The knowing carry seeds of uncertainty. The ignorant may have moments of clarity. There are seeds of goodness in the sinful, and dark thoughts among the pure. Things grew more ugly and rancorous on the streets as both sides growled with bitterness, fear, and resentment. But those growing wiser were learning to resist their own thirst for revenge. Even as they spoke against evil, selfishness, and destruction, they still tried to listen for truths in the other side's beliefs. They had a greater work at hand. They were finding their Indigo natures. Learning to heal by helping others to heal.

They reached out through social media to comfort and uplift the spirits of strangers. Had meals delivered to needy folks they'd never meet. Opened their churches and hotels to the homeless, or to help handle spillover from hospitals packed to overflowing with the sickened. They learned to sew masks for heroic health care workers on the front lines of this deadly and ever-changing epidemic. They learned foreign languages and caught up on current events. They reached out toward those with greater needs.

But all the while, others were burrowing more deeply into some very dark corners. Left alone with themselves, they turned against others. They poisoned their hearts with rage, and paranoia. Poisoned their communities and the internet with lies against anyone different. They took it out on their spouses and children. They accosted and murdered blacks. Carried weapons into capitols to attack anything unfamiliar. Thinking themselves patriots for White America, they became soldiers for freedom by stripping freedoms from others. Advised to wear protective masks or stay home, rebels for selfishness packed barefaced into churches and bars; they massed at beaches, sharing each other's pathogens in a war against experts and do-gooders. Gathering, shouting, coughing sickness all over each other; spreading disease as though demanding, "Give us liberty, *and* give us death!"

Political leaders with hidden agendas preached to the pathologically gullible. This virus was no worse than the flu. Nothing to worry about. Just a hoax to embarrass the President. His re-election depended on a thriving economy. He needed commoners to work until they dropped, keep paying their taxes into the treasury he was looting. Senators who had built their careers on denying truth and ignoring experts, now paid little heed to epidemiologists telling us to stay home, wear masks and stop touching each other. Instead, they held rallies where mindless followers gathered by the hundreds, spreading disease through their families, work places, and communities. As millions fell, the President fudged the numbers, hiding the death toll from his reign of neglect and incompetence. In the no longer quite-so-United States, the deadly pandemic slammed through clusters of his most rabid supporters like one of those selective plagues of the Old Testament after God had taken all He could tolerate.

It was Easter. As the President went golfing, his supporters crowded together in their places of worship. Breathing thick soups of contagions into their lungs and onto each other, they spread disease all over their clothing, pews, and prayer books. The faithful caught their death in their churches, and then carried it back home with them.

It was inevitable they'd use this to glorify themselves, their ways, and their leaders. The first Pentecostals fell, and were proclaimed martyrs for their Lord and the cause. They had been given this glorious death while in worship, their voices raised high in reverence. They had died for the cause, that they might join Jesus in Heaven. As more of them fell, they called it *The Lord's Holy Virus*, summoning the chosen home to sit beside their savior.

As this *Plague of His Glory* ate through herds of the devoted, others in their villages sprouted the faith. They rode, walked, or were bused in to die in their temples for all to see. True godliness had become a mighty and televised spectacle. They cried out that The Rapture was upon them, crowding and shoving together into prayer halls, falling in great numbers from their benches in reverence. Snake handlers all but begged to be bitten. Pastors declared for all to hear that Jesus himself had appeared unto them in their own private chambers, where he had spoken to them. And he had revealed unto them personally that he had called down The End of Days that his followers might be glorified in their suffering, just as he himself had suffered for their souls. Evangelist preachers cried out and were made mightily wealthy as even the unemployed and sorrowfully hungry tithed what little they had.

But then that great wealth couldn't save them, and they too fell.

Morgues, funeral homes, refrigeration trucks, even ice rinks were piled high with the dead until they could stack up no more. Huge burial pits were dug through fields, and at the edges of towns with great earth moving machines, where even the living were jumping in among the fallen that they would not be left behind.

They spread death through their own communities while those in other parts of the country stayed home, sharing their own religious services over the internet.

The President declared himself God's chosen as a plague of Old Testament fury ravaged his voting base with seeming vengeance. He launched death against his own peoples. No one could count how many were starving and being thrown out of their homes; how many had been killed by the virus. Viral, racial, economic, and psychological plagues devastated whole regions as they followed their President's every twisting mood, moving en masse however he bade them.

Health workers fell victim to the psychological and physical strain of fighting on the front lines of a continuous war with diminishing hope. Straining through long hours in hospitals, as colleagues who had been fighting right beside them were hauled away in body bags. Bags now being ordered by the thousands. Struggling to save lives even as supporters of the President cursed them with their last pain-wracked breaths. At the end of long shifts, hospital workers dragged themselves home, weary and spent. Dreading what they might be carrying to their families. Hearing reports about swarms of the selfish spreading disease everywhere, some couldn't take any more. For the sake of their own lives, families, and sanity, they quit.

The government refused to admit how many were falling sick or dying. Humans were herded back to their jobs, like beef to the slaughterhouse, and no one was allowed to tell them if someone working next to them was contagious. Leaders called workers, "Human Capital Stock" serving only to boost profits for investors. And yet, even then, on just a whistle from the White House, supporters massed in armed protest for their right to go back to work unprotected.

The great rectifying virus tore through every side of humankind; offering itself as a catalyst for change. Global, national, societal, familial, and personal. It dragged mankind through life altering choices, slamming in physically, psychologically, spiritually, culturally, and economically. For some it called out everything selfish, mean, and vicious inside them. Others began to awaken.

And this plague wasn't only about humans. Life on this planet had long been needing a break from man's countless destructive offenses. The air, sky, and waters needed healing. Nature seemed dead set on putting some of that right. Animals needed to breathe for a while beyond the reaches of those who found joy and took pride in wiping out entire species.

As humans took a timeout, the rest of the planet tried to regather. Pollution levels dropped. Animals roamed streets and strips of land that humans had claimed for their own.

Her mom had said Sylvie should've been starting first grade, but what with everything so crazy in the world, and now this disease going around, she had been giving that some serious rethinking.

Sylvie had been playing with the idea of being a nurse when she grew up. She could sense people hurting out there. That heavy feeling like the air was growing thicker. As a nurse she could help with that probably.

But she might have to go to school far away some place where they might make her wear shoes, so maybe she would have to find another way. And anyway, she thought, even nurses came here to take classes from her Auntie Ailana. They drove in from everywhere, and put chairs on the lawn so her auntie could tell them about the lights glowing through people that nurses can't see. They apparently didn't teach them that at nurses and doctors school. They had to drive all the way out here to have Auntie show them how to move that blue energy through their hands.

Well, Sylvie was already here! Why couldn't this be her nurses school?

Yes indeed, this was a very fine idea, even if she did say so to herself.

She had been walking, and laying out her side of things, but listening to the other side as well, when anyone else might have thought she was alone. Which she might well have been; she couldn't always tell; but talking with herself was fun too.

"Well now, that is interesting," she said a couple of times, just chatting with the universe and letting words fly where they may. She looked to be just a small child in the woods, chewing her nose through her thoughts, and waving her hands through her most joyous moments as though orchestrating her wonder. She thought probably a lot of the thoughts and pictures she found in her mind could be of major importance, but a lot of them wandered through just for fun. She couldn't always tell which was which.

It was a lovely day, she had a lot of exploring to do, the world danced along, and life was good. She caught some flashes and glows off to the sides of her eyes, which could of course have been fairies, or they might have only been lights. Her mom liked to tell her maybe she shouldn't just go around telling strangers everything she thought she saw. But Sylvie herself believed that if it was stuff they couldn't see for themselves, then she had obviously been shown them for a reason. And maybe people needed her to point some of this out. Maybe that was her purpose.

She thought back to before she became little, and figured she had probably decided to be born next to these gardens because she had important work she had to do here, but also because she still had a lot left to learn. And if big peoples ever decided to let her, she had a lot she could help them to see when they stopped by.

She came across one of those funny little whirleybobbles, and so of course she had to watch it for a while. Mama Nature kept bringing her new things to learn from, which of course had really been there all along, but she just hadn't known about them yet. Sylvie watched it for a long time, until something else caught her attention and so she had to wander off over there to look at that then.

As she watched, she was also pondering stuff. Like that sometimes what a lot of big peoples needed to learn most was to slow down and look around them and inside them better, because they seemed to keep missing a lot. She picked up a pretty leaf and then put it back down again. Like for example, why did they go around trying to be like everybody else if their everybody elses weren't seeing things much better than they were?

If they started doing their own thinking, and paying better attention, they could maybe understand a whole lot of things better. They might not exactly start seeing with their other eyes the way her auntie and her liked to do, but if they could feel with their other hearts, then maybe they wouldn't keep hurting each other so much.

The next thought that came to her was that maybe Mr. Mica had been listening in after all, because it felt like he was nodding along since he agreed with her on that. He just wasn't saying anything because he didn't feel like chattering just to agree with her on something she already knew she was right about. He didn't always feel like talking right at this very moment.

The first raindrops hit, but then just as quickly changed their mind. Sylvie was so deep in the woods she decided maybe she had better start heading back before she got herself any lost'er.

But you know Sylvie. She got distracted. She found a goopy salamander on a crumbling leaf beside a pond, and decided to stop by and say Hello.

It was quite a squishy little thing. She held her finger down beside it for a very, very, very long time before it finally decided to climb on. They were just not the two of them communicating at their best, she and this little gunky guy, she decided.

She held it up to her face so they could look at each other; tiny, squishy thing eyes to giant little girl eyes; and study each other. The salamander wasn't saying much, but neither was she.

Some of them had dots. This one didn't. He wasn't trying to get away as he rested on her point-at-stuff finger. She hadn't held enough of them to know if this was unusual or not.

She didn't want to try to hold him by his sides, because she was afraid she might squish him too hard. She tried to pet him a couple of times very gently, and he didn't seem to mind, but it was definitely not the same as stroking something bigger that had hair.

Like a big furry dog, or maybe a giraffe. She didn't know. She had never tried to pet a giraffe, but she would like to.

She wondered if he was studying her and trying to learn things, like she was studying him and trying to figure out what he was all about. Or was he maybe just only looking at her, thinking she was too big to be a bug and so he really shouldn't try to eat her.

Or maybe he wasn't thinking at all. Maybe he was only barely noticing that she happened to be there, and so what?

She moved her tiny digit around, pointing the salamander in different directions, and he did seem to turn his head a little to watch, but not very quickly, so he must not have been all that interested.

Or maybe he was just dull-witted.

She settled her slimy buddy back down onto the leaf where she'd found him, trying to face him the way he had been when she'd first come galumphing up through dry leaves. As dim as he seemed to be, he probably wouldn't even remember she had even been there after a while, and so he wouldn't have any stories to tell his friends about this great big giant girl later on.

She stopped to look around. She watched a big yellow and orange butterfly flittering about, changing directions like he didn't really know what he was looking for.

Sylvie could see that glow running through trees and bushes that flowed faster in the springtime, but now it had slowed down to rest inside them because it was winter. She could see how the lights in animals and peoples dulled to gray when they were sick, or when they got really, really sad, and then it pulled loose outside of them when they were getting ready to be dead. It might hang around their solid parts for a while after everybody was saying they'd passed over, but then it would always go away.

When she had been younger; like last month; life had been all about playing. But now she was seeing things more seriouser, she thought. Was this what it was like growing up?

She stooped down to pet her new slimy friend on his wet goopy leaf one more time. His life wouldn't last as long as hers would probably, but she had a whole lot of more growing up and learning to do, and so she needed more time than he did. You couldn't just live for playing your whole life. Not if you ever want to turn into a big people, and help out.

She wasn't quite sure if this had been her own thought she'd just had, or if somebody had put it there into her brain for her to find, but either way it was a nice idea and she figured she'd keep it.

She nodded and smiled just in case he was watching.

She wandered, and considered, and played. She could have her own school right here, and call it The Sylvie School of Learning Stuff. That would be a good name for now, but you could call it whatever you wanted to. And she could learn how to do that thing her Auntie does with her hands that all those nurses want to know how to. When the blue light comes down through the top of her head, and then it goes out through her hands, and whoever she is aiming it at starts to feel better. Sylvie would sure like to be able to do that, and Mr. Mica had already agreed that he might "someday" help her start learning it. And today was someday already, wasn't it? She could start learning it today.

She looked down at her hands and tried to make them glow, but they still just looked like hands to her. She really couldn't see any difference. She didn't know why she couldn't see light in her own body but she could see it in other peoples and animals and bushes and things. Even for a while after they died she could still see it there. It just wasn't hooked into their bodies as good after they'd stopped being alive was all. But then she realized she had already thought that before, and so now she was just repeating herself.

She stopped thinking about her own hands and started looking around for someone or something that wasn't feeling so good so she could help them. She thought of her Auntie Ailana and figured she was one person who could probably always use a little more energy these days.

She wanted to reach her hands out toward her auntie's house but didn't even know where she herself was, so how could she know which direction the house might be in? It was liable to be just about anywhere, she thought.

Then she felt something touch the top of her head very gently. But it felt electrical, so it wasn't like she'd walked into a branch again or something. It also wasn't like someone was standing there tapping on her with his finger, so she didn't turn around and look for anyone she knew wasn't there. At least not in his body anyway. Instead, she looked softer with her other eyes, and tried listening with her other ears.

The top of her hair felt like she was opening up a window in the springtime to let in that beautiful-smelling fresh air. But this window was in the top of her skull and all that lovely blue from the sky was coming in through it.

And then she felt her heart, and then she felt her hands, and she didn't even have to try to; they just woke up on their own.

She thought of her auntie. It was amazing how clearly she pictured her. She was in her gardens, petting her tomatoes, but she was also thinking about maybe making cookies.

Sylvie smiled at Auntie in her heart, and felt that smile coming out through her hands, and then after another moment still, she could feel her auntie was smiling right back at her.

And then the thought came; why did she have to just aim this good feeling at one person at a time? Why couldn't she just spread it out for everybody? The whole world was hurting and was going to be needing her smiles.

The virus locked people in with their shadows, where they couldn't help but take a long, hard look at what had been going so terribly wrong. It was as though all life on the planet was sharing one heart, fighting for survival together, and many now saw that.

Sometimes a body part grows cancerous and must be addressed or cut out. Mankind as a whole had never been necessary for survival of the planet. It had risen to the top of an experimental evolutionary chain, but then grown destructive. It was in therapy now but it seemed only part of it was healing. Everything was coming to surface, both radiant new flesh and pustules of rotting old tissue. Radical surgery might yet be required.

At first it was only a seeping. But then a few of those sores started busting wide open. Forced to swallow private, public, and officially sanctioned racism for too many generations, now came the time for America to cough it back up. Millions gathered on the streets, calling for justice, fairness, and compassion among all peoples. Filtering in among peaceful marchers though, there were often a few outsiders who looted, threw bombs, and set fires, hoping blacks would get blamed. As film crews caught fed up dark-skinned Americans smashing and burning police cars, raging against the murders of black citizens by white cops, behind the scenes white supremacist gangs had been bused in to bomb police stations themselves. It didn't take much to set government leaders off against those they'd fought so long to smash down. As millions cried out for an end to suppression and cruelty, the American President called out armies to drive them back. He called for attacks against non-whites now standing up strong and united, begging for the simple grace of being recognized as humans.

Peoples of many nations marched by thousands in support and camaraderie with those who had suffered lifetimes, even generations of abuse. For many, this was a time for reaching out. For the growing together of all ages, races, and cultures. But rabid forces against change struck back with savagery. Their hatred had dug in too deeply, anchored into their cores and core values. Forebears had given their lives to crush lesser races, and had passed this hatred along to their children. This latest generation did not dare let these people rise free.

Upstairs in his room, Benjie watched cops opening fire on reporters and TV crews. He watched a little girl not much older than he was, hiding behind a tree in someone's yard as police spilled over onto her street from a nearby riot. So they shot her too. She'd only been trying to carry groceries to her grandmother when all Hell had broken lose and she'd ducked behind a tree, not knowing what else to do. Benjie watched a cop shoot her in the face. He watched the child collapse, bleeding, and weeping. That poor, innocent little girl, he thought, his heart hurting for her. Lying there crying, no one helping. She hadn't even done anything! Benjie's barely contained anxieties strained to breaking. Everything was going so horribly wrong these days. He wanted to run off into a dark corner, curl up quivering, and never come out again.

But he already hated himself for all his cowering in corners. Just sitting around, studying; telling himself he was getting ready. But for what? And for when? When did that kick in? When would he finally stand up?

He heard a notification ping on his computer. He ignored it. Probably only someone wanting Bj. Who might not even be real for all I know, Benjie thought. It's probably just me spouting off like any other drunk, acting like I know everything when I'm only making shit up.

Even if he is real, I can't just whistle him up out of the shadows. Like Superman ripping off his shirt.

I'm useless.

I am no good to anybody. I'm too shy. I don't speak out. Not everyone can be a world changer, but I'm not even trying. Maybe I should give up and be a monk or something.

Nah, I'd probably screw that up too. I'm worthless. I hate it. It sucks.

And again with that flashing window on his PC. He slammed it off.

It came right back on again. Someone calling herself Donna Bliss. What a stupid fake name, he thought. She obviously made it up. I don't need this right now.

But then he noticed the logo under her name. A hand writing with a feather. *The Buddhi Connection*. That made her harder to ignore.

He opened her message so she wouldn't know he'd seen it. "I keep trying so hard. I try to be nice to everybody all the time and only say nice things but I get so frustrated sometimes! I get angry and want to say something nasty but then I hate myself for it. I am trying so hard to be how the spiritual books tell me to, but it just isn't getting me anywhere no matter how hard I try. So I get all pissed off at myself I am not getting anywhere!!!!!"

"Yeah, tell me about it," Benjie told her, knowing she couldn't hear him.

She wrote, "Sometimes everything turns against me like God and the universe <u>want</u> me to get mad! Things are going really great, I think I've got it all figured out, I know it I can feel it, but then everything starts coming all apart. EVERY TIME!!! I think I'm doing great, and I have every right to feel proud of myself for all the great evolving I'm doing, but then everything starts coming at me at once like someone flipped a switch. All the magic has dried up. It's like none of this has ever been real from the beginning. I mean what other way is there to look at it, right, and why shouldn't I get frustrated, who wouldn't get mad?"

She seemed to be feeding Benjie's own thoughts back to him. "I think I'm making contact with my Higher Self or with Gurus of some kind or something, and they should be recognizing me, because I am doing good service and they should be glad, but then it all shuts down again and I am all alone and there is nobody out there to help me."

Benjie wished he could. At least tell her she wasn't alone, that he felt the same way. But why should she care? He was just a kid.

He started pacing, in a high state of agitation. It was like she was watching him, waiting for him to answer. He kept sneaking nervous, guilty peeks back at his laptop. He tried fidgeting with other things, but couldn't drive that feeling out of his mind that he and this stranger had been connected in some kind of a way, and this was no time for him to hide in a corner.

She needed him. And he had heard her; he shouldn't pretend he hadn't. Even if he couldn't help, he should at least tell her she wasn't the only one feeling that way. At least let her know he wasn't ignoring her because she didn't matter. It wasn't that at all. He actually did know how that felt. It hurt. It hurt bad.

So tell her! Just try.

It reminded him of that first time he'd met Maddie. Shaking those papers at him like he should know what to write on them. And now here was this lady thinking he should know what to say.

Pick up. Give it a shot. Just try.

He was practically yelling at himself for being so insensitive, just leaving her hanging.

He tried really hard to think of something to tell her, but it kept sounding dumb. "Gee, I am really sorry about how you are feeling. Maybe it will be better tomorrow." No. Probably everybody told her that. They were just throwing words around and she knew it. Things could get even worse. Nobody knew. How did that help?

He wanted something to offer her that actually meant something.

He took another peek. She was writing, "And then Wham!!! I'm right back at the beginning again. I have to keep learning the same stupid damned lessons over and over again."

He wanted to tell her, "Tell me about it!" He wanted to say he had been there. But she needed to hear this from an adult.

She was writing, "He moved out, like all our love didn't mean anything. He says how it's been very healing for him, I am such a good person and how I have helped him stop giving up on himself, so he wants to try to go back to school and finish, and he thanked me and was real sweet about it but how could he do that to me?"

How could Benjie advise her? He hadn't even started dating yet.

"I had worked so hard for so many years to learn to trust in love and then this happens.

"I mean I feel great for him and all and want him to do that, but it still hurts me terribly. How can anything ever be the same again? I have lost him. I know I have. I have been through this with other guys that I have really truly loved and then for whatever reason one of us moved on. Why does this keep happening?"

What could Benjie possibly say about that? He tried typing some things, but they came out all wrong. He'd delete them and try again, but they'd still sound clumsy.

So then he'd want to tell her about that, about how bottled up he felt. How he couldn't ever think of the right thing to say. Kept cutting himself short, knowing he could do better. Waiting for everything to be perfect.

But what did that have to do with dating?

He wanted so badly to help her. He hurt so bad for her. Couldn't he *please* think of the right thing to say just this once? *Please!* He dropped to his knees, feeling so frustrated. "If not me," he said, "Then *somebody. Please* send somebody to help her. If you can hear me, please send somebody! Please!"

He thought, "It isn't just me, it's not just the two of us. A lot of people feel cut off and alone. They could be out there doing good, but they feel useless. If we find the right thing to say to her, then maybe some of those others could read it there and it could help them too!"

Thinking back through his books, he wondered if maybe this was more than her just feeling angry or depressed. Maybe she was going through a Dark Night of the Soul.

He felt a new confidence settling through him. As though he was becoming his own teacher, he told himself, "That's it! That is exactly what this is. And some part of her knows it.

"She is ready to be reminded. You will know what to say. Just open up. Listen more deeply within you."

And then he told himself, "Try."

He started typing, "Each of these seemingly catastrophic disruptions has been a stage of transition. A time for breaking free of what had bound you until that moment. Things feel like they are coming apart because they are. They no longer fit. You are ready to move on to something more than you have ever known or been before."

Okay, that sounded way too pretentious adult'y, Benjie thought. I can't tell her that.

And so, he didn't send it.

He tried, "Lessons that appear to keep repeating themselves are actually spiraling ever Deeper and Higher. You are indeed evolving, as you are mastering another layer each time."

But then he thought, No, she has the same books I do. She's read that in them herself.

So, he didn't send that one either.

This was wearing him out. He was getting awfully, awfully tired. He shut his eyes for a couple of minutes just for a little rest. And it did seem to help. He felt fresher and more clearheaded afterwards.

He tried writing, "This pain comes from the pressure of having outgrown your former self and old ways. It is like breaking through an old skin. These painful thresholds are reached at each stage when you have pushed up against your old walls, straining against them until one or both of you must break. What you had once believed had limited you can no longer hold you back."

If she's read everything I have, she could probably figure that out on her own, he thought. He still didn't feel confident enough to hit *Send*.

She kept piling up details about how everything in her life was coming apart. Fighting with her family. Friends saying mean things; telling her she wasn't acting like herself, and they didn't like it. She kept losing her keys when she was really, really in a hurry and that was the worst time to lose them. Doing stupid stuff like driving to the store and forgetting her wallet. Her brothers and sister were hardly talking to her anymore.

Folks on the internet kept repeating the expected cliches about closing doors and opening windows, and God never gave her more than she could handle. Some got all pompous and metaphysical, insisting that suffering was only illusion; telling her to just let it go; stop focusing on the dark side of things in a world that wasn't real in the first place, and crap like that. It didn't seem to be helping at all. If anything, she was sounding even more stressed now, because they weren't even listening. How could they not see how terrible her life was? Political arguments were tearing her family apart. She'd found out out her own siblings hated black people and Jews. You can't just ignore something like that, hope all those people they're hurting can see their suffering isn't real, so don't worry about it.

Suffering is real! Don't tell me it isn't, she was writing.

People everywhere are stressed out, living off their savings, don't know if they'll have jobs to go back to when they come out of quarantine. People are hating and killing strangers in small stores buying baby food. But they shouldn't take it personally? That's no cause for suffering? Everything was getting all torn apart. But what? We should just ignore that and talk about windows?

"Why have I even put myself through all this, trying to be a better person?" she asked. "Why have I even bothered? How does it help anybody?"

Weary, nodding off, only half awake, Benjie wrote, "By rising to your most hurtful challenges you have grown stronger not for yourself alone. Each conquest has been real, and truly personal. And yet, despite appearances, not won in isolation.

"Even then, we do not reach a certain plane and then stay at that level forever. Deeper growth is not stagnant. What has helped us this far becomes then itself another hill to be surmounted, and then the next. Relationships even with self, with those we love, with all we believe and have learned to trust in, become the ground from which we take that next step. All is now seen in in new light. We find nothing comforting and reliable because no <u>thing</u> can be permanent. All is in transition. We are barraged and set upon and tossed about on a changing battlefield where our true foe has always been ourselves. After each victory and each loss we find that we are no longer whom and what we once were.

"Seeing this, others may feel they have lost you because they have. They have lost the old you. They might feel challenged by this. But do they then rise to meet the new you, or try to cram you back inside the image they have held for so long? Dare they let you inspire them; take themselves on then, and see even their own lives in new ways? Or do they feel compelled to anchor down even harder into the familiar, wall themselves up inside what they would rather believe? Even as their own ways begin to chafe because they no longer fit.

"We move forward or fall depending on how we handle our darkest moments.

"And no matter how quiet some of us may appear to be; even to ourselves; we each of us do affect others. Your growth is not only for you, though you may not always see the connections."

He told her, "We do well to have faith even when we lose faith. You will understand what I say here, while many may not."

Benjie may have lost hours wandering in and out of great fatigue. So tired he couldn't even think clearly. But somehow the conversation kept going. He could tell by the stars outside his window that it was getting to be nighttime, and then that it *was* nighttime, and then the stars began to fade into a glow that told him it was getting to be daytime again. He was in bed with his clothes on and had not pulled the covers up over him.

He got up to take a pee, washed his hands, played with his messy hair for a while as he leaned over the sink. Decided once again that his morning hair was hopeless, and gave up on it.

Stepping back into his bedroom he saw his PC was still on. He sat down at his desk to check on how things were going for this lady. They had apparently kept writing much of the night, off and on.

He'd told her, "The world has outgrown the comfort of its previous ignorance, just as you have. With growth spurts often come growing pains. We might see these current times as a sort of a <u>Global</u> Dark Night of the Soul. A time of reckoning and breakage before the new dawning. Those who recognize these pressures for what they are, may still flow with them in a state of grace. That choice is always our own.

He'd told her, "This is not intended as punishment."

And then finally Benjie saw what should have been obvious before.

Bj was real.

He had shown up after all.

He'd written, "Your own heart has grown stronger through its trials. Each step of your development has offered you more that you could then share with others. The world is in great turmoil even as you are empowered. Humanity now faces a Dark Night both individually, and collectively as a species on this planet. As with Dark Nights of the <u>Individualized</u> Spirit, it will be our choice whether to grow as aware and compassionate beings, learn from our lessons and hurts, and become something better; or to let ourselves fall back into the swamps of confusion and unknowing, of hurt, self-absorption, and seeming helplessness."

Benjie noticed that Bj had then left this one message just sitting there. He hadn't posted it. He'd left it up to Benjie to decide whether to pass it along or fall short again. That decision would have to be his.

At first he fell into his old ways. He started stressing out again. This was too important. It seemed to make sense, but what if it had only been *he* who had written it, not Bj? How could he, Benjie, know if there was any deep metaphysical meaning to all this hurting and chaos?

But even as he quibbled with himself, something soft and peaceful was settling through him. Bathing him in an undeniable sense of clarity and confidence. Recognizing this deeper aspect of himself, he reached forward toward his keyboard.

He hit *Send*.

It was a time of great loss, shared suffering, and dire need. A time calling for change at every level. A pivotal point had been reached.

In chaos, nothing seems solid and reliable. And so, pretty much anything could be possible. And now chaos reigned through American politics and policies. Leadership was scattered, unfocused, and weak. Then came the plague, jobs disappeared, and civil unrest hit the streets. The nation was hurled through devastation. Everything we had come to rely on, or guess at, was so harshly and thoroughly torn apart that we could no longer even recognize the pieces.

And then, from scattered fragments and dreams, different types of people set about building very different types of worlds.

A hug would never again be just a hug. A casual smile from a passing stranger was now a rare and blessed treasure. The world would need to find other ways to love.

Chapter Thirteen

Maddie was exquisitely sensitive. Lately he'd been sensing darkness rising up and reaching through people everywhere. His own father had come home from work one night, and something had broken away. He'd been losing parts of himself ever since. Carrying shadows he wasn't ready to set down and walk away from.

Maddie wanted to help. He had to find a way to reach out.

Danni Beaufort shined creative, bohemian joy into life and the world around her. Her stylistic choices were often instantaneous and unpredictable. She enjoyed wearing huge glasses, strange hats, and from time to time cutting her hair oddly on impulse; carrying it all off with a certain confident and playful panache.

Even her son Maddie was susceptible to her charm. It wasn't obvious at first, and along the way each had some adjustments to make. She knew to respect his need for distance, quiet, and minimal contact, but had lately been learning to interpret his subtleties, catching hints of underlying needs and motivations he'd never tried very hard to explain. She'd begun to suspect he might be offering them hints into things he couldn't explain to them in words. So, she just let him have his space, softly communicating that she'd be there for him however he needed her to be. Then she went about adding lighthearted goofiness to the general mood of their home life.

Danni was playful and upbeat by nature. If she happened to be floating around near her son, doing something a bit off; and he happened to notice, and was glad she was there; then they could both of them consider that a connection. In that, it was a kind of a win.

Early on, he was more curious than anything about her creative, colorful way of finding joy in just about anything. It might catch him off guard as she swirled by, but it was his mom after all. He could trust her, and his mom could be goofy.

As his adviser from *The Buddhi Connection* had predicted, some of Maddie's "veils" had been lifting for more than a year now. They hadn't exactly blasted away in a great storm of revelation, but did appear to have been shifting a bit. He'd been coming more into himself. Or perhaps more *out of* himself and *into* the world around him. Other times, places, and possibilities still held his attention, but he no longer felt he needed to bury himself in his room and shut the door to explore them.

He'd taken up drawing; his walls and shelves were no longer quite so barren. Sometimes in black & white, or other times with only mild hints of muted colors; in pencil, crayon, ballpoint pen or markers in earthy colors; he drew mountains capped with snow. He drew horses and thick-horned beasts of burden saddled to be ridden, or laden with supplies for a long journey. He chose not to draw anyone riding them.

He was still basically quiet, but had opened his world out beyond the walls of his own rooms and begun wandering the house much more freely. When one of the workers felt ill, or a bit down, he always noticed, and stood near them, smiling until they felt better. The household grew lighter and happier for him being out there among them.

Now his dad was going through something intense that really bothered the man, but that he wasn't ready to let go of it yet. Maddie had seen how some plants grow lush only in sunshine, while others had to be allowed to root slowly through darkness. His dad was in some kind of darkness.

Laurence had come away from that horrendous office confrontation wanting more than ever to protect his son from the evil that was everywhere these days. Madison, like so many other kids, was in terrible danger. Beaufort's run-in with those thugs had changed him, and the way he felt about himself. It changed the way he stood; how long he could sit still; how hard he had to try to at least look like he was smiling.

Maddie noticed. He saw patterns in how things connected, and when they slipped out of synch. His dad had changed all his patterns. He was acting disconnected. From their home, and his family; even from himself.

Maddie had seen how harsh weather could make some plants stronger, but sickened and killed some of the others. Maybe what worked in plants sometimes hit people the same way. When things were going wrong it seemed to feed some of them somehow. Some plants you left alone. They did better in darkness.

Sometimes when someone was feeling so tight that it was hurting them inside, you only had to put a blob of ketchup on their arm. That probably wouldn't work with his dad.

For Maddie, everyone and everything was a puzzle inside a bigger puzzle that was only one tiny piece of an even greater puzzle still. Mostly we each need to move our own pieces. People who care about us sometimes have to just stand back out of the way and let us do it.

He was starting to remember some of what he'd learned in the old days among those shining white mountains. Healers never force anything on anyone. They just offer what they can, and let others use it however they're ready to. They might block it and not take it in, but that has to be up to them. Sometimes all you can offer is love, silence, and space.

Sitting on a window seat, looking out into the woods, Maddie had an open sketchbook on his lap and a fistful of colored pencils in his hand. He'd been drawing a dark, yak hair tent in a rocky terrain, pausing from time to time to gaze as though he could just about see one out there. He'd drawn a small forest of flags around this nomad's portable home, but then stopped to consider each color for each pennant as though each choice held its own special symbolism. Each connected this wanderer with special hidden beings and forces. Choosing each color had to be taken on as a very focused part of his project and must not be dishonored with haste or inattention.

He heard a giggle coming down the hall. It distracted him for a moment, but not in a bad way. It was his mom. His mom was goofy. Maybe he should find a way to work some of her joyful living energy into his drawing. It wasn't happy enough with just his own dull colors in it.

His heart caught a twinkle, and then his eyes caught a flash of movement. He watched his mom dancing past, wearing those same colors he'd just been sketching, plus some livelier ones

She seemed oblivious at first, dancing around to some music she was listening to through earbuds. But then she caught a sense that he was watching her. She dared in that moment to look back at him, to meet him eyes-to-eyes, and was happy to see he didn't flinch. They shared a very special moment of connection between mother and son. She let a little smile out, and softly offered it to Maddie. Simply her heart expressing itself honestly and purely, as it always did. He accepted, and couldn't help but smile back.

It released something between them. They began honoring each other with more smiles and special moments after that. This single instant of gentle acceptance turned out to have been a really big deal.

He started letting her stand off a ways and study his drawings sometimes. Then he started holding a few of them up for her to see better, in the process inviting her to step closer. Few words were exchanged.

Laurence envied them their deepening connections, but didn't try to poke his way into the middle. It'd be like watching someone nap peacefully on a rubber raft in an unruffled pool, but then you take a huge, splashing belly flop right next to them. So, he held back. He said nothing. He tried to not even let them see he was watching. He chose to stay in the shadows.

Still in all though, he would dearly love to share such gentle sweet times with his son.

Danika Beaufort exuded a clear, lovely warmth through anywhere she and her son stood or sat near to each other, even silently. Danni had always been active and playful by nature, but had been spending more time sitting quietly in recent months. Reading intriguing books and articles about the deeper ways of man. Maddie seemed to call that out of her. Sitting, and reading, and pondering.

But as she was growing quieter, he was moving out into the world. Helping the workers put cleaning supplies away, load the dishwasher, or sort the laundry. He was really good at anything that called for organizing. He was great at seeing patterns, or creating them.

Danni sat quietly near him some days, but didn't make any kind of disciplined ritual out of it, or force herself on him. She rarely forced herself, period. Free spirits were just that. They were free. Maddie had noticed this about her, and loved her for it, but found it curious to say the least. He was far from the spontaneous type.

There were days now when she'd be reading for a while, and he'd maybe be on his computer, or gazing out through one of the windows or into nothingness, and he'd feel that endearing warmth between them, and move in closer to her. Maybe pick up, move a couple of steps closer, and sit back down again. But then that would be that. He wouldn't feel he needed to actually say anything.

Laurence often marveled at how his delightful partner in everything still held such an almost magical effect over him. He still felt he was under her spell. He sometimes wondered if they might have been drawn together for some greater purpose. How else could he have managed to lure such a special, joyful being into his dull, corporate meetings and paperwork life? Had he been contributing his own share though? Had it been enough just to see that his family was well fed and comfortable? Walled away from the suffering outside their privileged community? Misery, anger, and fear were reaching their tentacles into his offices anyway; how much longer could he keep it out of their home? The world kept reaching in, and prying away at his grip on everything pristine and innocent he fought so hard to maintain. Was he wrong in wanting that for his loved ones?

He hadn't told them about the terrorists at work. How he'd buckled under to government thugs. Danni could probably see something was wrong. He'd come away brooding, angry, and hurt, but tried so hard to hold it in. He didn't want to dump those kinds of feelings on his family. But now it felt like he was only standing *near* them, wanting to participate, but holding back. Privately eating away at himself. He'd had that one chance to face evil down, but he'd buckled. He'd given the bad guys everything they'd wanted.

He carried the stench of that around in his guts. Every bitter, enraging, aching moment churned away inside him, but he held himself mute. When others at corporate laughed it off as their "little office party", he wanted to haul back and deck somebody. They hadn't been there. Not one of them had seen and heard those sick, disgusting bastards.

But he kept quiet. They joked about this just being the new rules of working with the new D. C., and he wanted to slam somebody, but held back. He kept it in. Building, and building, and building up inside him. He had to contain it. Didn't want his family knowing the danger just outside their walls.

But then everything started tearing open for all the world to see with that reporter and those doctors on that bus at the children's prison. Why should there even be children's prisons? Cage cities for young innocents? Why hadn't someone stopped these guys before it had gotten this bad? Thugs just like the ones he'd had to deal with. The whole world was crying out against these guys on every channel now, Danni could see how it was tearing him apart, but had no idea why he was taking it so personally. Side-by-side but not together, they watched every network but the President's propaganda ministry dig through each tiny detail 24/7. Driving it relentlessly into everyone's hearts just like hammering a stake. Flooding their lives until it was all anyone talked about. Forcing Laurence to look hard and honestly at everything he had been bottling up.

Danni watched him, and hurt for him. She asked, "What's going on, Laur? Is it Madison? Are you picturing him in those cages?"

He was. But that wasn't all of it. He wasn't being fair to her. She really needed to hear this.

He laid out the full story for her, pouring all his long pent up passions into it. Vicious brutes storming in; innocents terrified for their children and grandchildren. He watched all that pain tearing through her as he released. Shock. Terror. Anger. Disgust.

He cried as he told her, "I didn't want to drag that into our home."

But then Danni laid a truth before him that they would both need to take an honest look at. She told him, "This isn't going to be settling down any time soon, Honey. We can't just go shutting each other out every time things take a deeper turn into ugly. There's going to be a whole lot more waves coming at us from that swamp for a long time to come." He nodded in sad and discouraged agreement. "This didn't all start with one President, an uprising of newly empowered skinheads, or because the networks finally got around to figuring out that we haven't always been nice to other races. The world has always been this way. It's just that now seems to be the time for us to vomit some of these poisons back up and maybe start doing something about them.

"But you and I, Sweetie, need to keep in mind that we are in this together. So let's don't go shutting each other out over it, agreed? We have to work together."

"Agreed," he said, and nodded, and then they both stepped in for a hug.

"Not just you and I, but all of us," he added. "Together."

And then suddenly there seemed to be riots everywhere. In strange, often violent ways, the country started coming alive as Americans let themselves feel again. In a world of savage suppression, rich turned against poor, Christians against gays, whites against "servant races"; America's leaders grew more powerful from any infighting and suffering they could stir up.

Quaid Parker told the world, "Americans want their country back. They are telling the government, 'Listen to us. Tell us the truth. *You* work for *us*, and you *will* be held accountable'."

Citizens on every side of every issue had given in to a nationwide rebirth of passion and fervor. The President kept feeding the chaos, calling for armed civil war. He and his followers wanted to turn the world back to times when their race had been allowed to do whatever it had wanted; to any other race, animal species, or stretch of Nature; without having to answer for any of it. He told his supporters that wearing masks was a sign of the enemy, and so they beat or shot strangers they caught wearing them. They hijacked trucks carrying protective gear to hospitals, and burned their equipment in protest. Insanity tore loose on the streets.

On the 4th of July, America's traditional day for celebrating its freedom and independence, masses of its weakest gathered to celebrate their freedom from good sense, and their independence from concern for the greater good. They marched against compassion and common decency.

Armed cops and soldiers attacked innocents they'd sworn to protect. Government troops fired rubber bullets and teargas; charging mercilessly into scattered strands of peaceful protesters. They shot at reporters who were daring to show people the truth. Moms and dads with bicycle helmets, small town hockey players, and ordinary citizens with leaf blowers batted gas canisters back at police sent against them by the White House. The whole nation was coming apart.

Hit men broke into the homes of investigators and federal judges working on cases against the President and his alleged mob connections. They shot their families and eviscerated their pets. Heavily armed federal troops in masks and with their name tags hidden grabbed citizens off the streets of major cities; all records deleted. Children and disobedient girlfriends and wives were being found living in cages, or buried in backyards. Honest investigators and journalists could not keep up with all the carnage. Ultimate power seemed to be in the hands of the violent, the vengeful, and those who lived with no sense of remorse.

Laurence and his wife were in pain, they were terrified, but they stood. Loving and strong, beside one another, they held. They fought against everything raining in on them through the media, focusing more on their love than their terror.

"I do worry about Maddie," Laurence told his wife one afternoon.

She pondered a moment, then suggested, "I seem to think there might be more to Madison than either one of us has been able to see."

She suggested her husband try breathing a little more softly around his son. "He notices the little things," she said. "Try not to look so worried when you watch him. He can sense that. And anyway, it tightens you all up and makes your face look like you're afraid he's about to split open. Don't do that. You'd be surprised what he's aware of."

It was hard, but he tried. How could anyone so locked up in tension, living in a world like this, just stop worrying because someone said he should? He couldn't just snap his fingers and relax. And he couldn't just sit down and make small talk with the boy.

Maddie could see his dad was trying to break loose from what had been hurting him, so he started moving closer and sitting nearer to him. Sometimes then, he'd just close his eyes and smile softly for a while.

That did seem to help. Just to see his son smiling, Laurence thought. There was something contagious about that smile. And it meant so much, knowing he wanted to be close. Knowing he was reaching out in the only way he knew how to.

Maddie started leaving a few of his drawings around where his dad could see them. Sketches in color or black and white of what looked to be nomadic Mongolian huts and beasts of burden. Saddled horses with nobody on them, and exotic temples shown always only from the outside. Bronze and copper urns pouring out thick clouds of smoke from incense ropes, wads, and sticks. Urns sitting with flowers on some sort of an altar, but any framed portraits left fuzzy. Suggested only by soft-edged blurs and shadows.

"He really has a thing for the orient, doesn't he?" Laurence asked his wife one afternoon over tea.

"Seems to have," she said. Her tone and smile were telling him, "Gee; ya think?"

She didn't mention that he hadn't even seen Maddie's best stuff. She found some of it really intense. Almost spooky. If he saw some of them, he'd want to cross himself three times and gulp holy water. But she kept that to herself. She'd let Maddie decide what he shared, how, with whom, when, and why.

Laurence felt he was starting to know his son a little better. But Maddie didn't feel his dad was quite ready to see the whole package. He could share some of the deeper stuff with his mom, but couldn't even show everything to her.

Danni and Laurence began talking about whether they should maybe try taking Madison on a few outings. See how he handled himself in the real world.

But where could he move among strangers without feeling imposed on, or threatened?

Laurence had been gathering information on Nepal and Tibet, on nomadic Mongolians, yaks, and hidden temples. He was just basically trying to understand. It's not like he could just sit down beside his boy, slide him a beer, and start chatting about their travels in the East, but he wanted to know more about what fascinated him so.

There was a village of displaced Tibetans not too far from their community. Laurence had driven through it a few times, sat and sipped tea in their tea shoppes, had a look around. It was a quiet place. It had a small park where they could take Madison to hang out quietly if they managed to get him that far, and the drive hadn't been too much for him. Maddie might actually like it there.

Laurence suggested a little road trip to his wife only after he'd done his best to consider all possible outcomes and emergency change-ups. He was fully prepared to map out all the intricacies of his Plan B, his Plan C, and Plan D.

She didn't need to hear them. She leaped right in with, "Great idea! Let's do it! You've really been using your cookie on this one, Laur. I'm proud of you."

He had actually been hoping she'd be more circumspect about it. Give them both some time to reconsider.

But then late one Saturday morning, there they were. All three of them in one of their cars, Madison actually looking excited, and Laurence doing the driving himself.

He was feeling edgy as they headed out, his wife beside him, their son sitting well buckled just behind them. Laurence kept glancing awkwardly at each of them. This was a big step they were taking, and he wasn't quite sure they were ready for it.

But Madison did look calm back there. Acting like this trip had been his idea, and Laurence had only come along as the chauffeur. He half expected Maddie to tell him to keep his eyes on the road.

And sure enough, at one point he felt a small tapping on his elbow from behind. Leaning forward, Maddie told him, "We will want to make one special stop before we get to the village. I will let you know." Laurence watched as his son sat back again, closing his eyes.

He looked over toward his wife. She smiled at him without saying anything. He didn't know how to interpret that.

As they neared the little village he heard Maddie tell him, "Take this side road coming up on your left."

And so he did. He looked over at Danni, she shrugged her shoulders, maybe almost but not quite as confused as he was, but when that side street appeared, he did take it.

Following a few more curves and twists took them out to where they could see a rather odd looking building, maybe centuries old, rising up on the other side of a large field that may once have been farmland. Even from this far off Laurence thought it had an eerie feeling about it.

"That's the one," Maddie told him, then just sat back and smiled. His dad thought he said something then like, "She'll be expecting me," but must've heard him wrong, because that made no sense. He didn't feel up to asking Maddie what he'd really said, only to be ignored by a child who only spoke when he wanted to.

They parked near the entrance. Madison unstrapped and let himself out. He walked well ahead of his mom and dad but then couldn't open the heavy old door to the building once he'd reached it. So he just stepped aside and waited.

The sign out front suggested in more than one language that it was some kind of a home for children. Whether an orphanage or a place for kids with special medical or psychological needs, wasn't spelled out. By this time, Laurence wasn't expecting any immediate or satisfying answers for his many and tumultuous questions. He felt like he was just following his son, and doing what he was told; so when he reached the door, he opened it to let Madison and his wife pass inside.

The lobby didn't tell him much. A few small drawings similar to Maddie's had been posted on various walls, with no labels to explain them. Nothing bright and showy anywhere. The interior, much like the outside, seemed understated and sedate. And out of date. Like the twenty-first century hadn't reached this place yet.

The Beauforts hadn't phoned ahead, so no one here had known they'd be coming. They'd had no reason to prepare for visitors, and probably rarely got any. There seemed to be no one around. The place had a quiet, drowsy air about it, like falling asleep on a swing seat in springtime, your book just falling closed across your chest.

He didn't have time to notice much more than that. Madison hadn't slowed down since the moment he'd stepped inside. He'd marched in and kept walking. He was already trotting up the stairs.

"No, wait!" his dad called after him.

Laurence watched his little, non-communicative, allegedly autistic offspring just wave him off with a couple of quick flips of his hand backwards over his shoulder as he kept climbing. The boy was upstairs and heading down the hall before his dad could gather himself together enough to chase after him.

"Wait! Madison! No," he called to the second floor, but it didn't slow his boy down any. Laurence didn't want to just start running around uninvited in someone else's home, so it took a moment to talk himself into charging upstairs after his son. He looked around but still couldn't see or hear any signs of other adults being around. He looked over at his wife. She appeared mildly bemused but basically seemed to find this whole event kind of funny. She smiled for a moment before suggesting, "Guess we'd better go see what he's up to then, hadn't we?"

How could she be taking this so lightly, he wondered?

She laid her hand on his chest very softly but firmly. She looked directly into his eyes as she told him to "Breathe." And he did.

She set the pace up the steps. She was curious but not panicking. Laurence tried to feel the same way. It wasn't working.

He moved behind her along the upstairs hall toward the room at the end where they assumed their son had gone. He seemed to have left the door open behind him for them. The floor everywhere was thickly carpeted. They stepped quietly as they approached.

They pulled up before reaching the room. They might be invading the private space, maybe bedroom of some institutionalized child who didn't even know them. Their own child wouldn't have wanted them to do that to his.

They held, and listened, but heard nothing. No voices. Either Maddie's, or anyone else's. This might not even be the right room. Everything was so quiet in this place.

Danni took those next steps forward, stopping just outside to look in first.

She froze.

Laurence could see she was staring at something; watching someone. Her eyes had locked onto it and she wasn't moving. She didn't even appear to be breathing.

He took those last steps himself, pulling up behind her.

On the bed was the frail, twisted form of a Tibetan girl with terribly sad eyes. They'd find out later that this poor scrawny child hadn't spoken a word in what might have been years. She rarely left her bed, didn't eat well, and interacted with no one. She'd been traumatized by her adoptive parents, and so had been taken from them and placed here.

Danni and Laurence now stood witness as she and Maddie appeared to recognize each other. The tiny child brightened and reached for him. Danni and Laurence were there to hear it as she spoke her first word in a very long time.

In her weakness, she pushed away what she could of her covers, tried her best to turn toward their son and sit up. Her eyes and smile were alight, though her skin was gray and pallid and hung loosely. They could see how much she wanted to raise both of her arms toward their boy, but she needed one of them to stabilize and support her in her half-risen position.

Madison had his back to the door and therefore to his parents, but they could see he was standing strong. He seemed quite clear about where he was and what he was doing. He had raised both of his own arms only slightly, as though ready to receive her if she found herself capable of walking to him.

Her eyes brightened still more, and they heard joy in her voice as the little girl looked toward him and gasped, "Rinpoche!"

Within half an hour the two kids were basically talking; though only sparingly and in short, quiet spurts. Neither Laurence nor Danni could understand anything either one of them was saying, but they were grateful to be just standing there quietly, witnessing a miracle.

Visits from the Beauforts came more regularly after that. Danni and/or Laurence drove Maddie out there. Receptionists and care givers at the home said Hello to him each time on his arrival, but he just walked in, strode right past them, and went "on his rounds" as the adults liked to call them. Children brightened, came out to play, ate and rested better after one of his visits. Even those he spent no individual time with; sat or stood only generally near, with no one speaking.

Everyone there accepted him as one of their own. He marched right in like he knew what he was doing, barely nodding at attendants along the way. Some bowed their heads, placed hands together before their hearts, and called him Rinpoche as he passed. He'd come to be known affectionately and respectfully around there as Runt Rinboku, or as the Little Runt Rinpoche. They never tried to explain the title to his parents. Danni and Laurence tried Googling the words themselves, but felt they'd been left outside any real grasp of their subtleties.

Laurence set up funds to help this and other homes like it, but it wasn't just another business move for him. He took it as a kind of a calling. He felt he was helping out in something far greater than himself.

It was like cells dividing in the embryo of a new world. Life had never been clear, simple, and obvious. Now it seemed even less so. But it had grown urgent we find ways to sort these things through.

Everyone had been shaken loose from what they and their worlds had been. For good or for ill, most had been shocked through to their cores. Parts of the nation had beaten the virus back, though many feared it might never truly be vanquished. This plague or another could always hit again. This one seemed to have a mind of its own, and a spirit for vengeance. It kept changing its tactics and attacking from new fronts. It kept mutating, just as mankind itself seemed to be. The world had been wrenched and twisted into something intolerable that no one could get a really good grip on. Things could never again be as they had been, but could not be left as they were.

People at both extremes were determined to make sure of it.

The American Civil War was dredged up and fought once again between basically those two same original camps; and once again, on both sides, it was the poor and the ignorant who were falling.

It had been a long fight. Many had sunken into their positions generations ago. They couldn't just rethink matters now, and change sides. And as for the nation as a whole, divisiveness had worked its way into the system. Tinkering with a few scattered laws and painting slogans on streets might seem briefly encouraging, but couldn't bury all of those rusted and bloodstained old axes people still chose to grind.

States relentlessly supporting this President found ways to pull apart from much of the rest of the world. They started building real, imagined, and virtual barriers between their own kind and those who insisted on learning from scientists, experts, and history. Banning from their own communities any who kept their news media and internet open to voices from other countries, cultures, and colors. Speaking out proudly of their "Great Barrier Walls," they fought desperately to keep their communities pure and untarnished. They worked to censor or block outside influences even as much of the rest of the world was finding commonality. To force public news and private opinions into synch with the sometimes moment-by-moment positions of their often moody leaders.

They called their local and state governments, "The PolitiChurch." Renamed their political party, "The Family Values Party." Just as early Nazis had had their brown shirts, bands of terrorist thugs now roamed the streets and alleys of large towns and small behind these Great Barrier walls; brutalizing and often killing those they felt offended by, took a dislike to, coveted the property of, or whom they could claim hadn't been upholding PolitiChurch dictates. Abused citizens called these wandering and often drunken marauders, "rat packs."

PolitiChurch leaders had to keep their citizens ignorant, broken, subservient, and in a constant state of fear. Outsiders had to be seen as the enemy. Citizens had to believe all the way through to their souls that outside their Barrier Walls stood an army for the devil always poised for invasion.

And that Satan might already have slithered in right next door to the citizens themselves. He might be in their own homes, or those of their neighbors. It was their duty to spy on each other for God, country, and community. Report anyone with uncomfortable ideas. Citizens had to believe that the all powerful PolitiChurch had sent spies into every home, friendship, and grocery to report on them if they failed to report on each other.

The nation and the world needed to change. But changes that vast and forever couldn't be just slapped on like band-aids allowed to flap loose some time later. This was a pivotal moment in global consciousness. Maybe even survival. Humankind had to either take a full and meaningful stride forward in their awareness and evolution, or they would fall at the hands of Nature and history.

Indigo spirits were like the scattering of stars throughout the darkest night skies. Each perhaps a sun within their own solar system. Held together and interacting through forces we couldn't see.

Chapter Fourteen

Sunrise and sunset reach their peaks for only a moment. But when they are at their best they are glorious.

Ailana looked around. The air was steeped in that magical, sad sweetness she'd always loved at this time of year. It was autumn. The time of passing from one stage to another. A time for leaving things behind, letting them fade, trusting they'd grow bright and fresh again. Even if they had to take on new forms.

She'd seen so very many changes, and so many seasons. She'd watched children come into the world, grow old, and then die again. She'd watched centuries change. And all the while these gardens had stood curtained away from the ravages of time. For many, they had long stood for hope, and hope must never be allowed to grow old, wither away, and to die. The mystical life here kept this land forever young, it's healing energies renewed, even when those coming to drink of it must inevitably taste death. Many visitors had moved on from here in service to others. They'd helped heal broken bodies and torn hearts outside these grounds somewhere, often in other parts of the world. They had helped in so many ways with so many troubled souls. These gardens would soon be needing someone younger, more vital and alive to watch over them. More lively than she'd been feeling lately.

Everywhere through autumn came the rustle of leaves, and the stir of shifting spirits. Each morning the trees looked more spindly, and naked. The smell of greenery returning to dust. She caught sight of one brown leaf alone from all the others now, dangling in the air from a single thread of silk. She watched it move as though choreographed even when there seemed to be no breeze.

The subtle, swaying, interweaving moods of autumn worked their ways through her very slowly. Slowly, and yet so deeply that she felt their sadness all the way to her bones.

She noticed a good number of tomatoes still ripening even this late in their season. Life in these particular woods and gardens did seem to set its own rules. Bears had so far left a lot of the lower fruits and berries untouched. Animals here tended to share.

Ailana didn't like squatting to pick those fruits nearest the ground anyway, so she too left them there for the rabbits, raccoons, or whatever. Her knees weren't what they once had been, but there were plenty of critters around for whom that would present no real problem. She, and the fruits, and the vegetables, and all life in these gardens and woods coexisted in gentle and meaningful harmony. Here, Mother Nature was a friend and companion.

She'd also been noting that when she reached too high for too long she often got dizzy. Her body kept reminding her of her gathering frailty. She was much older than most would dare guess, or even imagine, but at some point all things physical must wear out.

This was her time.

She reached to press her fingertips against a beautiful, round, shiny red tomato. Paused to appreciate its fullness and perfection. Ailana felt gratitude, and offered her thanks. She applied just enough pressure to know its firmness. Hefted it on its stem a few times to marvel at its weight and know it would be juicy. Minutes may have passed before she plucked it.

This was one of those borderline days when she couldn't quite tell if it was starting to rain, merely intended to, or hadn't really made up its mind. Now and then she maybe felt a little drop, or maybe didn't. The air was either turning to mist or simply expressing the melancholy of autumn. Fallen leaves gathering into a jigsaw of countless colors and shapes. A puzzle scattered everywhere, forever in process. Broken but complete. Outer edges of the neighboring woods lay thick with crumbling leaves. That organic dust aroma hung like drapery through her senses. She felt it in her eyes, on her skin, in her hair. She inhaled it into her lungs, briefly forgetting that everything seemed to be making her cough these days. This body was getting very, very old.

She found another perfect tomato, paused to hold and appreciate it for a time, but then left it there for the other animals, and moved on. Autumn was a time for conscious sharing. Some would be in more need than she would through these bitter months ahead.

Ailana moved along from the tomato patch, and away from the berries growing along its edges. She checked the levels of suet and lard she'd put out for birds. This was going to be a cold winter. She had been forewarned.

Frank wasn't going to be around for his family into his ripe older years. Probably not even long enough to set those heavy loads of corporation stress down, and let his loved ones see his softer sides. If he still had any. Probably not enough time left to really get to know his wife and son. And hope that they would want to know him.

He'd pretty much had to let go of seeing anything in the ways he once had. He almost wished he'd never even gone to those bloody mountains and taken such a hard look at the harm he'd been doing. How had seeing that really helped anyone? How had his retirement changed anything? All he'd done was pass the torch along to others who'd care even less about all those helpless little guys out there they'd been stealing from. Nothing would change. He'd accomplished nothing. Not one damned thing. He should have stayed in, kept his gloves on, and fought the good fight. No one would listen to him now. He'd helped nobody.

No wonder he was in this damned wheelchair. Kinda said something for karma he guessed, didn't it? Condemned to a life of watching himself fall apart. Dying in the slow, degrading way he had earned through his neglect of so many other lives. This could take years and he would hate every stage of it.

Good. He deserved that. This disease was an ugly and terrifying thing to have to deal with, but ugly and terrifying was exactly how his corporate policies had made the lives of more people than anyone could count. How much of that could he maybe have stopped? His excruciatingly slow self-demolition couldn't have happened to a nicer guy. He really believed that, and it sucked.

His body was coming apart. System by system. Getting weaker. He wouldn't grow old with those he cared most about. He worried a lot over whether or not he'd done right by them, which then added even more to his stress, and then that tore greater chunks out of his health.

At least his wife had her social life, her circle of friends, and she would go on. She'd be okay. And Benjie was the kind of sweet, innocent kid any parent should be pleased with. Nothing like his father. Sometimes you teach your children, and sometimes you should try harder to learn from them. Or at least try to be better people because of them. Benjie was a fine and sensitive child. Frank hoped his own bad example had shown his son that money couldn't make you a man. The world needed more out of us these days. We had to be there for each other.

Frank sat up and braced. Taking firm hold of his desk, he pushed himself to his limits trying to stand. There would probably always be that part of him that refused to give in.

His head swirled, instantly on the very edge of passing out, but he caught hold before he could slam his head and do some observable damage. His family didn't need to deal with that on top of everything else.

He was left as always with that aching dizziness that seemed to ring through his teeth. He sat very still for a couple of minutes, rigidifying himself from every angle, but breathing very calmly and slowly. He sat, focused, in a kind of meditational state until the worst had passed. Until he dared turn his attention away from impending collapse.

When he finally could, he tried inching his "chariot of disgrace" across the room, bracing again when he got to the door. Trying to decide if he was ready to open it

It took him a while to work his way down the hall. Heading out to greet his loved ones.

It hurt Laurence deeply, knowing that Madison was the sort of child these extremists would gladly snatch off the street and stuff into one of their cages. Family Values "security forces" had been breaking into homes and schoolyards, hauling off kids they wanted to cull from the herd. Kids who didn't think like everyone else, didn't believe what their precious PolitiChurch wanted us all to swallow blindly. Didn't fit their leader's ideals for strutting, obedient, everyone-the-same mobs of armed zombies.

Madison was happily attending regular schools these days, where his offbeat nature was bound to challenge other students, and would definitely stand out. He seemed to be normalizing under his own steam, but doing it in his own quirky style. They were thousands of miles away from the nearest Great Barrier Walls, and Maddie was in a very good school, but you just never knew where or when someone might show up and start blasting or nabbing.

Laurence had been watching his sweet and amazing little boy, his little *Runt Rinpoche*, even more carefully since they'd first started visiting that strange, borderline mystical orphanage. Maddie could have an almost miraculous effect on some people. And sometimes the boy himself seemed to grow brighter; more knowing, and confident. Like he was connecting to something deeper that Laurence and Danni could only guess at. Acting like a kind of a doorway to other possibilities and worlds.

But Laurence feared this wouldn't be enough to shield him and keep him safe from all the dangers in this one.

It was dinnertime. The weather had shifted lately, and Maddie was wearing winter gear at the table. He had a Tibetan-style fur cap on, with one of the ear flaps down, and was having trouble picking up his soup spoon because of his mittens. Was this just his curious mind experimenting, Laurence asked himself? Expressing himself creatively like his mom liked to do? They hadn't told him the cook had made oxtail soup, afraid he would take that literally, as he did so many things. In those stories he painted of exotic times in faraway mountains, oxen might have been his close companions and friends for all Laurence knew.

It was a cold, blustering day. The help had dug out gloves, coats, and winter hats for the family. They had ironed or steam pressed scarves. But Laurence and Danni knew not to wear them inside. Particularly not at the dinner table.

Or at least Laurence did. What his wife was liable to wear at any given moment was rarely predictable, but usually delightful.

Using that over-sized spoon like some sort of steam shovel or excavation tool, Madison had set about re-arranging bits of food on his plate. He formed a river of gravy meandering through mountains of meat he'd capped like snow by shaping mashed white potatoes on top. Getting to know Madison often involved trying to interpret why he'd re-arranged certain details of his life, room, or plate the way he had this particular time. Those mountains of meat and potatoes might be some kind of pilgrimage for him to some sacred realm where deeper things were made clearer to a mind that didn't think like most others. Laurence studied each detail, eager to learn what he could.

Slowly, patiently, lovingly, and always cautiously, he was learning to communicate at last with his son. Now he asked Maddie if there were holy brothers trekking up any of those mountains he was forming on his plate. The child beamed with joy to be so clearly understood. Thrilled that he was openly communicating with his dad. Pointing to the second lump from his left he told Laurence, "This one!"

The boy smiled a smile that brightened the souls of his parents. Then he settled back down into his labors. His forehead was beginning to sweat a little, but he kept his hat on.

Danika sat, studying her son openly in awe.

When he was done with his earth moving responsibilities, Madison blessed his food, and gladly let them watch. He no longer felt the need to run off to the sacred private spaces of his own room to communicate with the invisible and perhaps questionable. He let them listen in as he mumbled strange, guttural sounds very quickly in an exotic foreign rhythm. Laurence wondered if he'd picked up a few prayers and chants at the orphanage. Prayers had never been required in their home. This was Maddie's own colorful addition to mealtime, and they honored that. Laurence had a strong urge to bow his own head in silence out of respect, but was afraid Maddie might take that as just pretending, and consequently dishonoring both the boy, and whomever he might be praying to. So they just sat and watched, but wouldn't begin eating until he'd finished.

Laurence had always been agnostic. He had never really given the possibility of there being any kind of God or gods out there much thought, and he really wasn't doing so now. And yet there was a part of him in this moment that almost felt blessed. Watching the deep reverence his son was offering to some unseen other or others was almost like participating in it. What a much nicer world it could be if every one of us came at every new moment as if it was special, the way their son did. If everything was honored with open gratitude this way.

Seeing little men trekking up their potatoes might be a bit of a stretch, but watching from the other side of the table, Madison's dad shared the reverential joy in his son's heart as he lost himself in even the tiniest details.

It was only once Madison began taking his own first few bites that his mom and dad thought to move, let alone speak. Danni asked her boy, "Are we done? Should we start?"

Madison beamed a goofy grin at her, raised up his hand, and wiggled his ear flap in her direction. It all looked so immediate, so intentional, and yet so bizarrely out of place. She snorted a couple of times with suppressed laughter. It was only later she realized that Madison had been playing the clown on purpose at least in that one moment. He could see how they must be confused, and maybe concerned about some of his odd ways, and though he felt no compulsion to explain, he could at least show them all was okay. That they just could dig in, enjoy, and not worry about him.

Madison had been carefully eating around one of his meat and potato mountains, leaving the one with elder brothers trekking it untouched out of respect. He stopped for a moment and just sat there, gazing off into the distance with deep compassion. Like he was telling somebody out there somewhere beyond the walls that he really understood what this other was going through, and that he cared.

It was easy to read that in his eyes. The boy was so open and sincere. Laurence had been learning that every gesture, every slight shift in his son's position, every change in his face counted for something. Madison never wasted a moment, a word, or an action. Now he caught Maddie's serious, deeply caring, far away look, and wondered where his son had gone off to. And whom he might be helping.

He was beginning to understand. This was all becoming real for him.

Sometimes Maddie's subtleties called out special levels of Laurence's perception and he wondered how much else he'd been missing all this time. How much he probably still was. He wanted to not only know and understand his son better, but be able to care just as deeply as his boy did. He wished he could find a way to help people as profoundly as Maddie could.

But then again, he thought, could anyone ever really understand what was going on inside this very special being? Probably not completely. Not all of him. In that one moment though, he considered it a blessing to at least be riding along.

He'd been rethinking everything lately. Had they really given birth to a small, troubled infant, and then raised him out of utter helplessness into what he'd become? Or had they been entrusted with someone who had already been strong, albeit strange, from the beginning?

Their first dishes were cleared and new treats were brought out from the kitchen as Laurence just sat there.

Wondering.

From his place at the table, Madison was looking off into the invisible distance again. His father wondered how often he did that. And what subtle promptings called it out of him.

The boy had such a look of deep compassion in his eyes. As though he was out there among the lost and the broken, holding one of those poor, starving children of the streets in his arms.

It reminded Laurence of how he responded to those poor kids in that orphanage. And how they all responded to him. With Madison, there seemed to be so much going on that most people couldn't see.

Could Laurence himself learn to sense, respond to, and help people far away? Was it something normal folks could learn?

He looked up again, and saw that this time his son was watching *him*.

In that moment, Maddie looked so deeply knowing. Like all things were just as they should be.

Then the boy bowed his head, thanked his potatoes, and smiled.

Sylvie was still only ten years old, which a lot of people would say wasn't a lot, but she had decided she wanted to commit her whole heart and everything to helping out, and hugging stuff, and dancing a lot.

Auntie looked like she was letting go of her body more than she was inside it these days. She needed help in certain ways sometimes, but for the most part overall she really didn't. Like picking things up when she dropped them and couldn't bend over. But then, once they were on the ground, they would be closer to Sylvie's level anyway, and so it was easy to just hand them back up to her. Sometimes trying to stand up made her dizzy, so Sylvie told her to just sit still and don't worry about it; Sylvie would get that for her. Or she helped her auntie wake up and get out of bed some mornings when she had gone off somewhere in her spirit, probably helping somebody far away, but now was having trouble getting back into her body again. Sylvie walked over there most mornings around wake up time just in case.

But today the little girl was out in the woods. Her one concession to the forest was that she was willing to wear shoes while she was in there. Just not any that fit her too tightly. She liked them being way loose on her so she could wiggle around inside them. She didn't like to keep stepping on all those pointy sticks everywhere, so shoes turned out to be pretty much called for, but if they were going to be down there, they really should have to be fun.

She also thought that way about watches. They looked like they could be beautiful and fun to wear around, and she would spend a lot of time looking at hers even if she never did really care what time it was. Of course, she didn't know any of that from personal experience, because no one had ever given her one. Which made sense when she really thought about it. Because who would ever in their right mind ever trust her with a watch? She would probably just go and fling the thing off somewhere when she was dancing some time, she thought. And it would go flying up into a treetop or somewhere, and nobody would ever see it again.

Unless she happened to see a big bird, or maybe a squirrel walking around the next day, looking all proud of himself because he was wearing a watch.

But he would probably have to wear it around his middle, like a belt, she thought, because even her tiny wrist had to be bigger than a squirrel's wrist, and it would just keep falling off if he tried to wear it the way she did.

Except she couldn't, because she didn't have one. Which was probably just as well.

She had been walking for a while, and thinking about all kinds of fun stuff, when she saw Mr. Mica wandering toward her from the opposite direction. He was already aiming his smile at her, but taking his time getting closer. Maybe because she was. Taking her time, that is. They seemed to like matching each other's paces.

She heard a mourning dove off in the distance somewhere and a woodpecker announcing itself against an empty tree some place else. There was a deer wandering around, but he didn't seem to notice her new visitor. Which made Sylvie wonder if maybe Mr. Mica wasn't in his real body this time, but maybe just coming to her in his light, or in a dream while she was awake. Because he did sometimes do that. She had caught him at it before.

She was carrying a feather she'd just found. It was gray with darker and lighter stripes. She waved it at him like she was saying Hello, and he wiggled his fingers back at her.

She pointed it at him as he came nearer those last few steps. He kept looking down at it and giggling like he knew what she was up to. He always seemed to know what she was thinking, and maybe even what she wasn't really thinking just yet, but was probably going to.

She asked him if he was really, really there this time, like this feather was, or if he was only pretending again.

He reached toward it, but didn't take it from her. He passed his fingers softly over it from the hard, pointy part to the other end, where everything was so soft that she liked tickling it against her face. As each bit passed between his fingers it turned a glowing, radiant, pure white, and stayed that way. She now had a perfect white feather.

He told her he could always be really, really with her, even if and when he also happened to be somewhere else at the same time.

When she thought about that though, she didn't think he had really answered her question.

So then the next moment it looked like he was walking toward her from every direction. He was everywhere.

And then the next moment after that one, it was like she was inside of him as he did that, and she could look at everything in the world from every angle without moving.

"Well now, that was interesting," she said when she got back inside her own self again. He laughed to hear her put it that way.

He didn't try to explain to her what had just happened, like Auntie Ailana always tried to. She helped Sylvie straighten out what she really could see from what she was only hoping she could. Like, was that *really* a fairy this time, or just another funny light in the trees? If Sylvie said she'd seen a unicorn, her auntie would tell her they weren't really actually real, but then they could pretend together and tell stories about them anyway. Everybody needed somebody like Auntie around to help them figure out stuff.

Auntie told her things sometimes even when she knew Sylvie wasn't quite ready to understand them just yet. She could just carry them around in her for a while until they were ready to tell her what they meant later on. And sometimes Auntie used big words, knowing Sylvie would figure them out eventually. The little girl might just look up at her at times like that, when she didn't seem to be making much sense, and tell her, "You can be very mysterious sometimes."

Auntie would always break into laughter again, like she always did, until it seemed to be rolling off the trees all around them, and Sylvie would turn around to watch all the plants giggling everywhere. Then Auntie sometimes told Sylvie something like, "Oh, I do try, Little Flitter. I certainly do try to be." And then they would both laugh.

She and her auntie really got along.

And now Mr. Mica was doing that to her as well. He was letting her not understand things until she was ready.

He stood there smiling and watching her think. When she was done remembering about her auntie, he happened to look down at her feet, and then giggled a little. With this, she knew he was admiring her footwear. She wiggled her tiny toes inside her great big boots just because she liked doing that, and because she thought it might be a charming way of saying hello, to wave at him with her toes.

A breeze stirred the trees around them for a moment. There was a smell of fresh mowed grass and blooming mountain laurels in the air. She looked down at her hand again and she was still holding that beautiful long white feather. It looked like one of those long, curly, writing plume pens she'd seen in pictures from the very old days of Benjamin Franklin and Sir Thomas Jefferson, back in the times when they gave you great big huge pieces of paper you could write on with them. Which made her think of another question to ask Mr. Mica. If he had been around back then. She decided to not ask it out loud though, to just think it real hard, just to test him and see if he heard her thinking it.

He didn't choose to address that particular issue though. She had noticed before that he didn't always feel he had to answer absolutely everything.

Instead, he changed the subject to something much more important. He told her, "I have come because you have been wondering if you will be big enough in time to help your Auntie Ailana guide those who come here, once she no longer can in the ways that she has been."

"Something like that," she told him back.

"We each offer whatever we can," he told her. "And through trying, we grow stronger."

"That is not much of a Yes or No," she told him.

"You are probably more ready than you think," he said. "Still not a Yes or No, but close enough for now, I hope?"

"I guess so," she said. "For now."

She was serving him notice that there would be more questions coming later when she could think of them. And that he might want to consider giving her a better answer next time.

Mr. Mica nodded, accepting her terms.

They wandered and played for a while. She offered to let him hold her feather. He took it as though he thought this was a very great honor.

She had decided to call him Mr. Mica because she could see the energy around people and his was really shiny. Like when you look at the dirt and some parts are really sparkling out at you because there is mica there. He was like that. He sparkled out brighter than anyone else. If you could look at everyone in the world from high above the planet, and you could see all of their energies at once, he would be one of the shining ones. He had never told her his real name. Or if he had, it was probably one she couldn't pronounce even when she worked really hard at it, and so she had probably just decided she didn't really need to hang on to that particular name in her memory.

Sometimes walking with him was like taking a nice drowsy nap under a tree in soft leaves, she thought. Except that you were standing up while you were doing it. You always felt refreshed when he was around.

They paused by long thick rows of milkweed swarming with every kind of butterfly. Their full round balls of purple flowers filled the air with Sylvie's favorite smell. Her nose drank it in, which made her heart very happy.

When their fat pods burst open with that white sticky stuff, they weren't much fun to try to play with, she had learned, because you had trouble getting it off of your fingers then. Or out of your hair if you happened to rub it. Which she couldn't help but do every time she told herself she shouldn't. They were a lot more fun when they burst open with all those feather-headed fly-away seeds, which she had learned right away not to put in her mouth. But now today, she and Mr. Mica stood, and watched, and smelled, and then moved to another spot after a while and watched some more. Neither one of them was saying very much, if they were actually saying anything at all. The butterflies were everywhere.

"I like watching stuff," she said finally, but it was really a very, very long time later.

"Moving through life attentively and respectfully is your second nature," he agreed.

"What's my first nature?" she asked, and she could tell that she had caught him off guard.

"You do ask the good questions," he observed. "You are a natural born teacher."

Very much later he added, "It would be a great gift to others if you could help *them* learn to attend respectfully to what is around them, and inside them, as you do. We each of us help through what we are, what we have been through, and what we have become. Even while knowing that we will continue to change. You ask if you will be big enough in time to help adults when your auntie has taken her next step. But there is no need to wait until we are bigger, or until we have learned more, before we start helping. We will always be learning more. We cannot wait until we know absolutely everything. You are even now ready for more than you suspect.

"And as for your auntie. You have already been assisting her greatly."

They stopped to watch a tiny minuscule green caterpillar so small you could only just barely see him. He kept dropping himself lower from a tree branch overhead by spitting a long silk cord out of his butt in short bursts. He did this part very quickly but then turned around and climbed back up very slowly. All the way up, he kept using some of his arms to gather that silk into a wad and hold it in front of him.

"Why didn't he just stay up in the tree and spit that string into his arms in the first place?" Sylvie asked.

"I don't really know," her friend said. "I suppose I could hazard a guess if you like."

"It is much better sometimes to just watch and not know, than to guess and get everything wrong," she observed.

"A natural born teacher," he noted. "And your time is clearly coming."

He then paused to consider before adding, "I suspect the world will want to ready itself for you more than you will need to get ready for the world. It might well be they who have the more to learn and to prepare for."

When they were finished walking, Sylvie saw that they had returned to Auntie's special gardens. Ailana was out there, petting her vegetables again. She looked up and waved at both of them as they approached, they waved and smiled back at her, and the whole world seemed to be happy.

March had come in like a lion, but was going out like a trout. Benjie was getting tired of sitting around inside all the time, but it looked like it wasn't going to ever stop raining.

He'd been drinking more lately. Mostly he blamed that on either the weather or hormones. He had always felt a little lost and out of place, but now these days he'd been feeling even lost'er. They'd been telling kids in health class that their emotions might go screwy sometimes as they moved into adolescence. Everything was sure going completely all crazy these days. But he didn't think it was completely just him and his personal, internal chemistry. Could the whole world have gone hormonal?

Another reason he was drinking more was because Bj never showed up unless Benjie was really out of it.

Benjie had been feeling disillusioned again. Even the woods seemed more empty. He had loved it back when he'd still thought there might be Indian spirits wandering around in them. But then no one had ever really shown up, and after a while he just hadn't felt like looking anymore. Why bother? They'd just leave him standing there alone with his heart hanging open again.

His books basically told him it was probably his own fault. Rule # One was that what he *wanted* shouldn't matter as much as what other people *needed*. Feeling all disappointed when things didn't go just exactly how he wanted them to was childish, and it was time he grew out of that, he told himself in some of his clearer moments.

But why did he have to choose to be *either* psychic *or* helpful? Edgar Cayce could do both. He was psychic, and he helped lots of people. Benjie wasn't gonna hurt anybody. If he was a really amazing psychic he could get his own TV show and help people every week. And anyway, what was wrong with wanting to be a little special if nobody got hurt?

Pretty much anything would do. Flip cards over using only the power of his mind, or change the dice and then give all the winning money to charity. That would be helpful, right? Tell people their dead friends still love them. He could cure cancer with just the touch of his hand as thousands lined up everywhere he went, cheering. And if he maybe got a little bit of a swelled head out of it sometimes, they were still feeling better, weren't they?

And anyway, probably not every psychic in history had always been a completely nice guy. Some of them might have been nasty and selfish even. Like what about Rasputin? He looked pretty mean. Check out those eyes! He looked nasty!

Why couldn't what Benjie wanted ever count for anything?

And so, he drank, even though he wasn't legally old enough to yet, and it wasn't always just to coax Bj out when someone needed help.

Despite his often moody and self-absorbed ways of dealing with things in these awkward first spats of puberty, Benjie really did care about others. His compassion had been coming more to the front of his many thoughts and few actions in recent days. The deep-seated nuances of pure altruism were having to work their ways through his basic nature very slowly, but he had definitely been wanting to help. He held back from that urge more often than not; just like he pretty much held back from everything; but at least it was there. Problem was, the process of reaching out to other people had trouble untangling itself from his much more elaborate thought processes. He sat around and tried to work through all the options first. That was just who he was. His intentions were good, and always getting better. He wanted to help; he just held back.

And it was all of it making him moody. Which then made things even more confusing.

He found a neatly folded note propped up against his pillow one night.

It told him, "You will work this out.

"You are not alone."

It told him, "You tend to react to challenge and pain by letting it shut you down. You choose to slide back into frustration rather than take any real step in dealing with it. You would like to see your life as an adventure, but then your actions suggest you would rather stay home. A true adventure tears one's heart open, forcing him to deal with that which he had never faced before. It pushes him past what he had previously held to be his limits. A real adventure forces him to reach higher and deeper. To grow into more than he had been. He must make room for a new way of looking at life.

"<u>Pain</u> can tear one's heart open as well, but not everyone thinks to search inside it for that which is higher than pain; not everyone thinks to reach deeper into his soul for greater truth while he is facing it.

"One must choose for himself whether or not to step forward."

Benjie was feeling frustrated that night, and maybe his hormones were acting up again or something, but for some reason, he got pissed off at whoever this was, thinking he could just shove bossy notes in his face whenever he damned well felt like it; telling him he had to change the way he looked at everything, but otherwise they all just stood around and ignored him.

So Benjie just wadded it up, and threw it away.

Laurence wanted so badly to connect with his son and the world he lived in. Get some sense of what he was seeing, and what it all meant to him. It was obvious there must be more going on in this world we all thought we knew, but had only been seeing from the outside. Was it the rest of us who didn't really fit in, while Maddie had been at home from the beginning? What had Laurence been missing all these years?

How can someone connect so instantly and deeply with strangers; profoundly change them and heal them without touching or speaking a word? What were the mechanics of that?

Laurence wished he knew how to reach deeper into the real truth of things. Instead of burying himself in his darkest emotions, shutting his loved ones out.

What did Maddie know? What could he see?

What was he looking at when he appeared to be gazing through walls? What was that gesture he made with his hands?

Laurence tried researching Tibetan healing methods, but that got him nowhere. He tried "Healing without medicine or touching", and "General proximity healing", and "Non-contact healing." He found sites on modalities like *Therapeutic Touch*, and *Reiki*, and an overall genre called *Energy Work*. That sounded about right. Energy exchange. That made sense.

A lot of the practitioners were apparently nurses. Some even did this sort of work in hospitals and taught it at major universities, which lent the whole matter a certain respectability as far as he was concerned. It wouldn't be just a bunch of New Age Wackiedoodles. He felt better about signing up for a few of their internet classes. There seemed to be thousands out there taking the sort of thing Maddie did seriously.

Which meant his boy wasn't alone. These weren't just symptoms of some troubling autistic aberration. Maddie had tapped into something real.

How had he learned this on his own? Maybe he'd been taking classes in his room.

Laurence found a quiet place in his home to settle out for a few minutes each day and try meditating. Sometimes Danni joined him. It wasn't as hard as he'd thought it might be. He actually liked sitting quietly, letting his tensions ease out of him. He got better at imagining himself in a forest, or glen, or by the sea. Listening to bird song, running streams, or ocean waves lapping the shore. He could feel the warmth of sunshine soaking through him. Smell the breezes.

Then came the moment he was to ask some even deeper level of peacefulness to help him open as a channel for healing. Surprisingly, in what seemed only minutes, he felt something softer, and brighter; something unseen, but truly good passing through him. He felt soothing but invigorating energy flowing in from all directions. All things were connected, he was a stream, and other streams were joining in from everywhere.

> *"No soul that aspires can ever fail to rise; no heart that loves can ever be abandoned."*
> —Dr. Annie Besant

"Consult not your fears, but your hopes and your dreams. Think not about your frustrations, but about your unfulfilled potential. Concern yourself not with what you tried and failed in, but with what is possible for you to do."
—Pope John Paul XXIII

Chapter Fifteen

"You seem a little lost tonight, Burrito," Frank told his son. Benjie looked up. He'd been staring at his food, but had basically stopped eating it. Outside their dining room windows, the air was blustering cold. He told his dad, "I've been thinking about all those homeless people out there in this kind of weather."

"You want to bring them some blankets?" Frank asked. "Maybe have the cooks fix a little something up and have someone take it to them?"

Benjie hesitated. "I was thinking more of maybe spending a little time with them myself. I don't know. Sit around with them awhile. Somehow show them they still matter."

"You could get hurt out there, Honey," his mum told him. "You don't know what kinds of diseases they might be carrying." She was more afraid of the psychological harm it could cause him, being exposed to that kind of misery. "He's never been in that kind of environment," she told her husband.

But Frank actually liked the idea. He told his wife, "It's a big world out there, Sweetheart. He will have to grow up to meet it some day."

"He... He could see things," she said.

"So he could," Frank agreed. "In fact, I'm sure he will. I hope he will. I'll be counting on it.

"Look," he told her. "These people haven't been shown proper respect, or even treated like humans, in probably a very long time. Hundreds may walk past them every day and not even make eye contact. How long has it been since anyone's stopped long enough to treat them with a little respect?"

Benjie told her, "They're dying out there, Mum. Everything just keeps hitting them harder, and hurting them worse. Everybody needs someone to care."

He told his dad, "I probably can't do anything much, but if even a couple of them feel like smiling for a couple of minutes, shouldn't that count for something?"

His father said, "Of course. Yes it does. It counts for a lot. That's a beautiful thought." He told his son, "You're a better man than I am."

Frank thought back to those long ago first days when he'd snuggled a tiny thing in such over-sized blankets, and had called his new son his "Little Benito Burrito."

He told Benjie now, "I am really very proud of you, Son."

Benjie said, "I'm proud of you too, Dad."

"Well, I'm afraid I haven't been earning that in the long haul, Benito. I haven't been all that pleased with myself lately," Frank admitted. "But thank you. Thank you anyway. I know you meant that, and it means a lot to me. It really does."

"Sure, Dad."

"But maybe sometimes we can be offered second chances. You want to help these folks, huh? Get out there and do some good?"

"I do, Dad. I really do."

"I understand," Frank said. He told Reenie, "I think it's a beautiful idea."

He asked Benjie, "Would you mind if an old, dying cripple tagged along?"

Reenie looked immediately and dramatically troubled. Even picturing it riddled her with horror and revulsion. She felt sorry for these people, but sitting right in the middle of them, passing germs around, wouldn't fix all the world's problems. Their job was to stay home and look out for their son. They could do a lot of good right from where they were.

Frank told her. "We can't hide the boy behind garden walls forever. We can't keep life out. We wouldn't be doing him any favors if we tried. There are some mean and ugly things out there for sure, Reenie, but if we hide from them, if we don't let ourselves see them, we aren't *really* safe because nobody anywhere is safe. I seem to recall you telling me that once, up in the mountains."

She blustered a little, feeling lost, not quite taking that in.

Frank told her, "Sweetie, the day is coming when I won't be around to help him, and at some point, neither will you." He leaned in on arms that seemed stronger in that moment. His hands steadied as he spoke. "Left to his own ways, don't we want him to stand up strong, and count for something?" he asked her.

"Look. I am not proud of all the ways I might have contributed to a lot of this. And it is not my son's responsibility to make things right. But I am proud of him for wanting to do get out there and show kindness."

He thought a moment, then added, "We are all in this together. I am thrilled; and, frankly, amazed; that he is seeing that so young."

Benjie beamed, though his mum still looked worried. There had always been traditions. She had always known how to handle things according to the old ways. Things had to be kept under control. You couldn't allow them to change. But now everything was coming apart. It had gotten so out of hand. She wouldn't know how to protect her son if she just gave in to this chaos. She didn't dare yield.

Benjie told her, "You don't dare think too hard sometimes, Mum. Just keep doing what you can, and hope it helps."

Benjie felt really good inside as he said it. Like he had finally connected to his own life somehow.

He looked out the window toward the old woods. Pictured natives thanking the storms for their challenges. Thanking elders for their experience, and Mother Nature for her guidance. Time bled away. He smelled crackling campfires. He was one with the spirit of his people again.

In challenging times to come, this ancient part of him helped him deal with his dad's degenerative disease. There could never be a cure; his body could only waste away one part or system at a time until all of him was gone. But when Benjie could manage to find his way in to this softer, clearer, openhearted space, he could draw on some renewed inner strength he found there, and offer some of that to his parents.

In compassion he found strength.

Great swathes of humanity were battling and succumbing to existential terrors. Alone and together, people suffered. Losing themselves to personal, national, societal, and global Dark Nights of the Soul.

But seeds of Enlightenment can take root even through the heart of debilitating Darkness.

Renaissance means rebirth.

"The Leaders of the Damned," as many called them, were being voted out of office, but then trying to rig the system so they could still hold all the power. They sent teams of their own in to make a big show of re-counting the votes of any communities that had gone for the other guys. They passed laws to keep the downtrodden downtrodden. To stop them from ever voting again. The President lost, but refused to concede. He called for violence in the streets, but then tried to find safe haven somewhere far away from it. He built formidable protective walls around "his" White House, sending rioters to attack those who opposed him. He fed his most rabid supporters lies, fanning the flames of their hatred. He told them to rise up against leaders in state capitals all across the nation, and they did. Feasting on his deceptions, they drove vans loaded with weaponry and homemade bombs into surging protesters wherever he bade them. He promised them he'd stay in the power, fighting on their side, in their White House forever; that he would never back down, and neither should they. But all the while, he was looking for some luxurious, heavily guarded, retirement community for millionaire white men he could settle into safely while his minions and lesser citizens were killing each other at his command.

As the incoming President gathered a team representing many races, areas of expertise, genders, and cultures, entrenched white males tried to block them from ever taking office. The new team worked out elaborate and detailed distribution systems to help vaccinate millions against this deadly plague, but those entrenched in power blocked the money to pay for it.

America was still broken.

But there did seem to be something rising up in the souls of a few. Forced to stare into the depths of raging, unconscionable evil, they saw how badly things needed to change. This was no time for the weak and indecisive. As one world was tearing itself apart, a better one had to be built, and all of life would need to work together. Young activist Greta Thunberg told the peoples of many nations, "Right here, right now is where we draw the line. The world is waking up." She told them, "We have run out of excuses, and we are running out of time. We have come here to tell you that real change is coming, whether you like it or not."

But under a constant, inescapable deluge of meanness slamming in from all sides, many may have carried things too far. They felt they'd been left with no recourse but hit back. They started picking fights with their own families; making trouble and finding fault where there didn't need to be any. It may have started out as understandable defensiveness, but had taken a turn for the ugly. They got stuck there, and couldn't turn it off.

Given time to think things over, some could see they weren't being fair. That matching anger for anger, both sides seeking vengeance and domination, could only leave us with a world in which everyone hated everybody, and nothing could ever be healed. They resolved to fight even harder against themselves and their own weaker natures. To become something better than they had been.

Randy Cuttering stood on that high, huge, stone pedestal in the center of town. He called out to the crowd that, "Raging on social media helps shine a light on what needs fixing, but raging by itself is not enough. Being angry can tear down the old ways, but do nothing then to build something better.

"If we don't replace some of our rage with compassion, then what we create could be just as hurtful and unfair as what we've torn down.

"First we must care.

"Our anger is worthless if we don't care deeply enough to try making this a better world for *all of us*. It gets lost in that darkness we blame others for. It *becomes* that same darkness. Anger without compassion destroys.

"But we who are here today, want to *build*.

"You can feel it in the air around us. Breathe it in. It is crackling, and alive with new hope. With greater possibilities for all.

"Breathe it in deeply."

Most of them did. He told them, "This is the springtime of a brand new era. A time for renewal.

"A time to make caring real, to bring it alive, and to build something with it.

"Get out there and *do* something."

He told them, "Get out there and do something that makes a huge difference. Stay home and do something that makes a small difference. Do something somewhere that helps even one single person in even some very little way.

"But do something.

"Help somebody.

"Care.

"Act.

"Now!"

Mankind continued to separate itself into camps. Many felt charged with helping to build a brighter new world. Others threw themselves, often violently, into attacking anyone threatening to let a little light into their old one.

And now stood the women who would no longer be tamped down, silenced, or sent to their rooms. There might have been terrible darkness running rampant through their families, their nations, and their lives, but these voices; these forces; still shone forth and would not be contained.

They'd been told they weren't good enough. That women were too emotional. That they could never stand up to the pressure. And yet, here they were. Being voted into leadership everywhere, set on turning things around. They wrote and passed laws offering fair pay and safety protections for workers, and health care for all. They worked with scientists and industry leaders in removing poisons from air, food, and water. They prepared for outbreaks of pandemics, cataclysms of Nature, failures of food crops, and the devastating but unexpected. They'd seen horrific demonstrations of how bad things could get at their worst. They knew we'd have to change quickly, and for the best interests of everyone.

In New Zealand, Taiwan, Germany, Iceland, Finland, and elsewhere, women leaders had been among the first to respond to the virus, had taken all the right measures, explaining each step honestly to their citizens. They had worked hard and earned greater respect for keeping their peoples safer from the disease than had weak and deceptive males in other countries. They set up interactive televised question and answer times with children, telling them it was okay to be scared, and responding to whatever they asked.

The children, and the women, and the hopeful urged us forward.

In some ways it seemed that the soul of the planet itself had been awakened.

And that there were a special few who could tap into it more effectively than others.

Sylvie didn't have to look very hard with her "special eyes" to see how the light in the gardens and the forest had been changing. Her auntie's aura colors had always been a rich kind of blue mostly. They were dimming around her now, but shining more brightly through the land she'd always loved. Like her energy was leaking out into the gardens somehow. Like the plants were holding on to it for her, since she was losing the strength to hold all of that wonderful blue sweetness by herself. Even if her auntie did someday leave her body forever, she'd still be here, Sylvie could see; because her living light spirit would be.

Her livingness would be everywhere.

Softly green leaves of early spring gently petted passing breezes. Madison listened in on the silent hum of distant holy ones in meditation. Felt the stir of them. He sat, and he smiled, but said nothing. His mom and dad smiled along, feeling something deep in their hearts newly opening.

Maddie could feel the world awakening. Being ground down to what each and all truly were. The world was coming more into balance. Everything was working just as it should.

Dry old roots were juicing up again beneath the soil. Reaching toward the light as they had in seasons past. Bulbs long lost in dark fields were only now finally sprouting. Seeds of fresh hope being planted. But this early, only the most rare of buds were fully flowering. Bursting courageously, magnificently into bloom.

Chapter Sixteen

It had been a very long night. Darkness had lain heavy and thick over everything for more years than anyone could count. It had all seemed so relentless. So futile. But glowing embers of something more kind could be seen if you looked for them now. Those who turned toward the heavens might have found a few gathering stars.

Others had grown so used to cowering, they couldn't bring themselves to peek out. They could no longer remember the times before the storms, or dare let themselves think that maybe the times ahead could be different. They could allow for nothing beyond their own dread. How many times could we be told to just give it another chance? How many fresh starts could anyone's heart really hold?

A new light might have been rising, but there was no great blaring of trumpets and stampeding of angels. Sunrise often only suggests its arrival in mere nuances. Maybe through a subtle buoyancy of spirit that not everyone feels. First light touches hearts very softly. Some drink it in with welcoming. Others tremble in anxiety over what they might be dragged into next.

There are those who reach forward, and those who pull back. And always a great many who cannot let themselves see that anything could ever really change.

Some traded one form of addiction for another. They had hated slowing down under quarantine, but now hated the thought of speeding up again. They had churned with anxiety from forced isolation. Now they dreaded having to go out in public.

Extremists dove even more deeply into crazy. Carrying weapons of war everywhere. Shooting cops, firemen, children, priests, even old folks feeding ducks in the park. Driving taxis, serving food, or delivering pizzas could get you killed. Conspiracy nuts kept voting each other into national and state leadership, but much of the world had had enough.

Foundations were being laid for a better world, and slowly a greater kindness was taking hold. Even as many fought it back.

After that great attack on human spirit, people crawled out of their private spaces very slowly. They took their time shaking off the dust of what they all had been buried in. Slowly they allowed themselves to look around with great caution, and very little trust of any kind.

For some, the air seemed fresher, though still troubled by what they carried within them. Skies looked brighter, and though many had been weeded out, humanity as a whole had survived. For now. They sensed an occasional passing wisp of possibility, but after all they'd just been through, would need to work really hard to trust in it.

Nothing seemed quite right anymore. Animals wandered the streets. Humans passing each other now made eye contact, and yet were still afraid to hug friends they had missed for so long, and so terribly. Even the simplest, most dependable things seemed a bit off. Very different kingdoms of Nature mingled as if in some kind of partnership. Something had shifted. Walls were crumbling. Birds sung more sweetly. Or maybe folks hadn't been really listening before. Rivers ran faster and laughed more heartily. Skies reached higher, spread wider, touching richer shades of blue.

Blinking in the light of new challenges, people felt their ways around this new world. Their hearts touched others, but their hands held back from greeting them. They no longer took anything for granted.

There would be new plagues coming, and these they would need to meet together. Many had learned this one crucial lesson anyway. Even as others still refused to. Those who now felt themselves citizens of a world shared with everyone, had to steady themselves under the weight of that responsibility. They'd been through a lot together and seen how selfishness could be fatal.

Indigos set about helping to heal those stubborn welts of separation between one community and another. Between those scattered chunks of gathering unity. Brilliant and inspirational children were popping up everywhere, reminding us of what beauty and goodness could look like in this fresh new springtime of rebirth. Inviting each and all to find and live their own purity. Women and children stood strong as the very brightest stepped out onto the shores of new land, inviting the world to join them in grand Renaissance.

Even time itself appeared to have twisted somehow. It was as if they, or we, had slipped through that spooky, crooked door into *The Twilight Zone*. Been transported into some other dimension. On archaeological digs way out in long-untrodden jungles, and under sands shoved around harshly through millennia, ancient temples and libraries arose. Carved figures of beings half man and half eagle reappeared, reaching out to us through very different times and cultures, and on widely scattered stretches of the planet. Bearded men dressed exactly alike stood tall among bowing ancients who had thought these men gods.

Ancient stories and messages broke to surface that could only be fully understood if considered together. And only now, in this century, when the whole world could share them. It also seemed we might need help from special children to interpret them.

There was, for example, the boy who could read and speak ancient tongues. By the age of five he was helping linguists and archaeologists decipher steles and painted walls in tombs and temples that were only just then being found. Many of them, he claimed, spoke of coming storms and new light. One reporter had called him the "tiny Rosetta Stone who chewed gum," and from then on the kid insisted on being called Gumstone.

In a tiny village in Uruguay, to a very poor and uneducated family, Micaela was practically born speaking numbers. Hearing music, she pictured it in mathematical equations. Bring her a flower, and her mind diagrammed the number of its petals, proportions, and how they were arranged. She saw how Nature formed everything into patterns, and how those had been applied through early sacred architecture. The ancients had once understood what we had since forgotten. It was all a matter of connections, cycles, and rhythms, she said.

Abeeku, from Ghana, spoke in rhythms more than words, but somehow made herself understood in several dialects.

A child in Japan drew astrological charts for Babylonian scientists, Egyptian Pharaohs, Mayan and Aztec priests, and a few early Greek philosophers. Not many could be confirmed, but he'd gotten at least a few of them right. He seemed familiar with the teachings of shamans native to cities just now being dug up. Quoting ancient prophecies, he said recent troubles had all been foreseen.

On a cliff face stretching more than half a mile through Central America, locals stumbled across what looked very much like those primitive cave paintings from back when humans could first be recognized as human. On many parts of the planet, archaeologists had been crawling through miles of hidden and often subterranean tunnels to study the ancient art and try to understand early man's struggling beginnings. But these here had been splayed out in open air like a gigantic mural for everyone to see. Many of the established elements of the earliest cave art could be seen on this rock surface as well. Similar hand prints, and stunning representations of long extinct creatures. From back in those times when tools had been made from antlers, bits of bone, and chipped flint. These strange cliff paintings showed small people or children riding and taming giant beasts. Animals and humans walking side-by-side, and working together. Those same bearded men we now seemed to be finding everywhere, walked among regular humans stretched across these cliff walls. Micaela read patterns in how they lined up, stood, crouched, and pointed as though they had been painted this way to be read as notes in sheet music. She sang along as she stepped through the beginnings of history.

Another youngster, studying at a nearby university, mathematically demonstrated how these could also be seen as astronomical positions specific to the 21st century.

Little Gumstone was at that time translating lines of cuneiform from the other side of the globe, which he said spoke of a time of trial for mankind that all of life on this planet must pass through.

Parents and specialists were learning to not be so quick at hanging labels on children who didn't interpret or communicate in expected or traditional ways. There might be things we should be learning from some of these special ones with unusual insights. Children often saw what we no longer could. Felt deeply what we had grown numb to. Could a few of them be connecting with some shared mind that reached beyond time and passing cultures?

Had such strange and exotic children been born into every previous age of mankind's history? Or had today's particularly destructive times drawn special beings to take form among us only now, when we needed them most? Incarnating largely to uplift and guide those who were lost.

No one could say with any certainty of course.

And yet, there they were.

They often seemed to bring skills and gifts from other eras in with them. But then again, during their long periods of isolation, a lot of even normal, everyday folks had found themselves drawn to ancient crafts. They'd taken up knitting, or basket weaving, or pottery. Some had grown curious about bookbinding, calligraphy, or blacksmithing. Once restrictions had been lifted, hundreds signed up for stone carving schools, apprenticing to restoration teams at ancient cathedrals and temples. Others were drawn to the careful, focused work of restoring old paintings. Many felt inspired to apply to medical colleges, while others learned to grow healing herbs in their own gardens.

The planet had suffered a long and grave sickness, but was healing. Growing stronger. Finding its voice, though much of humanity still was not listening.

The Old Boy's Club was losing its grip. Harsh and relentless, its leaders were still hanging on, but much of what they'd been building for so long was now cracking around them, and crumbling away from beneath. The most offensive and loudest were being driven toward what they dreaded most; desperate irrelevance. Snarling, spitting, clawing at anyone they could still reach; calling names and cussing as the world turned against them. Forced to take refuge in imagined glories that no longer made sense; they were determined to fight against that rising sun until they fell. Unyielding and rebellious, they waved their guns around for all to see, as they sank into the dust of attitudes and ignorance they could no longer make work for them. As their own supporters started turning away

For, scattered even among this Old Guard, a few minds and hearts were awakening.

It was dinnertime at the Squirrelmann home. From his wheelchair at the other side of the table, Frank watched his son plow through his meal with primitive, ravenous, gustatory lust. He wished he himself had relished every bite he'd ever taken, every rose he'd simply driven right past in their gardens. He'd squandered so much of his attention on battle and conquest.

Watching his capabilities drain away one-by-one, inevitably crippling and killing him, he imagined losing those few that remained. Would he soon be unable to speak? Was his tongue growing thicker, less responsive already? It would have to go eventually. Everything would. Was it withering even now? When he could no longer speak, would his wife and son understand what he *wanted* to say? Had he ever really let them know him that well? Was it too late? If he tried to open up to them, would they listen? Would they care?

Reenie noticed her husband just leaning in and staring, but didn't know how to respond. She'd always relied on established rituals; they had addressed each other with respectable manners on comfortable issues, but now everything had changed. None of that worked anymore. And none of that had prepared her for this. It was more than she could deal with sometimes.

She turned her attention back to her son. As she had so often before, she told him, "No need to Hoover your food, young man. We have more in the kitchen." She knew he wouldn't listen. This was just one of their comfortable traditions. One anchor still holding in this storm. They had so few left.

At each stage of their meal, as old plates were cleared and new dishes brought out, Frank thanked the help, giving each his full attention. Since what had amounted to his medical death sentence, he'd often told his family that he'd learned to appreciate life more. Misquoting someone whose name he couldn't recall, he'd told them, "Each sunrise is even sunnier, the wine even winier, and this meat even meatier." He knew he wouldn't be enjoying them much longer. In strange, unexpected ways he was finding joy in letting go of his old ways. He'd learned to truly appreciate the household staff, though he'd never paid them much attention before. Now he thanked them, and meant it from the depths of his heart.

Benjie might have seemed completely absorbed in his meal, lost in the rich, juicy roast with all of its trimmings, but mainly he felt overcome by the pain of having to watch his dad suffering. He looked up to tell his father he loved him.

His mum cleared her throat to redirect his attention. She pointed at a corner of her own mouth. "You missed a spot," she told him. Being a proper British lady, she lowered her voice out of courtesy, choosing to believe that others couldn't hear her just the same. They did that little dance for a while where he kept wiping the wrong spot, on the wrong side, until he'd finally cleaned off that wee glob of gravy.

"Ahhh," his mum said then.

Benjie lowered his head over his plate so she couldn't keep analyzing his mouth.

She heard a burst of scraping and grunting from across the table. Frank was throwing everything he had into cutting meat on his plate that had already been tenderized by their kitchen staff.

"Oh, Frank," she chided him. "Why don't you just let Henry cut that for you?"

Henry was a live-in carer, there to help Frank however he could. He was sitting just a little bit off to the side, watching and ready.

Frank told them, "No!" much too forcefully. "Not while I still have arms. Anything I *can* do for myself I damn well *will* do for myself."

"Frank!" she chastised him. Such an egregious lack of manners at the dinner table was just not on.

He lashed back, "I am not going to just lie down and let this damned thing roll over me. Not while I can give it a good fight. While I can still wipe my own ass I want to love doing it, and when the time comes that Henry has to help me, then you had just better damn well pull the plug, because I don't want to be around anymore."

"Frank!" she scolded again. "Please don't be so crude at the dinner table!" He should know better. One does not bring vulgarities to a meal.

But then again, maybe she really should try a little harder to see things his way, she thought. His whole life had turned against him. Maybe she should forgive him a bit of vile language now and again.

But then, he should try to understand how hard this was on the rest of them.

"That is all well and good from your side of things," she'd told him once when she had really had quite enough. "You will soon enough have gone off on your merry afterlife way. Leaving us to deal with the consequences all by ourselves. Without any help from you; thank you very much. Completely abandoning us. Do you ever think about that?"

He'd told her he thought about that all the time. Sometimes it was pretty much all he could think about. It hurt him terribly.

The sting of that still lingered. She felt guilty and ugly inside. But it was terrifying watching the man she'd always loved, her partner in all matters, being eaten away like this.

She'd had to change the ways she looked at everything, and change had never come easily for her. She was trying, but it was so hard.

She should at least try to understand why he couldn't always be courteous, or even civil.

"At the dinner table?" she suggested again, but much more gently this time.

"I am not going to just quit," he told her, and the subject was closed.

He started in again, hacking and grinding away at his meat, but even more loudly, almost viciously this time.

Reenie tried to soften, but was caught between warring and contrary passions.

"Honey…" she began.

Frank could see how even her anger toward him sometimes could be taken as an odd way of saying she cared. He smiled as he told them, "I may not be able to pull my own pants up without help any more, but I can damn well still take an ax to my meatloaf!

"It might just take me a few days to get it into my mouth is all."

He smiled warmly all over her.

"Frank!" she chided, but lovingly this time. He knew how much his newly dark humor had been bothering her. All his death jokes in particular. The language he'd been using, the ugly things he'd been so eager to bring up and make sport of that most proper people would take pains not to mention.

But she was beginning to see that this was pretty much all he had left, and together they were finding deeper ways to communicate.

The new administration was doing all it could to find parents, reunite families, and get border children out of those cages. Frank was working his connections to help set up halfway homes for them, stocked with everything they might need: clothes, good food, comfortable furniture, and well-equipped play areas.

Benjie said they'd also need therapists. He told his dad those poor kids must think the whole world sucks after what they'd been through. Packed away in cages with so many others, sleeping on cement, nothing they could say was really theirs. Pooping in buckets probably right in front of everybody, he imagined. They had to be thinking this must all be their own fault somehow, because that's how kids do. You probably hate yourself for your whole life, thinking that way, he told his dad.

Frank said the parents must think *they'd* failed too.

Dad and son decided clothing and feeding them would be only the beginning. They'd be needing help for maybe years, even decades yet. Whether we'd put them there ourselves, or just not tried hard enough to get them out; either way, we'd helped to destroy them, his dad said. We couldn't just dump them on the streets now and call ourselves done with it. We'd only be abandoning them again. Opening up new wounds on top of old ones. We'd keep right on tearing them apart.

Frank and Benjie worked together, talked things through, then called in experts to work out the details. They set up programs, created funds to finance homes and systems indefinitely, but then turned it all over to boards of directors that Frank took special pains to populate with only kindhearted trustees.

Sylvie gazed around The Gardens with her "secret spooky eyes." In the hours just before sunrise she could see more of the hidden lights and true nature of things. It was springtime. New life was rising up everywhere. She wished she could share some of this with people who couldn't see it for themselves. But some folks didn't want to hear about things they didn't already believe in. Their minds were made up, and they didn't really listen.

The world was changing in all kinds of ways though, and more people would be waking up. That'd be good enough. She didn't have to be the purveyor of all good news. She probably wasn't cut out to be a teacher, she didn't think.

But then immediately, as if someone was chatting with her, she heard her brain tell her she wasn't giving herself enough credit. Whoever was in there this time probably didn't want her being down on herself, which hardly ever happened, but she didn't want to be rude and just ignore someone who could throw ideas around the world, so she told them they could be right about that. And she thought it a little louder than she did most of her thinking, because it really couldn't be very easy listening inside somebody from so far away. Like if they were maybe in another country or something.

She started feeling sad then, because this wasn't as good as talking with her Auntie Ailana, which she couldn't do anymore.

Sylvie had inherited all of this land when Auntie's body had stopped, but she would really rather have Auntie herself.

Sylvie's mom told her she'd do the paperwork and take care of some of the more confusing matters for a while. No reason such a young child should have to start worrying about some of that just yet, her mom said. She also kept telling her it was important she not feel sad because her dear beloved Auntie wasn't there to talk to and play with anymore. She said this had to happen to all of us eventually. As if that was supposed to be comforting somehow.

But looking around through her special eyes this morning, she could see that Ailana had never really gone away. Everywhere around her was that lovely, ethereal shade of blue that had always flowed through her sweet auntie when she'd been sitting quietly, helping someone. The little girl stood a long time, watching it ease in and out of the plant life, sometimes floating over what had been her aunt's favorite resting spots, or where she used to squeeze tomatoes.

Frank held on for three more years than his doctors had predicted, getting to know his family, and setting up charitable trusts. Reenie died a little more than three years after Frank. Benjie did what he could to help out with the charities over the next few years, but business was just not in his soul. He turned it all over to professionals who could do some real good not just for the formerly caged, but for the homeless, and orphans, and others in need. Experts who could help without botching details.

Then he sold their family estate among the wealthy and pampered, moving up into the peace of the mountains. He bought a large rustic cabin and acres of land deep in the woods where he was alone but for animals that seemed to gather in around him from everywhere. He posted *No Hunting, Trapping, or Fishing* signs around, but there was no one to read them.

Television and radio could be pretty iffy this far out, but the internet seemed to perk up when some stranger needed help from Bj.

Natives of many cultures, eras, and nations had long been finding their shamans by sending young tribesmen off on vision quests, where they'd had to suffer greatly. Tribal elders knew how tough would lie the path ahead for apprentices who completed the training. Young folks couldn't simply declare themselves ready. They had to be tested to prove it, and those trials had to be long and torturous until something in them broke, and something better climbed free.

Then their unseen guides often sent them some little sign, like an animal behaving strangely. If the student saw this for what it was, he'd know his time was now upon him. He'd start seeing differently and more deeply. Taking on new responsibilities.

Benjie figured he'd been tested all through childhood, but found wanting.

So he had just let it go. In his early years he'd been all ego and neediness. Had thought he should be able to push Masters around. It had been childish, it had been stupid, but at least judging by the joy and peacefulness in his spirit these days, they seemed to have forgiven him.

Benjie found a young deer, little more than a baby, by his cabin one morning. She no longer had her spots, but was still tiny, and her ribs showed. At that age she would normally be tagging along behind Mom and maybe three or four others, but this one was alone. She wandered in again the next day, and the one after that. He started putting out corn for her, and some of his own vegetables and fruits. He tried cashews, but she didn't much like them.

Watching her eat, he saw that her face thinned to a point more than it seemed to with others, making her big deer brown eyes seem even more huge and compelling. Her chin was recessed maybe a little more than an inch, giving her a bit of an overbite. She didn't look exactly like normal deers, but she wasn't all twisted up, dragging limbs, deformed. She was actually cuter than most. But he did wonder if maybe just this mild abnormality had been why she'd been rejected from her family and companions.

He fed her, but knew to be sparing. She'd need to find her own food when he wasn't around, and even fight for it sometimes against stronger deer.

Benjie was standing around in an empty area one morning, gazing through the woods, smelling forest smells, sipping his java like his dad had.

Something went for his leg, and he leaped, splashing coffee.

It had only been that poor little deer, nudging him to say hello, but he'd screamed, and she'd torn off into the woods terrified, flashing her white tail to warn the world. They were all in great danger. She just didn't know from what.

Benjie kept calling out to her that he was sorry, trying to explain, but it took her a while before she came out of hiding.

Benjie sat down on a log then, and they had a nice little chat. It was actually him who was doing all the talking, but she really did look like she was listening. She even nodded at appropriate moments. When he came across something he needed to ponder for a while, she let him. She waited, looking up at him with those huge doe brown eyes.

His own eyes teared up, and his voice choked as he talked with her about his parents. He told her, "I miss them so bad."

The little creature moved in closer, sensing Benjie's pain. She nudged at his trouser leg. He wanted to pet her, but held back. He told her, "I try to sleep, but I can't. It hurts too bad they're not there. Do you ever feel that way about your folks? Do you miss your mum and dad?"

The young animal didn't say yes or no, but seemed to be listening harder than she had been.

It got so Benjie expected to see her every day, and would even worry a little when he didn't. Whichever door he stepped out of, she'd be there within minutes. He'd sit down on a log to scribble some notes, and she'd look to see what he was writing. Sometimes he tried to tell her, but figured she only liked the sound of his voice.

Benjie would get his tree lopper out to trim some of those branches threatening his roof shingles, and have to back her out of the way so they wouldn't hit her. She'd watch him drag fallen timber in from the woods, then stand close as he cut it into fireplace logs, but really wasn't much help with the actual sawing.

He stepped outside one foggy pre-dawn to sit on one of the decks with his notebook and coffee. The little lady had apparently been resting, nestled down into soft greenery. She stretched a little as she ambled in to greet him. He noticed several drops of dew sparkling in a line along her nose. Benjie had been wondering what to name her. From then on he called her Dew Nose.

He fed her often, but not always. He never tried to pet her, or force himself into what he imagined to be her private space. He let Nature be Nature, and was happy to just stand or sit around with her quietly. In this he found a wonderful deep level of contentment. Sometimes she came by, ate her food, nodded to him, and just wandered off again, and that was fine, too.

Sometimes birds joined in around him as well. At first he figured they only showed up to have him feed them, but then they often ignored what he put out. Sometimes they were hungry, and sometimes they were just having fun. Animals and human, just getting along.

The soft quiet of the land called, and he joined in. Breezes murmured, birds maybe chittered a little, and life was sweet. Benjie and the world around him opened their heart and soul to each other.

He felt something new inside him stirring just a bit. Like that moment you feel those first hints of sunrise beginning to glow from the other side of your curtains. Your heart smiles as it greets the new day, but you are not quite ready to sit up and step into it just yet.

> *"This is a simple religion. There is no need for temples; no need for complicated philosophy. Our own brain, our own heart is our temple; the philosophy is kindness."*
> —H H THE FOURTEENTH DALAI LAMA OF TIBET

CHAPTER SEVENTEEN

Benjie felt more drawn to Nature than to mankind and its often hurtful peculiarities. Had that been why Teachers had abandoned him early on, he wondered? Or had they never considered taking him under their wings in the first place? If he had been tested, found wanting, and dropped, he'd deserved it. Sitting out on his deck, thinking about what he took to be his unworthiness one day, he noticed a large white feather lying nearby, and went to get it. Turning it over and over, examining it from all sides, he wondered where one this big could have come from. He didn't know of any birds in the area that could have dropped one maybe eleven inches long. This was pretty far in from the sea for an albatross.

He thought about how Native Americans had considered feathers like this sacred. They didn't just grab them up, and pop them into their hats to show off. Grand white plumes like this one were cherished as special gifts from Great Spirit.

He pictured a young Native his own age finding such a treasure back in the old times, and feeling blessed.

But then he wondered if the elders would have let him keep it. They might have made him hand it over to someone more worthy. Benjie was slipping back into that familiar old funk again. He'd worked hard, but he had failed.

A chipmunk tapped his foot. Benjamin had named this one Chinky because he had chinks missing from his tail. Something had bitten him, or he'd caught it in something, and the fur hadn't grown back.

Benjie reached into his bag of peanuts, then bent way far over to hold one down to him. The little guy took a while perfectly positioning it in his cheeks to make room for another. Benjie had given him three before Chinky decided he had all he could handle for now, and scampered off with them. By that time, other chipmunks were standing in line waiting their turns. Benjie loved the sound of their tiny feet skittering up the steps, or scurrying away to bury their treasures. As he felt his joy radiating, little birds seemed to follow it in. The deck was soon swarming with life.

Titmice saw he had treats, but didn't come right after them. They gathered on nearby limbs first, happily singing their thrill to the world, until they'd called all the other birds in. Not everything had to be about greed, competition, and everyone bullying each other, Benjie thought. Why couldn't humans be more like this? Titmice grabbed sunflower seeds, and peanuts bigger than their heads. Chickadees went for smaller ones. Nuthatches wedged a few into vertical cracks in the tree bark for later. Juncos liked to hop about through the pile, kicking seeds around, and making a mess. But they all got along. They shared. Why couldn't we all?

He went back to thinking about vision quests again, how they'd inflicted such terror, self-doubt, isolation, and pain on special individuals, but in the process had opened them to deeper understanding. He wondered if all this disease, loss, and anxiety in the world today could serve as a sort of a vision quest for large numbers of people. Could we then maybe learn to get along a little better?

He sat there a long time that day, with such peacefulness, healing, and joy in his heart, that he began to believe it might reach a few others out there, and maybe help in some way.

It felt like things were finally just as they should be.

Benjamin had to drive almost an hour to stock up on supplies for himself and his forest companions. Groceries didn't deliver that far out. He kept a cooler in his 4WD, made his lists, and arranged his expeditions in detail, just as his mum had. He only left the cabin maybe once or twice a month, but made it count, handling all his chores in one trip.

Along the ride, he passed isolated locals in scattered cabins or small villages. Drawing water from their wells, neatening their land on huge rider mowers, or tractors. In such off-the-grid communities, folks tended to wave even at strangers as one drove past another, and Benjie delighted in that.

On one of his trips into town he found a handwritten note tacked to the bulletin board in one of the shops. Carefully lettered in pretty pastels, it read, "We sit alone in the woods feeding animals, afraid we're not helping the world enough. But if our hearts are really in it, we are radiating peace out into a stressed and troubled world. That just has to be helping a really awful lot of people and animals. Don't you think the world might be needing some of your peace and gentleness right about now?"

No one had signed it. Unless that little sketch in colored pencils of a fairy chatting with a salamander was some kind of a clue. Apparently there were others around there feeling like he sometimes did.

He started keeping his eye out for more of these snippets of insight, but they didn't seem to follow any regular schedule. One was, "They say when you're ready the teacher will appear. You have to be ready to let yourself see that you ARE this great teacher you've been waiting for. It has always been you. YOU are what you've been waiting for!"

Someone he'd never met was telling him just what he needed to turn himself around. "Connections," as Maddie used to say, like that one single word was a complete statement and explanation for everything just by itself. Reading messages from someone unknown, Benjie came away feeling much better about a lot of things. Seeing his part in the world differently. He started speaking to people in stores, and they relaxed into it as if they'd been chatting like this forever. He started making extra trips into town and heading right for this one shop in particular. They might not have anything he wanted at the time, but he'd buy something anyway.

Some thoughts struck home personally, like this writer knew him and what he'd been through. Even what he thought about himself on his most painful and private levels. He read some of them over and over again. Pulled out his journal and copied them into it. One note asked him, "Have you really been helping anybody by cutting yourself down? Saying you're not good enough? You might think that's humble, but maybe it's selfish. You're not radiating when you could be when people really need it. Have you been feeding even more negativity into this dark and troubling atmosphere? There is already enough of that. Knock it off!"

That one slammed him right in the gut. But the one that almost knocked him over was when they started with, "As the internet sage Bj once wrote…" And, SPLAMM! They'd slashed a whole bucket of ice water on him!

He stood there, not believing, holding his breath; this isn't possible; reading it again.

Nobody knew about him and his secretive companion. Nobody! And who could know they'd moved here of all places? Out in the middle of nowhere? It's not possible! Were they in this store now? Standing there, watching him read this?

He asked clerks if they knew who'd been posting these, but the only nibble he got was when one told him, "I don't know, man; anybody can put stuff up there if they want to. Could be anyone. Maybe it's that girl lives in those gardens a ways out. Where that woman just died."

After a while he started thinking maybe even him not knowing was just as it should be. It fit right in with all the other things he hadn't known, or gotten wrong, but that seemed to have been all tying together from the beginning.

And now here he was, living among strangers who had started off in very different worlds, and yet they all fit together so perfectly. They'd faced death, pain, and unnerving challenges separately, but <u>together</u>. They could see much more intimately inside each other now, without knowing anyone's history. Even when all that showed above the masks were the eyes of a stranger, those eyes spoke a deeper truth they held in common.

Folks were being gentle, and respectful of each other. Saying, "Excuse me" in stores. Stepping aside to let someone with fewer packages into line ahead of them.

The gas station guy always ran out to clean Benjie's windows along the drive home, and he did a really good job of it, smiling all the while.

And when Benjie got home, when he pulled up and parked in front of his cabin, his tiny buddy Dew Nose was there to welcome him.

But he still had to wonder. Who was this new mystery being who had punched her way into his heart? The girl who loved fairies and salamanders?

Sylvie had driven out to pick up the mail and was now sorting through it on the table of what had been her aunt's dining room. Students still wanted to come by, even without scheduled classes. Others just wanted to wander the gardens. Some drove all the way from wherever to lay their troubles down before Ailana; even though they knew she had passed. A lot of them said they still sensed her here anyway.

Sylvie did her best to help them however she could, but knew she'd never fill her auntie's shoes even a little bit.

The two of them had always been very different forces of Nature. Ailana had been like a gentle lakeside breeze when you were lost in your thoughts. A breeze you hardly noticed as it softly helped you sort through to what was important, and ease free of your troubles.

Sylvie you noticed. She was more like a whirling little dust devil that had suddenly spun in out of nowhere, and right across your picnic table, scattering your paper plates everywhere.

But the two were alike in many ways as well. There was a sweetness and purity to each of them, they both loved to laugh, and at least in Sylvie's case, there was more than a touch of delightful goofiness. They each had great clarity and compassion. And with clarity and compassion come true power.

Ailana allowed people all the time they wanted to tell their stories, reveal themselves gradually; to either come to the point, or keep sidestepping around it. To either see themselves deeply and truly, or refuse to even take a good look. Sylvie respected, even admired her beloved aunt's ways, but had no time or patience for any of that. She only knew how to be direct, and call things as they were. Sometimes Nature offered just a soft little nudge. Other times you really had to be thwacked.

The earth had been through a great shock. People had been pretty much hit with everything at once and come away changed. Nowadays, for example, it wasn't as easy as it had been to find room in a workshop at a spiritual camp like Green Man's Glen. Sylvie could no longer just assume there'd be plenty of slots open and she could just show up at the last moment when she was suddenly in the mood, and they'd just fit her right in. Classes might be filled up or even over-booked sometimes these days. A lot more people were being drawn to mystical centers since the Global Enlightening had begun.

But at least Ailana's Gardens still seemed hidden and protected from all that hubbub. She could feel quiet and basically alone here anyway. And even when somebody did show up, they didn't all need her to help them find what they'd come looking for. The gardens offered their own form of comfort, and sometimes it worked best if she just stayed out of the way. Sometimes you can help out more by not doing much of anything. When folks came to chat with Ailana's lingering spirit for a while, maybe even seek her advice, they generally left feeling they had gotten what they'd come for, and this high-spirited young lady hadn't had to get involved. In Sylvie's heart, The Gardens of Ailana would forever be Ailana's.

But she too had fused her soul with this land, and its many life forms, from very early on. And so she too had become a part of what this special center now was.

As she sorted through the mail that day, she spent time looking over a schedule of classes from Green Man's Glen (printed on recycled paper of course). She was really thinking about signing up for the weekend on *Native Healers and Teachings*. She'd heard rumors Madison Beaufort might be guiding a post-conference meditation for workshop leaders that week after everyone else had left. Maybe something about the connecting of lives and events. She'd heard some amazing things about this guy. He was said to be a rare treasure as presenters went. Not just somebody forcing himself into every conference he could, like all those authors pushing their latest books that seemed pretty much like everyone else's. Beaufort rarely even showed up at these things. Rumors had it that strange stuff happened around him when he did. Sylvie wanted to be there to watch.

Shirley Spears had asked her a while back to maybe do a little talk about fairies around one of their campfires one of these days. Shirley knew she had to be nonspecific with Sylvie. Maybe, Sylvie thought now, she should call and see if she could do one at this shamans workshop. She wouldn't plan anything detailed; just show up, and play with whoever came by. Invite a few fairies in from the woods that night to play along and maybe dance around the fire. That'd be fun. She'd just say whatever flitted through her head.

She stopped to make a mental note in her brain to call Shirley when she was done with the mail. Tell her she would definitely be coming to this workshop on Native stuff, and ask if she had a night open for some fun-with-fairies storytelling.

That'd be a good thing to call it, she thought, but then she didn't write either idea down, or stick either one of them very hard into her memory. She was too busy poking another letter out of the pile. This one interested her because it had been addressed by hand, and covered with stickers of chipmunks and small birds. She didn't recognize the handwriting, but already knew she'd get along with whoever this was. She found an actual letter inside, penned in ink. People didn't do that much these days. She loved that there were apparently still a few out there who took the care to write real letters to each other instead of just dumping out emails.

This was from someone who said he'd heard about The Gardens of Ailana, but didn't know much about the place, and had never actually been here. He wanted to know if he could stop by at Sylvie's convenience if that would be okay. Seemed an awfully gentle and unobtrusive sort of fellow. His penmanship was a bit challenging to read, but she could tell he'd tried his hardest to scrawl each word out as neatly as he could anyway.

He said he didn't know her, and she didn't know him, but she kinda felt there might be more to it than that. She had instantly found this person intriguing. She'd had an inkling this was the start of something special. And anyway, when somebody new popped up wanting to spend some special quality time here, she never just took them for granted. They might be someone gifted, being readied to make a difference in the world. People might *think* they're only coming because they need a breather, a little peace and quiet; they just want to get away from it all for a while; but then find out they're only digging themselves in deeper.

She began to wonder, since he said he lived out in Nature, could he too see strange lights and invisible beings? She should invite him along for her little fireside fairy chat. Maybe they could take turns pointing out what they were seeing to other campers around the circle who couldn't. Or if he couldn't see fairies and fire imps himself yet, maybe she could start teaching him how to.

She should maybe write him back and suggest that, she thought.

But then she didn't right away, and she forgot to.

Instead, her mind wandered off to someone who had really, really, *really* known the fairies and living lights, and even written some of Sylvie's favorite books about them. She had lived to a very old age, but even as a young child had been fairly well known, considering how such miraculously gifted beings tended to stay hidden. She had seen things and known things adults couldn't believe, and yet she had proven them. Some kids were born to change the world, and then grow up and not let it change back. Most people had just called her Dora. It must be cool to be known by only one name, Sylvie thought, and whenever anybody hears it, they know it's you. Dora had spent a lot of time in these very hills, even set up a camp for the special ones, not all that far from 3-G, as distances went around here. They said she had known the Masters personally. She'd touched and helped thousands of lives, and then died before Sylvie had even been born, but Sylvie had always been drawn to her. Especially when her "other ears" picked up the sound of someone laughing with the fairies, and with the spirit of her Auntie Ailana.

Had she known Mr. Mica? He would probably be evasive if she asked him. Probably change the subject, but he might get that certain twinkle in his eyes suggesting he knew more than he was saying.

She'd tried to challenge him on that once, how he kept changing the subject when she was asking her most important questions. She'd started right off by telling him, "I have a bone to pick with you," but then he'd said, "Oh, I do wish you wouldn't; I'm a vegetarian," and they'd laughed, she'd gotten distracted, and they'd started talking about something else entirely.

She was also curious about this Madison Beaufort. He was clearly not just another of those full-of-themselves, research-laden, quoting-old-books, egos out on lecture tours. Flaunting themselves for all their great wisdom, but really not doing much more than repeating what someone else had already said. No, this Madison Beaufort was somehow different. Just the mere mention of his name shot right past Sylvie's verbal mind, hitting her directly in her deeper heart.

Special beings seemed to be stepping out into the world more lately than they had been for maybe centuries. Or at least you heard about them more. Maybe it was just that since the quarantine, more people had been waking up and seeing them there.

Of course, places like The Gardens of Ailana, and beings like Mr. Mica, would probably for the rest of all time need to stay veiled. It was important you only be able to find them after you'd developed way beyond most people, and done most of the work by yourself.

She turned her attention back to the letter. He could come a week early and just hang out a few days. Then, when she went to 3-G, he could either tag along, or just chill here by himself while *she* went. That should work.

He might actually prefer that, she thought. He sounded like kind of a loner type.

She made herself another mental note to write him back and ask how he'd like to play this. Tell him he'd be welcome to stop by either way.

But then she got distracted again, thinking, "He might even change so much while he's here, I'll want to find him a new name.

"And besides," she thought, "He might even be grateful. He has got to be tired of being called Benjamin Jay Squirrelmann his whole life, for Pete's sake."

And then she heard that laughter again.

Sylvie stood barefoot in a room at the edge of the forest, opened up, and laughed right along. Her heart was light, connections were being made, and her friend Mama Nature was at peace.

That better world was coming alive.

Most of Benjie's life, he'd wanted nothing more than to be psychic, chat with spirits and masters. To see fairies, or move things with his mind. Offered that opportunity now though, he hoped he'd turn it down. He could finally let himself see that this had always been a weakness with him. Trying to develop psychic gifts now would only feed that and start stirring things up he'd fought so long and so hard to work past. Maybe he'd grown up. Just grown out of it. More likely he'd had to turn away from all that because he knew he could get lost again if he wasn't careful. He felt more at peace these days, and wanted to keep it that way. And if his inner spirit did happen to be radiating some kind of healing, doing some good where he couldn't see it, that was okay too. He didn't need feedback. He only wanted to help.

What a mess he'd been. And it had been his own fault. He could see that now. He'd never felt more alive, felt Spirit more clearly than he had since letting all of that go.

He sat with the forest one very early morning, marveling at how his senses had developed since he'd been living out in Nature. Native Americans must have been able to see and hear the most incredibly subtle shifts in pretty much anything. Even if only for an instant, the subtlest changes spring out at you. The merest flick. Even the merest suggestion of a whisper.

For just a fraction of an instant, and then gone.

That night then, gazing up through the heavens, Benjie could almost hear the sighs of countless others out there. Dreaming up through the stars from wherever they were. He felt their peacefulness cozying up with his own. All of them loving beyond the capacity of their everyday hearts. Sharing a sea of twinkling radiance through the darkness.

Benjie grew drowsy from all the beauty. He faded away, thinking, "Helping each other is not reaching outside of ourselves. We are touching other fingers on that same hand that we sprout from. It is all one. We are all one. Helping each other is merely that inner life flowing."

Benjie got the urge again one afternoon to try sketching a Native American on a horse. This time he was finally able to finish it.

Studying it then, he realized that this was not just any Indian, but a keeper of the ancient wisdom. Benjie was startled by the beauty and perfection of what had just flowed through his hand. It had been worth all the practice and failures. Every line and shade in perfect balance. A powerful Native Spirit sitting with such strength and confidence astride his mount, exuding a sense of timelessness, beauty, and grace. A sense of great depth and clear knowing.

As Benjie studied every nuance of what he had just lent his hand to creating, every detail of this magnificent being; he suddenly saw that he had drawn his own face.

Mr. Mica told Sylvie, "Emotions are fragile. They are easily bruised, twisted, or broken. Passions rush in and out, flick on and off, often seem to make little or no sense. They linger when we would rather be rid of them.

"Spirit holds true all the while, but it may be difficult for some to sort through the racket and chaos to find it."

He suggested she might sometimes "try to be a little more patient and understanding with those who appear to you to be lost. You may see only that aspect of them that is caught up in the messiness of their outer lives, while there might be more going on that you can't see. They may not even credit themselves yet with the strength to step free of their own stubborn disorder. They may think themselves incapable of looking deeper and standing in true strength. In the grips of great stress, many turn to more troubled emotions for the sheer comfort of their long familiarity. They are not ultimately wrong in this. We must all search in our own ways and get lost on occasion. In particularly challenging times, it might seem to some that they have no other choice.

"But we all learn to express Spirit eventually. We will likely not accomplish this in one single lifetime, and some might wander into some very dark corners. They may need to starve for a while in the depths of their self-imposed darkness and futility. But they will get there."

"You're right," she told him. "I get impatient with people sometimes. I think things I don't really mean deep inside. My brain flies around a lot faster than my better sense does."

"That could get messy," Mr. Mica observed.

Then he added, "You will also be learning soon that there are some who might do well to be more patient with *themselves*, and how they handle their own struggles. Even as they see Spirit, they may not always let themselves reach for it, and then their rage against themselves may be crippling."

She had a feeling he was preparing her to meet someone who could be way too hard on himself, and Mr. Mica wanted her to try to be nice to him.

"All we have to do is wake up and change."
—Greta Thunberg

Chapter Eighteen

Some find power and magic in the night. Others find pain, dread, and distance. The world needs all kinds. Those lost in darkness, those beginning to question, and those set on evolving. Those who see, and those locked in denial. It needs those in the trenches, and those climbing out of them. Those who are starting to find the bliss wrapped inside all that sadness, and those who know only to weep. It needs people walking the same fields, but through very different worlds.

Elena Francesca hardly remembered "the old country." Only the long, dragging agony of blisters, and famine, and misery; trudging through one nation after another; being passed from one set of hands to another as first her parents, or some other relative took sick, fell back, had been abandoned, and maybe died. Some of those hands charged with caring for her hadn't been much larger than her own. Some of those carers hadn't been much older than she. And that caring itself had often amounted to little more than keeping her moving, pushing her along, maybe sharing a few crumbs of their bread when they could find any.

She remembered the internal, eternal aching. Until she welcomed those long bouts of numbness. Until she would have invited death had she been old enough to know how to draw it to her.

And then finally, after what had seemed the better (or worst) part of her lifetime, they had arrived. America. She'd been torn from that last set of hands. From any heart that had even pretended to care about her just a little bit. Shoved into a cage already packed to throbbing with hundreds of other hungry, foul-smelling, often diseased children.

Had this been what her long, wearying horror of a life had been about from the beginning? Why they had all trudged so far? To wedge her into a cage? Was the whole world like this everywhere? The strong abusing the weak? All that jeering and scorn. Fat, overstuffed soldiers taunting you because you were hungry and they weren't. Hurting you in ways that didn't even seem human.

Crammed in a cell until time no longer matters, you tear yourself apart. Why were they treating you like this? What had you done to deserve it? You want out. You look for ways to escape. But then, after a very long time, you just stop. This is all there can ever be. You have no say in your own life. You are no more than just some stain on somebody's wall, waiting to be scraped away. Eventually, inevitably, a part of you has to give up. You yield, and let it take you.

What had once consumed you is dead. Leaving no ash from what had once been your heart. Dragging, pointless eternity had left behind only dark, sucking vacuum.

Elena Francesca had survived, though. With a change of government, she had been released. And now it was like the whole planet wanted to hear about those lost years. People everywhere seemed almost rabid for anything she had to say, but that only left her feeling caged in different ways. A lot of them were only using her. Some were feeding their own seething hatred for that failed government. They could fume, despise, and rant until it consumed them, but still need to keep fueling those flames of bitterness. They would always need more. She understood that. She had been there. But still she felt used. Penned in by publicists who'd just showed up and pushed themselves at her when all she'd wanted was some quiet, and a little time to heal. They kept rushing her between studios, standing or seated on stages, before small groups and full auditoriums. Shoving her into everyone's face. She had never had control of her own life.

When she could get her handlers to arrange a little time for her somewhere she actually wanted to be; she was drawn to quieter, softer, more gentle spots. Out in Nature with fresh breezes, clear sunlight, and open spaces. Shadowy trees, or waves lapping shores. No crowds. Maybe just a few, special people who could rest with her for a moment in peacefulness. Maybe sit by a stream. Listen to birds. Breathe deeply and soak in the sunshine.

Wandering the woods at Green Man's Glen one day, drinking in that fresh woodsy air and easing up a little on old troubles, she caught sight of a young lady in the distance with hair like a rolling thunderstorm. Hair matching Elena's brooding darkness.

She'd been watching this lady around camp though, and didn't see how two people could be much more different. This childlike spirit seemed to radiate sunlight from her smile. Elena had watched her bouncing about the camp like a child. Following her own arcs and whims. If ever there had been anyone who had never been in any way caged, it was this one. Whether despite this or because of it, Elena felt strangely and powerfully drawn to this delightfully odd little woman. She needed to know this person. And now here she was, flitting through the forest alone, but acting like she was partying with her very best pals. She seemed so happy. Overflowing with open silliness that seemed to reach out and tickle Elena's own heart, as though she'd been invited along.

Stepping a little bit nearer through the trees, but then holding there, she watched this child spirit chatting with a bug on her finger.

Elena held herself back. She cut herself short. That had long been an instinct with her. A protective shield against any whispers of hope that must inevitably be dashed. In these past few days at the Glen, she'd been starting to see that though the actual physical bars and locks from her childhood were gone, she'd been finding new ways to hold herself back ever since. Maybe, as she had told herself from the beginning, she wasn't meant to ever be free.

This one time though, she did manage to push such thoughts back. Just this once she managed to wrestle free of that darker part of her that had always insisted she never dare let herself believe that maybe something, maybe someday, could possibly get a little brighter.

She took another step. And then two more. Drawn by something more than just her own curiosity. She sensed a gathering thrill of connection. To life, to the world, and to this other being. She felt enriched in ways she'd either long lost, or never really known. Suddenly hungry for a world filled with things she'd never felt, considered, touched, or maybe (the image came to her) even put on her tongue and actually tasted.

She watched, and listened in as Sylvie chatted with that bug.

"They call me Sylvie," this strange one told her as they finally stood maybe only ten feet apart.

"And no, I don't expect the bug to answer."

They watched as the beautiful green katydid spread its wings, had a good stretch, and then took its time flying off into the forest.

"Ciao, little buddy," Sylvie told it. "Maybe I'll sing with you tonight."

Elena was sure the insect must have felt like smiling back. How could it not? Even her own lips really wanted to.

She told her new friend, "I bet some of them do kind of understand you, and maybe respond in their own ways."

"I guess I do get along pretty well with bugs," Sylvie told her. She thrust out her hand, and Elena took hold of it. Sylvie had found elbow-bumping cute for a while, but had grown tired of it. Elena had never known the luxury of personal space, social distancing, or healthy isolation.

"Elena Francesca," the young teen told her slightly older companion.

"I know," Sylvie told her. "I've heard you talk a couple of times. You've been through a lot."

But she added, "Maybe we can help you let go of some of that."

Elena and Sylvie didn't use many words early on, and yet somehow they bonded. They shared smiles. Elena even experimented with laughing. They played, and magic opened before them. It reached into them through everything they touched, examined, and learned to appreciate. They grew to be friends, though they had so little in common. Elena had been fighting hard for years, under impossible conditions, to dig her way through to where Sylvie had been all along. She wished she too could be goofy. Just let go and play like this whenever she wanted, with no fear of consequences.

Sylvie's joy was contagious, and Elena was beginning to catch it.

They wandered, sat by streams, dunked their feet, and giggled when tiny fish came to nibble. They talked of things vast, and inconsequential. Or sat in silence. Together.

Sometimes Elena couldn't manage much more than to just ease up a bit, maybe not frown quite so intensely inside for a moment. All that grit left behind in her heart maybe didn't rub her quite so raw for a while. And there were times when her all-too-familiar tears came more from overflowing giddiness than from that relentless grip of her suffering.

Birds darted, squirrels frolicked, butterflies popped about and fluttered. When the urge struck, Sylvie would often dance along. Elena tried to a couple of times, but felt embarrassed, and stopped.

Life came more alive all around them. The forest called. Their hearts answered.

But still there was a part of Elena's that held back.

Elsewhere in the camp, Benjie was struggling to break free of his own self-imposed cages. But he had no one to play with. So he went off looking for his new buddy, Sylvie. He figured she'd be in the woods somewhere, but there was a whole lot of woods around there. He might try using some of that developing intuition of his to try finding her.

He set off, stepping between shadows that reminded him of times as a young boy when he had almost let himself believe, but always talked himself out of it. He'd stood ready, pen in hand to take dictation, but had only listened with his desire, not his soul, and so heard nothing.

Now he heard the sound of distant laughter. Birds twittered, and leaves rustled, as though they were trying to sing along. That pretty much had to be Sylvie, he thought.

He came upon her with Elena Francesca. He asked, "Do you mind if I join you?"

A part of him was still holding back in self doubt, and so he added, "You can say no if you like, and I'll leave."

A chipmunk ran up and sat on his foot. As if to tell him, "You ain't goin' nowheres yet, buddy!"

Figuring the little fella had probably mistaken his boot for a rock, Benjie sucked in his breath, and then tried not to move.

"You seem to have found a friend," Sylvie told him after a bit.

The three of them held very still for a long time.

Well, maybe Sylvie let out a couple of snorts.

And Elena really wanted to.

Time passed as they all settled into their wonder.

Then the little guy just hopped down and skittered away.

The forest breathed magic that day. Nature reached out to embrace them, and invite them along. Elena jumped back terrified when she saw a bear, but Benjie settled his hand onto her shoulder. She calmed, and then he kept it there. He'd chatted with bears on his own land. But this was nice too, he thought, hanging out with humans.

A hummingbird zoomed at her, stopping inches from her face. She flinched, but Benjie's hand brought her back to a world that meant her no harm. The tiny thing hung in the air for a moment, looking her over, inspecting this newcomer to forest life. He flew off, and Elena just stood there, feeling anxieties melt. Four blue jays gathered on different limbs of a tree right in front of them. The air tasted fresh, and cooled her troubled spirit. Old cage bars were softening.

They listened in on an occasional chirp. Or a tweet. Or a rustle. Maybe heard a low murmur. Messages spoken and delivered in some realm beyond words. Sylvie, Elena, and Benjie flowed and sparkled with their love of Nature, and knew that Nature was loving them back.

Benjie felt everything in his life from the beginning sliding together so perfectly; so magically, even miraculously; that he half expected to find another huge white feather falling to earth or materializing nearby. Maybe a neatly folded note propped against his pillow that night.

But then again, that chipmunk would more than suffice.

As for Sylvie; she was finally taking in what Mr. Mica had been telling her. That it takes most people a long time to wake up, but we really need to love them anyway. For where they were now, not just where they were heading.

In her talk the next day, Elena told those gathered, "You can do an awful lot of thinking when you're in a cage so long it breaks you. You tell yourself that if you ever get out, you'll be happy all the time no matter what. Your life will be beautiful, and you won't ever let yourself be miserable ever again." She looked around at campers hanging out in quiet communion. Gentle breezes stirred the greenery. Their hearts flowed gently. All was at peace.

"But then that day comes that you'd long feared could never be. Armed guards who'd held you in there for so long, treated you so terribly badly, finally unlock your doors. They tell you you're free. And you believe them." Campers were listening more intensely. "And maybe," she told them, "You honestly do think at first that you can leave all that behind. You've been offered a fresh start. You're going to grab it with both hands and run! Your life can really and truly begin! You will fill it to overflowing with great joy, and success in all ways! You can't wait to get started!"

She paused.

They waited.

"It turns out though, that you really don't feel that way for very long," she told them. "Not if you're still carrying that darkness around inside you. Not if you keep building new locks and chains out of how you look at everything new that comes your way. If a part of you keeps expecting things to fall apart. If you are just waiting for others to start turning against you, because this is how your life has always been. This is all you've ever known.

"Well, I want to tell you all a little secret here, that you probably already know. If you keep expecting things to turn bad, they will. If you keep looking for trouble, you will find it."

People around her were nodding in agreement, following her every word closely.

"It might take a few troubled years or even decades before you realize that you've been doing a lot of this to yourself. But then you start watching for it. Self abuse through unnecessarily dark expectations. You learn to see it for what it is when it pops back up again. You find ways ways to work through it, though life may still be a struggle.

"But then, after you've been working on this for a while, when you look around, you start to recognize it in a whole lot of other people who are putting their own hearts in cages. They're imprisoning their own spirits, and you ask yourself, Why? Why treat themselves this way? They didn't have guards poking at them through bars when they were kids. Refusing to feed them. They didn't have to go through what I did! Not by a long shot. Why are they acting like this? Don't they see how much worse *I* had it? What those *really* bad guys did to *me*? You guys have it easy, you might think. It feels almost like, How dare you?

"And there you are; back in resentment again. What you've been fighting so hard for so long to crawl out of and be done with.

"So now you learn to recognize *that* little twist, and you see all these other folks caught up in resentments of their own, and hear them telling each other, 'Don't you see how they treated me? I've had it much worse than you! I shouldn't have to put up with this shit!' They say it, and they believe it, because most people's lives offer them their own personal, often cruel challenges. Things they don't think they can deal with.

"Maybe because… that might be part of what life is there for?

"That's how we grow.

"*If* we work at it."

Elena Francesca paused to let her gaze wander out over her audience before adding, "We have probably a lot of us been there. Our jobs, families, and relationships can sure feel like prison cells sometimes, can't they?"

Several of those gathered on chairs, or sitting on blankets spread out on the grass around her, nodded their heads in agreement.

"Even beliefs we've created ourselves can pen us in if we let ourselves get stuck in things we no longer need to believe, or might have *never* been true in the first place."

She and Benjie made particularly focused and meaningful eye contact. They'd been talking this through, just the two of them. Each had been learning a lot from the other.

She told them, "Our whole lives can be cages if we let them. We form bars out of everything and anyone who has ever held us back; even out of every time we have held ourselves back. It can get so we're grumbling over every little thing that didn't go our way just exactly as we'd wanted it to."

She took a clear, full breath of Green Man's Glen air. She gazed off into the woods where she knew that somewhere, little Sylvie was smiling. Then she told those gathered around her, "But I hope maybe I've begun to wake up just a little bit, anyway.

"And so; at least for now; this is me breathing fresh air. Shaking loose from my miseries and sorrows a little more. Leaving a lot of my regrets somewhere behind me.

"I am in process.

"And, I hope, taking some probably still pretty early steps toward truth, and fulfillment."

She had another thought then, so she added, "And this is me, learning to smile."

She did, and the whole camp smiled along with her.

Maybe even a couple of the forest creatures.

It was nighttime. Sylvie, Benjie, and Elena sat together under starry skies, listening to crickets. The evening danced with fireflies. It was a new world for each of them to just be quietly hanging out with their buddies. They had never really had buddies before. But now tonight they felt surrounded by their very best pals. Human and other. Breezes. That peaceful, soothing, unspoken bliss. Finding utter contentment deep in the darkness of night.

Sylvie had long been wondering how her goofy, spontaneous ways could ever help anybody. Benjamin had been attacking himself for being more comfortable with forest life than with humans. Elena had felt broken to the point where she had doubted she could ever grow strong and step free of her childhood angst. But now, around a group campfire at Green Man's Glen, this special night reached in through each of them, helping ease some of that loose. An owl hooted somewhere, and even Elena joined her friends in hooting back. Magic called, and their hearts followed. All the world sang along.

Tiny flickers of Heaven, glowing sparks from the campfire, like fairy lamps wafting about. Pausing midair. Lingering. For a thought, or for a dream. Caressing both murmurs and silence. Spits, and floaters, and embers below. Flames leaped, danced, wavered, and vanished.

Flashing heat, and waves of cold.

The popping and drifting of sparkles through bliss.

Snuggled in next to Benjamin, Sylvie reached her blanket out and around him, and then nested in against his shoulder. Elena Francesca sat to his other side, but preferred lots of open space. She hated being crammed up against people.

Only a few yards farther around the circle, a Native American sat with his wife and their son, Denis. Benjie couldn't help but lean in a little closer, and listen a little harder to catch snippets as they openly chatted with each other about their memories from previous lifetimes, and how they had always loved each other.

Now and then, flames softened to cast mild, glowing shadows as though others might be seated or standing in open spaces; beings whose forms couldn't actually be seen.

Benjie sighed, and held Sylvie warmly, finally trusting in the spirits of the woods.

* * * Back at Benjie's own place, Dew Nose settled into soft grass for the evening, closing her eyes in rich contentment.

* * * In Sylvie's Gardens, a couple of the overnight guests heard rollicking laughter. They recognized one laugh as Ailana's, but the other, also a woman's was a mystery.

* * * Laurence Beaufort had been reading a book by Dr. Dolores Krieger and Dora Kunz, about channeling healing energies. It had been changing his outlook, and his openness to deeper matters. Now he sat in meditation beside the woman he had long considered to be the real mystery and joy in his life.

As if on cue, he and Danni turned toward each other in the same instant. They felt true magic in the air, their eyes met, and they loved each other more deeply and with sweeter purity than perhaps ever before.

* * * Night settled over an archaeological site deep in the jungles of Peru. A young student apprentice watched the glow from her lamp dancing across a figure that had been carved into that wall many centuries before. In the eerie lighting, their eyes seemed to meet; hers, and this ancient one's. If she hadn't been among scientists dedicated to cold objectivity, she'd have sworn he was reaching out to her.

This ancient elder had the eyes of a child.

* * * An American writer and his British partner sat together on a swing seat in her gardens. The night before, they'd watched the storm riding through. Now they delighted in the wet, reflective peace after its passing. Masses of leaves hung heavy and low from the rains. Grass sparkled. The world appeared to be resting for a moment. Drinking in. Getting ready.

Passing veils of mists were thinning, the earth climbing free of dense shadows. Nothing was clearly defining itself yet, but freshness, aromas, textures, and colors were slowly stirring. Coming more alive.

These two lovers, partners in everything, with homes on opposites sides of an ocean, snuggled into each other as they felt it all going right. One heart rested in the other. Everywhere was silence, and yet it all seemed so rich, and so full.

Scattered elsewhere around the planet, a few of his readers paused for a moment. They held his books to their own hearts, and loved with each other through the silence.

* * * The American President set his paperwork aside and decided to play with his dogs for a while.

* * * In Africa it rained over a long-dry village. Children came out to dance.

* * * Watching down over that beautiful blue globe from the International Space Station, two astronauts from different nations couldn't help but smile.

* * * Benjamin told his two very special new friends, "Ahhh; this is nice," and they murmured in drowsy agreement. In that one heedless moment of reverie, he invited them to come visit at his own place; where birds gathered on the deck, only wanting to share, and you felt the peace rolling in waves.

Before he'd had time to reconsider his social anxieties, look for a way to take his offer back, Sylvie had jumped at the chance. She told him, "Sure!" and the deal was settled.

Elena said she couldn't make it. She was scheduled for some whirlwind speaking tour that seemed bent on dragging her pretty much everywhere. She told them she was sorry, but she just couldn't break out of it. There were contractual agreements. Plans had already been made.

She felt privately relieved, but kept this part to herself. She wasn't sure she was quite ready for close and binding friendships just yet.

And besides, she'd been discovering some wonderful new layers of herself, and reality. She was feeling a strong pull to get out there and share them.

Sylvie told Benjie, "Well, I'm sure coming anyway! I want to meet Dew Nose!"

And then, Benjie sensed a stirring in the space they'd gathered into. A voice he'd known long ago, but which had deeply matured. His old buddy Madison had returned and was standing behind them. No one had seen or heard him step in through those dried crispy pine needles and forest debris. He must have walked in while Benjie had been listening to Waters, Emmy, and Denis, Benjie figured, because how else could he not have noticed?

Maddie asked him, "May I come along? I would like to meet Dew Nose as well."

Deeper forces were gathering.

Much of the world was awakening.

Renaissance had begun.

Thank you for reading our story.

To share your feelings with others, please visit www.amazon.com: Edward Fahey

Like/Follow me on Facebook at www.facebook.com/edwardfaheyauthor

Even the briefest comment would be appreciated.

Thank you.

About the Author

Edward Fahey writes mystical tales for those struggling with darkness in their everyday lives and who ache for connection with something wiser and stronger than they see themselves to be. Something ancient and eternal that can guide them toward hope. His stories touch magic—those reading them can find hidden doors and step through.

For more information, visit
www.bobedwardfahey.com

Like/Follow me on Facebook at
www.facebook.com/edwardfaheyauthor

Other Books by Edward Fahey

THE MOURNING AFTER—Three souls reincarnate through lifetimes of tragedy and romances cut short. They're offered one more chance to get it right.

ENTERTAINING NAKED PEOPLE—A lonely young man born too sensitive wanders America at a time of protests and racial unrest. Searching for God, romance, or at least a little companionship, he dives into mysticism, theosophy, rampant sexuality, and tragedy. He slowly learns what love truly is.

THE GARDENS OF AILANA—The place seems hidden behind a mystical veil. You're drawn here only when ready. Taking a hard look at childhood traumas still crippling you, you might have to let go of any family and friends holding you back. But then you can learn to work miracles. The healed are taught to be healers. Those who had thought themselves lost now find themselves open to deeper and brighter levels of reality.

THE SOUL HIDES IN SHADOWS—Horrors await us in the near future if we don't face down the ugliness and hatred tearing America apart now.

www.ingramcontent.com/pod-product-compliance
Lightning Source LLC
LaVergne TN
LVHW091533060526
838200LV00036B/588